The Bone House

To Fern
With much
love & gratitude!

Suanne

OTHER BOOKS BY LUANNE ARMSTRONG

Annie (1995)
Bordering (1995)
Arly and Spike (1997)
The Colour of Water (1998)
Jeannie and the Gentle Giants (2001)

THE BONE HOUSE

LUANNE ARMSTRONG

NEW STAR BOOKS

VANCOUVER

2002

New Star Books Ltd.
107 - 3477 Commercial Street
Vancouver, BC
V5N 4E8   CANADA
www.NewStarBooks.com
info@NewStarBooks.com

Cover by Rayola Graphic Design
Typesetting by New Star Books
Printed & bound in Canada by AGMV Marquis
First printing November 2002

Publication of this work is made possible by grants from the Canada Council, the British Columbia Arts Council, and the Department of Canadian Heritage Book Publishing Industry Development Program.

Le Conseil des Arts du Canada | The Canada Council for the Arts

Canada

BRITISH
COLUMBIA
ARTS COUNCIL

NATIONAL LIBRARY OF CANADA CATALOGUING IN PUBLICATION DATA

Armstrong, Luanne, 1949–
  The bone house / Luanne Armstrong.

ISBN 0-921586-91-4

I. Title.
PS8551.R7638B58 2002   C813'.54   C2002-911139-0
PR9199.3.A547B58 2002

This book is for my sons

*With thanks to the Canada Council, K. Linda Kivi,
Dorothy Woodend, Carolyn DeMarco, Doug Toner,
Mary Woodbury, Jean Rystaad, the Berton House
committee, Jane Hamilton, Ellen McGinn, Evelyn and
George Armstrong, Greg Bauder, George McWhirter,
Rolf Maurer, and Audrey McClellan.*

As a dare-gale skylark scanted in a dull cage
Man's mounting spirit in his bone-house, mean house
dwells —

GERARD MANLEY HOPKINS

If they do this thing in a green tree, what shall be
done in the dry?

THE GOSPEL ACCORDING TO ST. LUKE

The Bone House

I

THE CITY LAY DREAMING under wisps of smog and smoke and rainbow light from the morning sun. The abandoned high-rises by the city's harbour had water lapping up to their foundations, higher when the winter tides came in. Some of the more accessible empty apartments had been taken over by squatters, kids mostly, although there was a large and constantly changing population of unemployed, homeless, mentally ill, illegal immigrants, gypsies, fortune tellers, drug sellers, people on the way up and, much more quickly, on the way down, who washed in and out on the tides of fortune and the city's shifting landscape.

Lia sat up from within the nest of blankets, pillows, and shawls she had made on the floor. She sat there for a while, rocking back and forth, moaning softly under her breath. She hated mornings. No one came near her in the mornings.

Lia and the others had taken over one of the lower apartments in one of the towers. They had it fairly well organized. They had made strict rules for their group, or rather, Lia had made strict rules. She had seen enough of the quickly shifting way that groups formed and broke up. The group she wanted to create would have leadership and rules. She was eighteen now; she had survived long enough that people listened to her.

They used buckets for shit and dumped them in the public

toilets at night instead of in the ocean. They had stolen enough solar panels to run a small stove. This worked when the sun was out. They had a wind-up radio, a wind-up disc player, and a motley assortment of couches, beds, rugs, and blankets. In the winter, to keep warm, they huddled together around heaters powered by stolen hydrogen fuel cells. It had taken some risk to get these. They were supposed to be dangerously radioactive, but Lia thought that was probably just old people's propaganda. They had stolen them from the storage bins at the garages for the city bus system. Members of the group worked for weeks, figuring ways to get through the wire, disable the alarm system, make friends with the guard dogs, and break the code on the electronic lock to get into the storage system. But they had managed. They felt good after that. They felt that almost anything in the city might now be accessible to them if they had the guts to go after it.

Lia had even bigger plans. Staring out the window at the water, she fantasized about windmills, tide pumps, methane cookers. Even when Star was curled up next to her, the mornings were private, times for thinking, dreaming, planning — sometimes mourning.

This morning, all she could think about was missing Star. Lia hadn't wanted to go wandering, but Star was restless. It had all started with Lia's endless homesickness, stories of growing up in the woods, of fields and trees, flowers and animals. Star fell in love with a place she had never seen. But that wasn't what pulled her out of the city. Star had gone looking for a fantasy, a foolish dream.

The rumour had been around for as long as Lia had been on the street, which was five years now. She couldn't remember when she'd first heard about it. Lia was skeptical — streetlife bred rumours like it bred lice — but Star had believed it. Star believed a lot of things.

"Star, it's just a dream," Lia said.

"But Mika said he had a friend that went there, and it was true. It was the Kind Place. They gave him what he wanted, just like everyone says."

"The Kind Place," Lia snorted. "Every fucked-up asshole in this city thinks all he has to do is find the Kind Place and his troubles are over. Who are they? Where are they?"

"They're in the mountains," Star said vaguely. "Somewhere. People know where they are. You have to go looking. That's part of the deal."

"What deal?"

"What they give you. You have to ask. You find them and you ask for what's most important to you and they give it to you."

"But who are they?"

"They're like — angels or something. No one knows."

No matter what Lia said, Star hadn't listened. So Star had gone and Lia hadn't heard anything for months. She sat waiting for the fog to clear from her head. She'd been dreaming of home again. She loved that dream. Why did she have to wake up from it to this shit-smelling mildewed hole? She could hear the water chewing at the walls outside. Some of the other high-rises had started to sag on their foundations, but people went on living in them. This one would go too, eventually, but they'd be gone by then. Long gone.

When Lia was growing up, she had lived on a small piece of land with her grandmother. Caila, Lia's mother, had been sixteen when Lia was born. Sixteen, rowdy, doing too many drugs. Caila came and went in her life until Lia was five. Lia had a vague memory of raised voices, of her grandmother crying, of doors slamming. Finally word came that her mother had died in a spectacular car smash-up on the narrow highway that ran from their house to the nearest town.

After that, there was peace in the house until Lia was thirteen and needed to go to high school. She and her grandmother talked over their options, sitting at dinner while the light from the kerosene lamps flickered gently on the log walls.

Lia's grandmother had already survived a difficult life. She'd knocked around — cooking for tree-planting camps, restaurants, ranches. At a ranch in the Cariboo, she met a guy who promised her they'd buy a house, settle down. He stuck around for the birth of his daughter but disappeared soon after.

Eventually, when her daughter was supposed to be going to school, she had a piece of luck. She finally acquired a house. It was more of a shack when she got it. It was too far out of town from the restaurant where she'd gotten a job when tree-planting finished for that season, but she went on living there anyway because she'd fallen in love with the place.

The guy who said he owned it had told her to live there, look after the place. She met him in the restaurant. She was trying to work while she was still living in her van. It was October. There was frost on the grass in the mornings, but she hadn't yet found a place for the winter and Caila was whining about how embarrassing it was to go to school when she was living in a van. The guy came in one morning, ordered coffee, looked around the restaurant, and announced to no one in particular that he'd had it. Living in the valley was fucked, he said. No work, no money, plus the world was going to hell, and what good did it do for anyone or anything, hiding in the mountains and pretending things were just fine? If anyone wanted his place, they could have it until he came back.

It needed some looking after, he said. He'd be back sometime. But he hadn't come back and so she'd gone on living there until everyone assumed it was her place.

There were fruit trees, a garden space. Over the years, with more determination than skill, she and Caila had fixed up the house. There was no electricity or plumbing, but there was a creek, there were kerosene lamps, there was privacy and silence.

Now she was getting old. The death of her daughter had cut the heart out of her life, but she was determined to raise her granddaughter, so she hid her sadness and worked to keep them warm and fed, which was hard enough.

In August of Lia's thirteenth summer, her grandmother said one night, "I think we should move to the city."

Lia stared at her grandmother. She had never thought about living anywhere else.

"I'm not sure I can handle another winter," her grandmother went on, looking at her hands, which were knotting grotesquely from arthritis. "The cold — it's so far from doctors — and you need to go to school."

Lia had grown tall that summer. She was brown haired, green eyed, and strong for her age. She had secret dreams of adventure, and now she was excited by the idea of the city. She'd never been to the city. There would be real schools there, other kids, access to computers, maybe even real books.

In the valley where Lia had grown up, there were no schools anymore. They had started disappearing when she was young, first the smaller rural schools, then the high school in the nearby town of Appleby. The schools were owned by a corporation that said it couldn't afford to run such isolated schools. As the highways got worse and medical services were cut back, teachers began demanding extra pay to live that far from a major centre. The place was almost totally cut off all winter. Besides, EduGreat pointed out, kids could still do school over the internet. But as Lia and her grandmother knew, that also cost a lot of money.

They got a ride to the city with the trucks that were leaving that fall to sell the valley produce. They wandered for a day or two after they arrived until they found a tiny one-room apartment on Cambie Street that her grandmother's pension would just barely cover.

At night, Lia and her grandmother sat side by side at the small wooden table they'd found in an alley. They wrote or drew pictures by candlelight to save electricity. The candles reflected in the black glass that hid the grumbling city.

Lia was shocked by the city, although there were things she liked. She couldn't get over the proliferation of stuff in the stores. Only the necessities had been hauled into their small valley by truck. The price of gas had risen steadily over the years, so fewer and fewer trucks rolled into the valley. People had gotten used to doing for themselves, growing food, trading and bartering in used stuff.

Every day, Lia walked five blocks down Cambie, crossed at the light, and entered the school. It was one of the few schools that still maintained a library. Lia loved books with a hopeless desperate passion. There had been a few books in her grandmother's house, and a lot of the neighbours had books they had saved which they let her borrow. But there was never enough.

When it dawned on her how many books had actually been written, how many she had never read, she set herself to catch up, knowing she would never make it but determined to try. Not many other people used the library for books. They spent their time on the internet, in the interactive webcam rooms, or playing games. The teachers laughed when they saw Lia with her nose in a book. Books were useless, they said. They had too much information in them. They were just confusing. The books were still in the school only because there was a law insisting that the school had to keep some. EduGreat was trying to get the law dumped, but hadn't managed yet.

One night Lia was sitting with her grandmother when she

heard a knock at the door. When her grandmother went to answer, people in masks, carrying tasers, laser pointers, and pepper spray walked into the apartment. They didn't have to bust in. Lia and her grandmother were too stunned to resist. The people who came in had painted faces and bright strips of cloth tied in elaborate patterns around their chests, legs, and waists. Their hair was either shaved or dyed in rainbow patterns.

They herded Lia and her grandmother out into the lobby with the rest of the people from the building. All the apartment doors, normally closed, stood wide open. Light shone from the open doors, music flooded and jangled into a snarled noise, the smell of food cooking mingled into a soup of odours. The raiders went from apartment to apartment, turning everything off, methodically and neatly cutting wires, carrying out anything of value: stereos, TVs, interactive VCRs, solar cells, hydrogen cells. They took these out back and loaded them into a waiting truck. They went from person to person, taking jewellery, phones, beepers. They were quick and cold but almost polite. Most of the people in the building were old. They stood there shaking, crying quietly. Some couples stood with their arms around each other. This kind of raid was becoming more and more common. The gangs targeted apartments full of old people. Sometimes, if there was no trouble, they let everyone go.

Lately, however, there had been raids in which everyone was killed and the apartment lit on fire. One of these gangs had posted a manifesto on the internet, stating that old people should be killed. They were destroying the environment and the economy. There were too many of them. They were a drag on the medical system. They had outlived their usefulness and should go. Moreover, they deserved to be punished. They had left a world stripped of natural resources and desperate with uncertainty about the future.

Lia held her grandmother's hand and tried not to shake. One of the raiders looked at her. He grabbed her arm.

"You don't belong here," he said. "You shouldn't be with these parasites." He shoved her towards one of the other raiders, who dragged her out the door and threw her into the back of the truck.

"Grandma," Lia screamed, and the raider backhanded her across the face, abruptly, impersonally.

"Quiet," he said, "or we'll just have to shoot old granny."

They all climbed in the back of the truck with Lia and drove away. It was pitch-black. Lia kept inadvertently leaning into the person sitting next to her, though she sat bolt upright, her arms around herself, trying not to touch anyone. The truck swerved, and something heavy fell onto Lia's feet.

"Jeezus fucking Christ," someone said in the dark. "Fucker can't drive worth shit."

"Shut up," someone else muttered. "As if you could do any better, asshole."

"Anybody got a smoke?"

A match flared, and for a second Lia could see the others in the truck.

"Hey, why'd we grab the kid? What the hell is that about?"

"Dunno."

The joint went around. Lia reached and took a deep drag when it came to her. Maybe it would steady her nerves. She had been smoking dope since she was six or seven. She and her friends used to steal it from their parents' gardens, meet in their treehouse, and lie there watching the patterns of sun, shade, and cloud within the tree branches. She wrapped her arms around herself again. Her feet hurt from the weight of the box and she shifted her body to move them.

"Goddamn, I'm hungry," someone said. "Anybody got food?"

No one answered.

"Chocolate," the voice went on. "When was the last time you tasted chocolate? Or really good coffee? That shit we drink ain't nothing like real coffee. God, I'm starving."

"Coffee trees are all dying," someone said. "Can't take the shitty fucking weather. And it costs too much to ship it. Get used to it."

"We got some of that wheat stuff left at home," someone else said hopefully.

There was a general groan. "Wheat shit," a voice said. "Every fucking day. More fucking porridge."

"Hey, be glad we got anything to eat at all. All praise to the mother," a deep voice growled.

There was silence after that. Another joint was lit and passed around. Lia was shaking hard now. Her teeth clattered and she clenched them together. The back of the truck was freezing. She had no coat. Finally, the truck stopped and everyone stood up as soon as the doors were opened. The stolen materials in the back of the truck were quickly and efficiently shifted into the basement of some dark building. People had tiny flashlights that gave hardly any light. Lia started to back away in the dark, but someone grabbed her arm.

"Stick around, kid," said a woman's voice, softly in her ear. "This ain't the time to run. That's for later if you got the nerve."

The woman stood holding her arm while everyone else finished the unloading. Then they all filed into the basement, went up some stairs, following the little tiny lights, and came into a room where, finally, a lamp of some kind was lit.

Lia stared around, kept her arms wrapped around herself, tried hard to stop shaking. The woman was still beside her, but no longer holding on to her. It was a huge dusty room, obviously part of an old house. There was a torn and dirty carpet on the floor, black plastic taped over the parts of the walls that must have been windows, and a wood stove in the corner. The floor around the stove was covered with ashes, sawdust, and wood chips. A pile of wood was heaped in the corner. At least the room was warm. There was a wooden table in the middle of the room and another in the corner, covered with dishes.

Someone made tea, and someone else thrust a hot cup of minty-smelling tea into Lia's hands. No one was looking at her.

"Go sit," the woman said, low voiced, in her ear and shoved her towards a chair. "And keep your mouth shut."

Lia sank into a chair, away from the table but near the stove. She curled up in the chair, her knees under her chin, her arms wrapped around her knees. She finished the tea and put the cup on the floor.

She watched the people in the room. She had thought there were a lot of them, but now she realized there were only five. They all looked young, not much older than she was. There didn't seem to be a leader. There was a tall black kid with his hair braided and tied behind his head; two blond girls; a person whose gender seemed indefinite, although Lia thought it was probably a girl; and another guy, tall, red headed, and who seemed older than everyone else. So far he hadn't spoken a word, merely poked wood in the stove, poured tea for everyone, then went and flung himself onto a heap of blankets and sacks in the corner. It was the black guy who had grabbed her, thrown her in the truck.

"So what the hell are we doing with a stupid kid?" one of the blond girls snapped, not the one who had been holding

Lia's arm. "Whose bright idea was that? And now what the hell are we supposed to do with her?"

They all turned to look at Lia. She stared back at them. They were a lot less scary now. They had seemed huge and terrifying at the apartment. Now they were normal, almost ordinary, except for their dye jobs and strips-of-cloth costumes.

"I want to go home," Lia said. "Just let me go home."

"Can't. You've seen everything," the black guy said.

"Why do you wanta hang out with those old freaks anyhow? They're disgusting."

"That was my grandmother," Lia said, "and I wasn't hanging out with her. I was living there and going to school."

"How fucking cute," said the other blond woman, who was standing uncomfortably close to Lia. "Families suck, kid, you get it? We hate families. We hate school. We hate old stupid parasites that eat everything and don't leave no fucking place for us. So don't give us some stupid shit about school and grannies. We don't give a fuck."

Everyone was silent after this outburst. Lia was shaking. She wasn't afraid anymore. She was furious. These stupid shits. Wrecking her life. Scaring everybody. Living in some dump with no food.

"I'm not staying here," she said. "I'm leaving. Just as soon as I can."

"Shut up, kid," the black guy said, not unkindly. "You don't know what you're talking about. You'll change your mind after a while. After we're done with you, you'll understand. You're just ignorant. You think your nice old granny and those nice old people are your friends? Forget it. They're the enemy. They're the reason we don't have no fucking future on this planet. They're the reason why everything is so fucked up. You ever notice that most of downtown is underwater, that you can't breathe the fucking air, that the food we eat is shit? That's their fault. So shut up about it."

"Let's eat," the other blond woman said. "Christ, all we do is argue. I'm sick of it. I'm hungry. Where the hell is some food?"

The red-headed guy got off the pile of blankets and trudged to the stove, lifted a pot, and carried it to the table. He slammed it down, got a pile of bowls and spoons from the other table. "All praise," he grunted, then dished a bowl for himself and went back to his corner. The blond girl brought Lia a bowl and sat on the floor next to her with her own bowl. Lia looked at the food. It was boiled wheat, something her grandmother used to make in the late spring when food was scarce, the root cellar was empty, and nothing yet was coming up in the garden.

"My name's Christy," the girl said. "We'll get some better food tomorrow. We been eating this crap for days."

"It's okay," Lia said. "My grandma used to make this sometimes."

"Oh yeah? Don't you got parents?"

"No," Lia blinked back tears, "I don't have parents."

"You're lucky, kid. That means they can't hit you. Can't fuck you."

Lia was suddenly eager, desperate to talk. "My grandma and I had a farm up north. We came here to go to school." Tears were rolling down her cheeks now. "We were gonna go home again next summer. I was gonna go swimming and riding." She couldn't stop crying. She put the soggy bowl of wheat on the floor. "We pick stuff in the summer, berries and garden stuff. I help my grandma with everything."

"A farm, eh? Jeez, that sounds good. I never been on a farm. I never been out of this city. I thought maybe there weren't no farms left anywhere."

"There's lots. Our neighbours are farmers. They grow all their own food."

"Oh yeah? Lots of food, eh? Maybe that'd be a cool place to raid. Where is it?"

"A long ways," said Lia, alarmed. "A really long ways. Up north."

"Oh," Christy said, losing interest. "Too much work to get there. Besides, I don't know nothing about farms. Aren't they really dirty?"

"No," said Lia. "Our place is beautiful."

"Hey, hurry up and finish eating. Study session," the non-gendered person called.

They all got up, took their bowls to the table in the corner, and gathered on the floor in a circle in front of the stove. Christy gestured for Lia to sit by her. The black guy talked about some book they were all supposed to be reading, some book Lia had never heard of. She tried to listen but sleep overcame her. When she woke in the morning, she was in the middle of a heap of blankets and cushions. Christy was beside her, snoring gently.

Lia closed her eyes again. She said her name over and over, Lia Harper, Lia Harper, Lia Harper.

She decided to think about home. Deliberately, she imagined every detail: the colour of the sun on the lake, the smell of water, the faint blue mist on the morning hills, the jagged black firs along the road coming up the hill to the cabin. Tears rolled out from under her eyelids and dripped down her nose.

As soon as she heard Christy stirring, she pretended to be asleep, wiping her eyes under the cover of the blankets.

Lia spent the next few weeks desperately looking for a way to escape, but someone was always watching her. There was only one door to the room where they stayed, and it was usually locked. They peed and shit in a bucket in the corner. People brought food, went away again. Lia grew desperate for sunshine, fresh air. New people came and went away again. Lia wondered if her grandmother or anyone was looking for her. She wondered if the police would come someday.

They had a study session every evening, talking about books and ideas and the new world and revolution. Lia tried to read the books, but they seemed long and dull to her. She sat in the study sessions night after night. The group seemed fondest of repeating horror stories about the end of the world, the world economy collapsing, the ocean covering the land, earthquakes, volcanoes, sunstorms, and other catastrophes. Meanwhile, life went on from day to day in a deadly sameness. Only the food improved.

Lia still slept beside Christy. The first time Christy's arm had gone under her head, the first time Christy's arms wrapped around her, Lia had been stiff, terrified, holding her body still and far away. But Christy was the only friend she had, the only one who paid any attention to her, the only one who wanted to listen to her homesick weepy stories of the farm and her grandmother. Christy held her, stroked her hair. When she kissed Lia, her lips were warm and soft and light. She stroked Lia's soft skin, the skin on her belly, her shoulders, gave her massages with perfumed oil, brought her special food, brought her tea in the morning while Lia lay in bed, confused but pleased.

After a few mornings of this, Christy's demands increased. She took Lia's hand, guided it between her legs.

"Kiss me back," she said. "Kiss me, kiss me."

She began to twist her hips, began to force Lia's hand to move.

"Use your fingers," she hissed. "Inside, go inside." Terrified, Lia tried to figure out what Christy wanted. Christy turned over, keeping Lia's fingers inside her, and rubbed and humped and moaned into the rags that passed for a pillow. Eventually she lay quiet and Lia pulled her bruised and sore hand back to herself.

The first time Christy fucked her with a dildo, Lia almost screamed with the pain. Christy put her hand over Lia's mouth to keep her from crying out. She made her turn over, fucked her from behind, keeping one hand on her mouth and the other kneading and twisting Lia's small breasts. Lia was sore for days, but the next day Christy put her mouth and tongue on Lia's sore vagina and clit, and for the first time Lia felt pleasure build within her. She resisted it. She didn't want pleasure from Christy. But her body began to twist and cry out without her inside it.

She let it do whatever it was doing and took part of herself off to the farm, imagined herself sitting in the sun in her favourite place, a mossy sloping bench of rock just above the lake's edge while somewhere far away her mouth cried out and her body convulsed.

The others in the group didn't seem to care what they were doing as long as they didn't make too much noise.

After a while, Lia realized she could make Christy do things for her. She got good at fucking her, making her beg, making her sweat and cry out. She knew now what Christy wanted and how to give it to her or withhold it. She got demanding, pushing to see how far she could go. She made Christy steal food, made her save the best food for her.

One night she whispered, "Christy, when are they going to let me go? When can I go back to my grandma's? She doesn't know what happened. She'll be looking for me. I hate it here. I want to go home."

"Forget it," Christy said, "they're not looking for you."

"What do you mean? Why not?"

There was a long silence.

"Why not, Christy? Why wouldn't they look for me?"

"Cause when Raz got picked up by the cops a while ago, he told them you were dead. He had to, or they'd have come looking for you. They might have found this house. We couldn't risk that."

Lia had noticed the black kid's absence, but people were always coming and going. She couldn't keep track of them and no one ever explained anything.

"Raz is in jail?"

"Juvie. He'll be out in a few months, maybe a year."

That night Lia cried herself to sleep. For the next few days she was sullen and weepy, wouldn't let Christy touch her, wouldn't look at anyone, barely touched her food.

Finally Christy said, "Look, would you like to go outside? Do you want to come on a run with us?"

"Yes," she said.

They took her out. She stared greedily through the windows at sky, sun, flowers. The whole city looked different. They didn't go anywhere near anything she recognized.

That night she was lying next to Christy when the police burst in. Lia huddled under the blankets, terrified, while rifle fire ricocheted off the walls, while people screamed, dove under furniture. Chairs and tables overturned, dishes crashed to the floor.

When it was over, most of the other people were dead. The police took Lia downtown, listened impassively to her story. They kept her overnight in a cell by herself and the next day they led her to the door, took her outside, left her on the sidewalk, went back inside, closed and locked the heavy iron door. It took her a day of wandering to find her grandmother's apartment. She had no money for the bus, and she couldn't remember the address. When she found it, it was a burned hulk. There was no one there.

She went to the school. She was weak with hunger. They hadn't fed her in the jail or let her have a shower. She hadn't been really clean for weeks. In the squat they washed out of bowls. They were always short of water.

"I'm sorry," the school counsellor said. She looked terrified. A security guard had followed Lia into the office and stood with his hand on his gun. "No one has paid your school fees." She frowned, peered at Lia. "We're not even sure you are who you say you are. That girl was reported dead. There is very little I can do. You'll have to go to welfare. Maybe they can put you in a shelter somewhere. They'll look after you. Stay here and wait. Someone will come."

Lia knew better. A lot of the stories in the squat were about kids fleeing FosterLove, the Christian corporation that ran child welfare.

"They feed you shit, then you have to work ten, twelve hours a day to pay for it," one girl said. "You don't work, they got all kinds of ways of fucking you over — drugs, solitary, tasers. Then you have to fuck them to get food."

"Scary place," Raz had shuddered. "Don't never go there, man. It's worse than hell. Man, they hate kids, hate us all."

Lia left the school, walked down the street, stunned and disbelieving. Two people who knew her from the squat found her sitting on a street corner downtown, begging. She moved into a new squat that night.

Every night she dreamed of going home, of leaving the city, of going back to the cabin. She would find it, she would find her home, and her grandmother would be there waiting for her. She would never, ever, as long as she lived, leave there again. At first she tried to find someone to hitch a ride with, or someone to come with her. Then one day she left by herself. The police picked her up, took her to a FosterLove CareHouse.

It took her months to get away. She had learned a lot from her time with Christy and the others. She had learned to flirt and tease to get what she wanted.

She let one of the male caretakers fuck her. He'd bragged to her one day about his control over the alarm system in the house, how he was the only one who really knew how it worked. He'd shown her how he could get in and out of the house anytime. He liked to have sex with her in the basement of the CareHouse, in an alcove created by the several lines of constantly drying laundry.

One night he fell asleep. She eased herself off the narrow pad and knelt on the floor, listening to his heavy breathing. He was an older guy, running to fat, addicted to pot and tranquilizers. He liked to fantasize about how he and Lia could live together when she got older, how they'd get a place and she could look after him.

He was snoring. She went through his pockets, and even though he grunted, he didn't wake up. Maybe it was the tranquilizers, she thought. Maybe he'd taken too many.

She slid his keys out of his pocket, then eased her way out the basement door. The house was surrounded by chain-link fence, topped with barbed wire. But once, while she was working in the garden, she had spotted the place at the back where the wild dogs slipped in and out to steal food from the compost pile.

Now she wriggled and fought her way under the wire. She slid down alleys and slipped under overgrown hedges and shaggy brush until she was far away.

It took her a while to find another squat she liked. There were lots of them, she had discovered, some better organized than others.

But she kept her dream of leaving the city. She'd met Star at the second squat she tried, an abandoned warehouse on the edge of the downtown. Star was beautiful, her long blond hair braided in multiple tiny braids, threaded with beads. What attracted Lia at first was that Star had read books as well, books full of ideas that fired her mind with energy. They fired Lia's mind as well, and she was surprised to discover that her body could follow, that sex with Star didn't hurt, didn't cost her anything except giving up some of her carefully guarded privacy. They'd been together for three years.

Except now Star had left without her, angry at Lia's disbelief in her cherished dream of the Kind Place.

Lia was awake now. She reached under her mattress, wrapped a length of chain around her arm and clipped it on, slipped her knife into her boot sheath. She ran her fingers over her shaved head. The stubble grew so fast.

She stood up and went to the window. A wind was ruffling the harbour. Even though it was October, it was still hot. It wouldn't cool off until late November. The weather was violent, erratic. Everyone talked about it all the time. People talked about an ice age coming or the earth getting too hot for anything to grow. But nobody really knew what was happening. None of the oldies knew shit. Climate instability it was called on the NewsNets. They said it was normal. They said the climate was always changing. Maybe. They also said it was hotter than it had ever been. They had been saying that as far back as she could remember.

It had been October, five years ago, when the invaders had taken away her life. She stretched, went to the table, poured herself some tea. Then she pushed aside the tarp that covered the hole in the side of the building and went down the rickety slimy planks to the streets that, however familiar they became, would never be home.

2

THE SLANTING SUN from the brilliant October day was hot on his back. He'd been wandering along the highway shoulder in search of bottles, pop cans, anything he could sell, trade, or recycle. He found odd things: hubcaps, tarps, once a perfectly good chair that cost him immense effort to carry on his back to his cabin, but which now sat by his stove, a bright soft spot amid the dust and sawdust and spiders.

He saw the blood splattered on the pavement and he searched until he found where the doe had crawled up the bank off the road and into the brush. She was lying on her side, her head thrown back and eyes wide open. One hind leg was crushed. What was left of the leg was dangling by a flap of skin. There were flies around her eyes and muzzle, but she was still breathing in short spasmodic gasps. Big patches of hair had been torn from her side and shoulder. These patches were red and bleeding. Matt didn't have anything he could use to kill her except his pocket knife. He pulled the knife out of his jeans pocket and crouched beside the deer. She scrabbled to get away, pulled herself onto her two front legs but couldn't get any farther. She struggled there, scrambling furiously, then fell back onto her side. Air spurted from her nose in a high thin whistle.

He looked around for a stone, something to bash the doe's head to stun it, quiet it. He had flung himself out of the shack, unable to bear sitting there any longer, staring at the sun on the leaves, unable to bear the dirt, the smell of himself. He hadn't expected to have to kill something. He had a rifle back at the shack. He kept it in the rafters, wrapped in a blanket, but it was too far to go get it. The deer would be dead by then.

The deer was dying while he watched. She heaved a huge breath, tried again to struggle to her feet, almost made it, but the crippled hind end collapsed, the feet scrabbled anyway, running in the leaves and the dirt in one last desperate effort to escape. Then she shuddered all over and went still. He thought the deer must be dead, but she drew one more shuddering breath and then, after a while, another. He began to cut her throat so the blood would be pumped from the meat while the heart was beating. His knife was dull and he had to saw away at the velvet-soft throat. He cursed himself and his fate while he sawed. He cursed cars and roads and people in general. He wanted to lie in the dirt and beg the doe's forgiveness, but he went on sawing at the meat and gristle inside the doe's skin, while his hand grew slippery with blood.

At last blood fountained out, spilled onto his boots, pumped by the deer's dying heart. It was an astonishing red against the ground. It made a puddle that looked like red plastic paint. He pulled his hand from its neck. He'd have to go home for a rope, a butcher knife, a sack to carry the meat. He should hurry, before the meat grew cold. But he went on sitting there. Flies gathered on the blood. Occasional fine shudders ran through the doe's muscles while she went on dying. Once she even kicked all her legs, but finally she lay stiff. He stared, tried to catch the moment, the transformation, from when it was still a live thing to when it became a pile of meat, lying in the dirt. But it was too fast. It was instant.

He went on sitting beside the deer. His hands dangled over his knees and his heels were propped on a lump of moss. After a while he got out tobacco and rolled a cigarette. The smoke rose straight into the air, like a thin pillar, and joined with the other pillars of smoke from fires high on the surrounding mountains. His bad leg began to ache and he had to stand up. He still didn't feel like moving, but he had to get back to the cabin.

He began to feel frightened. He had been away too long. The dead deer, the calm and silent afternoon, began to seem like omens. He swung back down the bank and along the road. The leg dragged behind him. When the occasional truck passed him, he tried to walk straighter and not limp.

Back at the clearing he went around the shack, checking that everything was the way he had left it. The clearing dozed gently in the warm sun. There was a chill in its rays as it sagged towards the mountaintops. Flies churned on the grey boards of the walls. Cedar bugs crawled their slow blind way up the logs. The heaps of bottles that he had dumped in various places were slowly being covered by gold and brown leaves from the alder and maple around the shack. His feet shuffled through leaves as he walked. He had to give his leg a rest before he went back. Then he would find a rope and a butcher knife and go back to get the deer. He settled himself on the stump he had positioned by the front door and dozed a little in the sun.

The deer kept inserting itself into his thoughts. When a local person hit a deer on the road, the deer got skinned, butchered, and hauled away as fast as possible. Sometimes the deer weren't killed. They crawled off into the bush, still alive but crippled, and died slowly.

Once he had seen a deer hit by one of the big trucks — a road train — so hard that it had literally exploded, blood spraying all over the road. The truck hadn't even slowed down. The highway maintenance guys used to pick up the carcasses and take them to the dump, but they didn't bother anymore. The few guys that were still working had enough to do just keeping the roads open. So these days, more often, the coyotes and ravens cleaned the carcasses. The bones got dragged back into the brush where they were slowly covered with moss.

It was the bones that bothered him. The meat got recycled, but the bones were left, bones and teeth and the black cups that covered the hoofs.

So many bones. So many dead animals.

Who cared? he thought. Who even wondered about the goddamn innocent animals, like the doe this morning, whose death was just another useless accident? The animals that people had run over with useless bloody cities and civilization and look at the mess people had made, the mess the world was in now.

He had never thought much about things until his accident. But now he worried all the time. Things were getting worse. Even as isolated as he lived, he could tell that. And there wasn't much he could do about it, though he tried.

He stood up, crossed the yard, and got the wooden box he had made. The sides were thick four by fours, the bottom was a piece of curved metal off an old car fender. The box was full of shards of broken glass.

It had taken him a while to figure out how to smash the glass with some efficiency. He had tried a flat rock, a regular hammer, and a block of wood. Eventually, he had found a meat hammer from the old butcher shop. The hammer had been thrown into the dump, where Matt spent a lot of time.

Now he balanced the box on his legs and began to pound with the hammer at the shards of glass in the box. He found old bottles in the dump and along the road, brought them home, and pounded, pounded, pounded the glass back into the white sand element from which it had come. It was a small gesture, but it was what he could do. When he had enough sand, he carried the box down to the river and threw the sand in a sparkling rainbowed arc over the water.

He brought home other things that could be fixed up or sold or recycled in some way, but a lot of it he never got around to. Parts from machines piled in rusting lumps around his shack.

But what could you do with bones? He knew that in cities, factories ground them up, made them into fertilizer and animal food. But he wanted something special, something to make people think.

He sat on the ground, rhythmically chunking at the glass. He had learned to do it slowly, hit the glass just right to keep fragments of it from flying up into his face. But sometimes, when he was finished pounding glass, it took him twenty minutes with tweezers to pick all the glass slivers from his hands. He had tried wearing gloves, but it didn't feel right, just like sitting on a chair no longer felt right.

As he pounded, his vision began to take shape. He saw a wall, a monument of bones, wide and tall and high. No, not a wall, but a house made of bones, white and shining, bones made useful, made solid, made as a mark, a monument to waste and stupidity and death and the living wild creatures all around him. He liked it. It had sense. It felt like the right thing to do, he thought, as if it came in a vision, an order from elsewhere.

He refused to believe in a god. That would be a kind of giving in. But still, there were spirits. He knew that. He'd seen them and talked to them and they were nothing to be afraid of. If this was a spirit-given idea, all the better, and all the more strength his house, rising from shit and blood and death, would finally have.

He sat in the autumn sun, soaking it in while it beat down

on his head, a steady regular heat thumping him into drowsiness. Finally he fell asleep sitting on the ground, and his head fell forward onto his chest. His mouth fell open. A thread of drool silvered his beard and the front of his shirt.

He dreamed about his house

The house stood like a shining crystal palace, full of wind and voices. The bones shone white as quartz. The house seemed endless. It was full of rooms. On one side of the house there was a fireplace and a bright fire burning. He couldn't find the door into this room. He wandered around looking for it. He went along the wall, which was full of the faces of animals, grotesque and gibbering, their bright eyes watching him as he felt for a door. He knew there was a door somewhere, for he had built the wall himself and he had put it there, but now it was gone.

He woke abruptly, jerking himself upright. The sun had gone behind a cloud and a cold breeze had risen. He stared around the clearing, at the gold birch leaves that fluttered in front of the fringe of blackened rusty hemlocks beside the creek.

The dream flavoured his waking for a long time. He believed in dreams. That was something Star had taught him. She had taught him so many things, much of which he didn't understand, but he believed what she said. She told him about crystals and auras, prophecies and meditation. How could he, looking into her green eyes, her smiling, dancing, elfin face, not believe her?

But this dream had the weight, the feel, of prophecy itself. It was a message, that was clear. The girl herself was the fire, the source of warmth and creativity. When he built the house, she would come again.

He closed his eyes, wanting to see Star, wanting some kind of vision to hold onto, but nothing came except flickering opalescent blue and green shadows.

When he opened his eyes again, the sun was setting. He went inside. Grey blankets were crumpled in a heap by his bed. The chair by the stove was partly propped up by a broken apple box. Most of the furnishings in the room he had brought from the dump or from people's backyards. The blankets and sleeping bag on his bed had come from the dump. The shack itself he had built with old windows, plywood, scrounged lumber, torn tarps, and pieces of plastic. It looked like an igloo from the outside; he had made a frame from old lumber and then covered it over with whatever he could find. Part of the roof was covered with rotting cowhides, also scrounged from the dump. He had made a stove out of a barrel, but a hole had rusted through the side and ashes kept leaking onto the floor. He had put a piece of tin under the hole so that the floor wouldn't catch on fire.

He was suddenly desperately hungry and cold. What he needed was a fire, some hot food. He went outside to chop kindling. He had some dented ancient cans of beans he had found in the dump for supper, and some eggs he had gotten cheap from a farm on the way back from town.

After he had the fire lit, opened the beans, cracked two eggs into them, and chopped an onion into it all, he remembered the deer. It was too late and dark to go back for it now, even though he needed, his body craved, the meat. His leg still ached fiercely from the long afternoon walk. He told himself he'd go first thing in the morning, but the smell and feel of the dead deer lingered in the cabin, a thin bitter smell. He opened the door to let it out, and the night came in instead. Cold came in. He could see the stars, harsh bright holes in the black sky. It would freeze tonight. He would have to sleep with the spirit of the dead deer hanging around the cabin, and the frost and dread of yet another long winter to spend alone.

He took off his boots and socks and got under the blankets in his clothes. There was blood splashed on his pants, and after a while it bothered him enough that he took his pants off but left on his plaid shirt. He pulled the book he was reading out from under the pile of books. It was a book Star had given him. He fell asleep with the book on his chest, and in the night, when his leg began to ache enough to wake him up, he turned over and felt the book slide to the floor. Worried that it might get ashes on it from the stove, he shoved it under the bed.

He lay staring at the rough boards next to his head and worrying. He knew about these nights. Lately it had been getting worse. Tonight, pictures flicked and jittered behind his eyes when he lay down to try to sleep. Over and over again he felt the softness of the deer's throat, felt it jerk against his hand when he cut its throat. He only wanted to save it, to keep it from pain. The truck driver who hit it likely never gave it another thought.

The deer faded, turned into faces, each one with blood fountaining from the throat. God, he thought. Please stop. Please make it stop. The faces turned into Darlene's face, her pleading sad face.

"It's my leg," he tried to tell Darlene.

The last time they fought, she had cried. "You're all I got," she said. He knew that was true. She lived in the little white house that had belonged to their parents. It belonged to both of them now, but Matt figured the best thing he could do was let her have the whole thing. He'd helped her with the taxes when he had a job, but now, however much he wanted to help, he could barely look after himself.

He had tried to tell her how much his leg hurt, how it kept replaying in his head for such a long time: the skidder tilting into the air, the realization that it wasn't going to settle back to earth the way it was supposed to, that it was going to keep going up into the air, up and over, rolling like

a demented soccer ball down the mountain. How he'd
thought about it all in that moment, realized clearly he had
a choice. He could stay with the machine and ride it out, or
he could jump. He wanted her to understand what it meant,
how miraculous it had been, that he'd weighed and considered those options in the second and a half he'd had to think
and he knew he should jump, that he'd have a better chance
that way, that if he stayed with the machine he'd get shot
out of the thing anyway, flung like human ammunition out
of a catapult, probably hit a few trees and rocks and stumps
on the way. But if he jumped, he'd be taking his life in his
own hands, taking control.

He'd stood up. He remembered that. He remembered
looking over the side of the skidder, trying to choose a place
to land, even while the thing was still rising in the air,
preparing to fling him out, and he'd balanced on the edge of
the cab, taken a deep breath, and gone flying. He would
have been all right too, he was pretty sure of that, but something caught his leg at the last moment, maybe the edge of
the treads, he wasn't sure, maybe a stick or log caught in the
understructure. Something flung him ass over teakettle. He
felt the leg shatter and the next thing he knew he was coming back to himself and the foreman was bending over him
to see if he was dead.

He hadn't fainted, he just lost track of things. After his leg
went, there was just a lot of confusion, a lot of air and a
sense of flying, even spaciousness, and a black place where
he hit the ground, though he remembered hitting it, but his
memory was all browns and greys there, nothing clear.

The pain didn't start until they got him on a stretcher and
into the shit-stinking crummy, going down the goddamn
mountainside, swerving around corners while he tried to
brace himself, sweat rolling off his forehead, trying not to
groan and cursing instead.

That's what he'd tried to explain, but Darlene wouldn't listen.

"I've heard enough excuses to last me a lifetime," she said. "If you won't help us, I'll find someone who will."

He folded his hands under his head, folded his huge tired shoulders around himself like wings, and curled his cold legs against his belly. He pulled the book out from under the bed. His hands were cold, but as he read he forgot all that, he slid back into the story, the story that was more like a dream, like something he had heard long ago, his eyes gliding smoothly over the page with no effort, the words showing up, one after another, like good soldiers.

3

HE HAD MET STAR several weeks after he'd finally hitched a ride back to the valley from the hospital in Vancouver. At first he'd stayed a week in the medi-centre in Appleby, which was two rooms, a nurse practitioner, and a helipad out back. The real hospital was a charity joint in Vancouver, to which they'd medivaced him after they had x-rayed his leg and seen what a shattered mess it was. He'd lain on his back there for a month. As soon as he could walk they sent him home with a cast on his leg, and crutches.

It was late afternoon. He was limping up the hill from the old library, which was being maintained by a tiny group of grimly dedicated volunteers, past the patch of burnt-yellow grass and a couple of benches that made a desultory sort of park beside the bakery. He was on his way to the bar. It brewed its own beer these days, lousy sour stuff but drinkable.

"Hey, big man," she said, "got any bud?"

He ignored her, went limping on by like a giant crippled bear. He had lost a lot of weight in the hospital, but he was still a huge man, blond haired, with brown-grey eyes. His long hair straggled down his back. He knew he stooped a little when he walked now, and he hated that, was forcing himself to stand up straight. He didn't want to talk to anybody. He had spent the whole day alone without talking to anyone. It had become a hard habit to break.

"What's your problem?" she yelled after him. "You could act human, at least say hello."

He stopped, swung his head around, looked at her. She was young, but it was hard to tell how young. She had long blond hair tied into a mass of twisted braids, streaked with bits of red and purple dye. Her face was thin, her slanted eyes very green. Her pack lay beside her on the bench. There were always kids these days, travelling around. They were always showing up on the NewsNets. Usually they travelled in packs and people were terrified of them.

With good reason. They were angry kids. They had grown up with a lot of craziness, disasters, and now a lot of them were saying out loud they wanted revenge for the way things were. They wanted the things their grandparents had had, cars and big houses and lots of different kinds of food. But they usually didn't make it this far into the mountains anymore.

"Hello," he said. His voice sounded harsh and rusty.

"You look sad," she said. "It's okay. Everyone's sad. It doesn't matter. It doesn't mean anything."

"That's bullshit," he said.

"They're just feelings. They come, they go. It's all part of the dance, like the old book said. It doesn't matter."

"You're nuts," he said.

"And you're sad and lonely," she said, "big man, big sad man, big sad hairy man." He hadn't cut his hair and beard for a while. He kept meaning to get around to it.

She stared at him, laughing a little.

"Go to hell," he said. He turned and started to limp away again. Then he turned back.

"I suppose you're hungry?" he asked.

"Of course," she said. "You buying?"

"I guess so. C'mon."

They walked together in silence towards the Appleby

Hotel. But he didn't want to take her into the bar. She was too young and too pretty. Everybody would stare and afterwards they'd give him a hard time.

"I'll get some food," he said. "We can eat out here." She didn't want anything with meat. The hotel menu was pretty limited these days anyway. He got some cheese sandwiches made with fresh bread and local cheese. There was apple cider as well.

They flopped in the tall grass and weeds behind the hotel parking lot and ate the sandwiches.

After eating, she lit a joint. It had been made legal years earlier, but he still never smoked in public. It made him nervous, sitting there where anyone who knew him might see him with this crazy girl.

"You got a place to sleep?"

She shrugged. "Park, under a tree, anywhere. I got a tarp, sleeping bag. I'm fine. Anywhere I am, that's fine. Sometimes I sleep in a tree," she giggled, "or a cave. Sometimes I scare people. Boo!"

In the faintly greenish evening light, she did look gnomish. Her cheekbones were high, her green eyes slanted, her wide red mouth spread across her face. She had a sly way of looking out from under her hair and giggling when she talked. Freckles spread across her face. She looked about sixteen. He couldn't decide if she was pretty or actually kind of ugly.

"How old are you?"

"Oh shit, who cares? I get the same interrogation every time. How old are you, where do you come from, where are your parents? Who cares? I live nowhere, my parents are no one. I'm old enough to keep moving."

She lay back on the ground, stretched luxuriously. "That was pretty good," she said. "I gotta go pretty quick, find a place to sleep. Been on the road too long. Thanks for the food."

"You can sleep on the couch at my sister's," he said. "I'll sleep on the floor."

"Yeah, right."

"No, I mean it."

"Forget it," she said.

"Then meet me here for breakfast. We can eat and maybe walk around. You could come to the library with me. I usually go there and read."

"You got a library?" she said. "With real books? Hey, that's great. Sure. See you then."

She slipped on her pack, stood up, and was gone before he could say anything more.

He went back to Darlene's and lay on his cot in the back room where he'd spent too many months already, cursing his luck. But there was one good thing. He couldn't believe now how stupid and ignorant he'd been before the accident. He'd never read anything, never bothered with school, paid no attention to the NewsNets. But he was catching up now.

It was the bad dreams after his accident that got him reading. Maybe it was the damn drugs they gave him. Maybe it was the nights of staring into the darkness, wondering what was going to become of him now, and then dozing off, only to wake, sweating, from terrible dreams he barely remembered.

He'd started reading at night because it was the only way he could get to sleep. He discovered he could lose himself for long periods of time. Anything was better than the present he was trying to live through.

But this night the girl's face and voice intruded into his dreams, got twisted up with them as he was in the long process of falling asleep, where his dreams took on a mad life of their own, no matter how he tried to control them. In the morning he couldn't remember anything, just that the girl had twisted and twined herself through his sleep all night long.

She was waiting at the restaurant when he came in the next morning, sitting in front of a cup of tea, writing in a notebook. She smiled when she saw him. He'd combed his hair and tied it back and trimmed his beard with scissors. After breakfast she followed him to the library, which was a musty basement room smelling of mould and old paper.

"I been reading, oh, history and stuff," he tried to explain, boasting mixed with embarrassment. "I had some money left from the accident."

"What happened?" she asked, glancing at his leg. Sometimes he used crutches, sometimes he said to hell with it. Today he was trying his damnedest to walk normally, not limp, not drag the leg behind him like a dead log.

"Skidder," he said. "Piece of junk. Rolled down a hill. I jumped but the edge caught my leg. Threw me a ways. Hit a tree. Buggered up my back but it's okay now. They put a bunch of pins and stuff in the leg."

"Does it hurt?"

"Now and then. I can't go back logging. I got some free time out of it anyway."

She shrugged, dismissing the leg. "You're lucky," she said. "You got some time, you sit here, maybe you'll get to learn something. Me, I'm never gonna sit in a school again."

"Why not?" he said. "Maybe you could get those people — what are they called? FosterLove — to help out."

She shrugged again. "Those bastards," she said. "I wouldn't ask them for anything. They want to control your whole life. I like to read," she said. "That's good enough."

He paid the library fee for both of them. Inside the library, she surrounded herself with books on palmistry and astrology, industriously making notes in her journal. He read his way through a couple of NewsNets, then spent some more time looking up books to order. Even though he couldn't afford to order them, he wrote them down anyway.

Today he couldn't lose himself the way he usually did. He was too conscious of the girl. His skin next to where she was sitting had grown a life of its own. It prickled and itched. He kept shifting on his chair, trying not to scratch.

At lunch they went to the bakery and bought soup, and honey pastries for dessert. She called herself Star, she said. Her parents worked for some high-tech corporation that produced the NewsNets. She barely knew them, she said. She had been raised by a succession of babysitters. She hadn't been home for years. She had left home at thirteen, bored to death. She hated school. She hated the way everybody pretended things were okay and no one seemed to know what to do about anything. She had been on her own for five years now.

"My parents were so shit-scared of what was happening. We had security all around our house. They watched the NewsNets all the time. They believed them. So all they did was complain how everything was somebody else's fault. The ocean eating the fucking city, cars and gas costing a fortune, too many old people, all that shit. We had this stupid boring house in the burbs where nothing ever happened and they just went on living as though nothing would ever change. So I left. I had to sneak out, but after that it was easy."

"Aren't you scared, hitching rides?"

"Look," she said impatiently, "sex is just sex. You give it away, you trade it, what the hell. It's not that big a deal. Some trucker wants to get off with me, what do I care?"

After a while she went on. "I'm just trying to figure things out for myself. That's why I read when I get the chance. If I can figure out a way to live that makes some fucking sense, that's cool. If not, boom, well, there's lots of ways to go, overdose on something good. Go out high."

"That's chickenshit thinking," he said. He was afraid for her. She was so young, sitting there with her sad green eyes. But he knew what she meant. "Things aren't that bad. The weather's pretty fucking weird, but it'll straighten itself out. We've had shitty weather before."

"You don't know anything," she said. "You're just a dumb fucking redneck. You believe everything they tell you."

"Any dumb fuck can kill themselves," he said. "That's just giving up, letting them win."

"No way. That's winning."

They sat in silence. He was only silent because he had so much to say and he couldn't decide where to start. He wanted to talk about the weather. He wanted to tell how much everything had changed since he was young and how no one ever talked about it. He wanted to tell her about all the stuff he'd thought about in the hospital, the long nights lying awake while the pain in his leg bit at his nerves, how he'd seen things, how pictures and stories flowed through his head. Sometimes he thought he must be crazy, that maybe the accident had broken something in his head as well as his leg.

He wanted to tell her everything, give her his life, let her hold it in her lap. The words tangled and clogged in his throat so he could barely swallow.

When they were done, he paid, and together they walked back to the library. He wanted to tell her about the story he'd been making up. He'd even thought of trying to write it all down. But he wasn't sure how to start. She walked beside him, but she'd gone distant somehow. He could tell she was thinking of taking off. He wanted to say something that would make her want to stay, at least for a while.

"Hey, you like hiking, wandering around in the woods?"

"Sure, that's where I been hanging out. I been trying to learn about gardening, shit like that. Work for my food, you know? I don't like towns much. There's lots of people glad for the help."

"There's this place I found," he said, too eagerly. "Most of the land around town here is chopped up or logged or it's got somebody's trash on it. But this place looks like no one has ever been there. It's up a logging road a ways. We'd have to walk. Not sure how it'd be with this lousy leg."

She looked at him. The sun glinted off her green eyes. "Sure, let's go. We'll take some food, camp out."

"We'll have to hitch," he said, "or maybe I can get us a ride."

She shrugged. "Whatever," she said. "I don't give a shit what you do. Getting out of town sounds cool. I got nothing else to do. Let's go."

It took them a couple of hours of walking and hitchhiking short rides with farmers to find the place. It was west of Appleby off the old highway. When their last ride let them out, they shrugged on their heavy packs from the back of the truck and then hiked up the hill. Matt was sincerely worried about his bad leg. He'd got the cast off only two weeks ago. The leg still felt new, raw, exposed. He wasn't sure he could really depend on it. The nurse hadn't wanted to take the cast off, but he talked her into it.

It'd be a stupid thing to fall down in front of this girl, he thought. But he didn't, and they found the place at last. It involved some climbing, but not too much, and there it was, a flat bench on the mountain overlooking the valley; a creek beside it running through cottonwood, birch, alder, and aspen; and beyond that, a steep open meadow full of bunches of beargrass.

They made a camp under some big firs on a knoll by the creek. The ground was matted with needles. They could see the meadow, the creek, the nodding tops of the trees far below them.

Matt had a sort of tent, old and saggy, and he had a sleeping bag that had definitely seen better days. They didn't have much food — canned stuff they'd bought and some stale bread bought cheap and apples they'd scrounged from an abandoned orchard along the way. They couldn't afford real coffee, but they had some of the fake grain stuff that was everywhere these days.

Matt wondered if maybe he should have brought a gun. He had his father's old guns, stashed in the attic at Darlene's. He figured he might have to get them sometime soon. Maybe when he ran out of money, he'd have to go hunting. He couldn't afford a hunting licence for himself or a licence for the damn gun, but Darlene would like the meat. He knew that.

The first night they lay side by side without touching. Matt had promised himself on the way there that he wasn't going to make the first move. She fell asleep instantly. He lay there listening to her breathe. His leg ached so hard he had to clench his teeth to keep from making a noise. He kept moving, little tiny movements, trying to ease the leg and not wake Star.

When he woke in the morning, she was gone. He got up, lit the fire, put coffee on to boil, made toast in the frying pan from the stale bread. She showed up then, coming up from the creek. She'd washed her hair and face. She was only wearing a torn T-shirt and shorts, coming up the faint path with the sun on her bright gold hair, washed and shining. She came into his arms as naturally as air moving.

"Hey, big man," she said, pushing away and laughing when his embrace got too ferocious. "Slow down. I hardly know you. I want my breakfast."

But then she came back again, kissing him hard and furious in sudden need, and they left the toast and coffee to cool while he dragged his sleeping bag to a space under the trees with a clear view of the pond. They smoked a joint first. He hadn't smoked for a long time and it made him feel dizzy and afraid. They kissed until they were both breathless. He thought he'd be impatient and in too much of a hurry. God, it had been months, two years almost.

But it was nothing like that. She wouldn't let him hurry. She was demanding and imperious, showing him where to put his hands, his mouth. When she was ready, she let him move into her, but even then she controlled the pace, going slow, slow. She seemed far away and listening to something. He was vaguely conscious of the sun on his back, the birds calling overhead. He was vaguely conscious that his knee hurt, that his heart was pounding, that her body was slippery and shiny with sweat, that she felt like a piece of silk, come alive and twisting in his arms, that he was afraid of coming too soon, that he was being dominated and bossed around by this slip of a girl, that he was losing his head and falling, falling, falling into something new and terrifying, that all the blood and warmth in his body was gathering and rushing to his groin in an agony of need and pleasure and urgency, and that he had never, never felt quite like this before.

After, they lay side by side on the blanket, teasing each other and being silly. All the tension was gone, the sun was hot on their nakedness. They were lying on a mat of pine needles. A breeze came up and brought the scent of hot pine toasting in the bright sun, and mud and water from the pond, and the deep mouldy pungent earth underneath them.

They lay there most of the day, only getting up to eat and make tea over the fire. They ate most of the food they had, they ate and toasted their own bodies, and he promised to hitchhike to town soon and get some more food.

He slept that night with his arm around Star, even when it hurt him to lie so still. She slept as deeply as before, breathing with funny little fluttering snores that he found endearing.

They spent the next day lying in the sun and making love. When they got too hot, they went and played in the creek.

"Man, this would be such a great place to live," she said wistfully. "You could put a house right where you could see out over the whole valley."

They spent the rest of the afternoon talking about their house and how they would live and what they would do.

"There's no place for a garden, though," Star said.

"Don't need a garden," Matt said. "We'll sneak down at night, steal everything we need. We'll be outlaws. We'll do whatever we want. We'll have a whole posse of kids and they'll do whatever they want. We'll be like, what did they call them, hoods."

They smoked another joint and lay half dreaming in the sun. That night, for dinner, they had some burned bits of bread and the last of the apples.

The next morning he got up while she was still sleeping and hiked down the road to the highway. It took a long while before he got a ride into town and an even longer while before he could get a ride back again. He was exhausted, hot, and pissed off by the time he got up the hill. But he knew even before he got there that she'd left. He tried not to believe it, went down to the creek and around through the woods and back to the tent, but she was gone. Her pack was gone. The fire was out. She'd obviously left not long after him. She hadn't left him anything, not even a note.

He made supper and sat by the fire until it was very late.

Owls were speaking through the thick blackness. He kept hearing things moving in the woods, and once or twice he got up and called her name.

"Fucking bitch," he said out loud. His voice sounded faint, stupid, feathery, like something the wind might eat. His heart felt heavy enough to fall right out of his chest and shatter at his feet.

It was early dawn, and he was half asleep, before he realized how right she was. If she'd stayed, he would have grabbed on like a tick. He would have fallen hard as a hammer bouncing off concrete, and what could be more ludicrous than a crippled useless fool like him falling for someone like her? She was wise, so much wiser than him. He was amazed at how wise she was. He thought of the books she'd been reading in the library. She knew too much for her age, that was sure. He'd go back, get some of those books, see what it was she knew, see if maybe he could learn some of it too.

He wandered moodily around the clearing all that day, ate the food he'd brought, and lay beside the fire that night, on his back, staring upwards. A star fell across the sky, and another. He held to the taste of her, the smell of her still on his fingers.

He thought about going back to Darlene's small white frame house with the room in the back, the cot, a piece of stained rug. His clothes hung from nails in the walls.

It was good to be back out in the trees. He'd always loved the smell of trees. When he was a logger, he had loved the smell of dying trees. It meant work and woods and freedom of a kind. Now it was such a relief to be out of the town, away from the stink and noise of people. The smell of rotten burning lard from the grill in the hotel and the rank smell of brewing beer hung over the whole town. He had forgotten about being alone.

He thought about it later, after he made it back to Darlene's. He lay on his spring-squeaking cot with his leg propped on a pillow. What he wanted was to get the hell out of town and live in peace and quiet. He couldn't afford a piece of land, but there were lots of places where he could squat and not be noticed. Maybe even the place he had stayed with Star.

Rural areas had been gradually emptying for a while now. It was hard to live here unless you were a farmer or a gyppo logger. There were a few jobs still for people involved in what was left of the health or education systems, but the corporations didn't usually hire local. They brought people in and moved them out again in a year or so.

Farmers couldn't afford to get their crops out of the valley, so they traded locally. People had resorted to a complex system of barter. A couple of farmers had a solid market trading barley to the bar-brewery and taking their payment out in beer and meals at the restaurant.

He'd started to figure some stuff out when he was stuck in the hospital in the city. He didn't have a lot to do except read, stare out the window, watch the same boring News-Nets over and over. The hospital was crowded. People roamed the halls. A lot of the beds were full of old people dying slowly. The lucky ones had families who came in to care for them. The few harried nurses did the best they could.

Matt had sat by the window for long hours, watching the parade of buses, bicycles, pedicabs, even the occasional horse-drawn wagons pass by below. The street was loud with the noise of street vendors, beggars, and buskers. At meal time, many of the vendors roamed the halls, selling from trays or ancient shopping carts.

He was amazed by the vitality of the city, by the many odd wheeled contraptions that people used to get around.

Especially popular were jazzed-up versions of the electric scooters that had once been used by handicapped people. The city suffered less from the lack of cars than people in Appleby did.

Matt had been just a kid when gas rationing started. He remembered his dad bitching about it. Gas prices had been climbing for a long while; then there were restrictions on driving. Rural land prices started falling and kept on falling. People began to move away to places where there were still doctors, schools, ploughed roads in the winter. When people in rural areas complained about services disappearing, the government told them it was their choice if they wanted to live there.

Then there had been the onslaught of environmental laws forbidding every damn thing. He'd started working as a logger when he was fifteen. Most of the big mills had shut down, but there were still lots of small outfits getting by as best they could, scrounging for gas and dollars to keep going. A lot of guys experimented with alternative fuels, some of which worked some of the time. No matter what, people still needed lumber, still needed wood. For a long time the price of lumber kept pace with the price of gas, so the business was manageable.

But it didn't take long until everyone hated the Green laws. Logging got more and more regulated, along with hunting. Some people shrugged and tried to ignore the laws, but you couldn't just grab a gun and go hunting. The Green Protection officers were armed to the teeth, and they got to confiscate your gun on the spot if they caught you hunting without all the right paperwork. Sometimes they got to keep your house and land as well. They were paid by the corporations.

More and more huge chunks of land were licensed by the corporations. You were supposed to pay a fee to hunt or fish or cut firewood there. People argued and worried about whether to pay the fee or take a chance.

In the hospital, Matt realized he had always taken the way things were for granted. Now he had a million questions, although he didn't know how to find the information he needed to try and figure it all out. One day, when he was finally mobile, clumping around the hospital in his cast, he found a room in the basement full of boxes of books. Most of them were cheap mass-produced romance paperbacks, but there were a few old pre-millennium books that he pulled out and carried back to his room.

He asked the nurse about books. She brought him a palm reader with a bunch of books already loaded on it. They were new junk, and when he asked about changing the books, she pointed to the station in the hall. But he couldn't get what he wanted. He went back to the basement, dug out the oldest books he could find, the ones whose pages were stuck together and spotted with mould and fungus. He read and read, late into the night, until his eyes ached and burned.

The more he read, the more complicated it all got. It was obvious that things were a mess, and he decided he should at least try to figure out why. He should know something, try to get some control over his life. Christ, he was still a man, even if he was crippled.

It was time to quit leaning on Darlene, get the hell out. He could still have a life that had some independence and guts to it. He still had a bit of money. He was only about half crippled. He could work at something. He could take care of himself.

And someday he'd see Star again. He didn't know how or where, but he would. He was sure of it, as sure as he could be about anything.

4

MATT WAS SITTING dozing on the stump by the door when he heard the truck. He had spent the morning scrounging for late-season apples and plums at a deserted farm several miles away. Stuffed on fruit, he had fallen asleep in the heat from the late afternoon sun. He fell asleep too easily these days, wherever he was sitting. It worried him. The pain from his leg bit at him as soon as he woke up. Although he'd heard the truck turn off the highway and start up the logging road, he knew it wouldn't be able to get to his shack because there was no bridge over the creek. The driver would have to stop there and walk the rest of the way.

His rifle was sitting inside the door. He picked it up and slid into the bush behind the shack, climbed the sandy slope behind the fringe of alder and birch along the creek. On the top of the bank was a hollow into which he fitted, the rifle resting lightly on top of the granite ledge in front of him. He could see the shack, the clearing, and the road from here.

To the east, he could also see out over the broken, scarred land below him, then the flat land and swamp along the river, and the town beyond that. He had sat here before, pondering the rumpled tree-clothed land full of secrets. He was getting to know the hollows, the creeks, the places where the creeks emptied into the marsh, the places where cattle trails rambled along through the cottonwoods, under the tangled willow.

He was another secret. He was a secret these people in the truck didn't need to see or know about. He could hear their voices far below on the slope, voices ringing through the cold air. They were coming up the creek instead of following the road. Then they stopped somewhere, maybe by the rotten logs that had once made a bridge. He couldn't hear what they were saying. He gripped the rifle, aimed it at the green wall of brush.

"Pow," he said softly, "pow, pow, pow."

When they came to the edge of the clearing and saw his shack, they stopped, surprised. They didn't go inside, just walked around, looked at things. They laughed as they kicked the leaves covering the building materials he had dragged back with him, old boards, broken bits of plywood, tin cans full of nails he had spent days hammering out of the boards.

Matt's fingers clenched tighter on the gun. He hated the intrusion, the noise the men made moving through his woods, his clearing, as if nothing they did mattered, nothing made any difference to them.

They were close enough now that he could see one of them was a stranger, but the other one was Luke, his sister's useless sometime boyfriend. Luke was actually a distant cousin. Luke's father had been a cousin of Matt and Darlene's mother. Matt and Luke had been on the same crew when Matt had rolled the skidder. Before that they'd gone to school together, when there was a school, played pool sometimes. Luke and Matt went after the same woman once. She picked Matt, and after that, Luke hated his guts. He told people in the bar he was going to get Matt, but it was an empty threat. Luke was like that. Matt had stayed out of his way for years and then one day, there the bastard was, screwing his sister.

These days, Luke was another gyppo, scratching a living from it but doing better than other guys. He always seemed to know how to get around the rules. He was always sucking up to the GreenPro people or the corporate bureaucrats.

Hell, he'd told Matt, there were still trees on the mountains and more growing all the time. There was still a market. People always needed lumber and it might as well be him that supplied it. The men who owned the trucks and the small portable mills turned out semi-legal lumber that went out of the valley in the road trains.

Legally, the contractors could only sell to certain corporations that controlled the price so they didn't make much money. The black-market guys made more money, but it was risky because if you didn't have the right paperwork, corporations came after you. Still, it was a way of staying alive.

The two guys stood by the door of his shack. They looked for a long time at the pile of bones Matt had collected.

Matt came up behind them, said hello quietly, but they jumped anyway.

When they turned around, he saw that the GreenPro guy was wearing a green shirt with the shiny lapel button that they all wore. He was a young guy, blond hair, good-looking, blue eyes, well fed.

"What're you doing here, Luke?" Matt asked, ignoring the other guy. His stomach hurt.

"We're just looking around is all, Matt. Just looking at the country. Checking stuff out."

"What's to check?"

"You know this is a protected area?" said the guy in the green shirt. "You're not supposed to be living here."

"Just camping for a bit," Matt said.

"Sure," said the guy. "It looks like a permanent kind of camping."

"I keep an eye on nature," Matt said. "I like to help out if I can." He grinned, showing his teeth.

"We're looking for poachers, tree thieves, dope growers ... You see anything like that, you let us know, eh? And next time I come back, you'll be gone, right? And take your junk with you."

Matt nodded.

They stayed a little longer, but Matt didn't have much to say to them. He sat on the stump and stared at the trees while they wandered around, then flapped their hands at him and went back down the hill.

After the two men went away, Matt sat by his door for a long time. He was shaking, he couldn't get calm. He prowled around his shack, around the clearing, went down the hill to the road and came back up. They hadn't touched anything, but the silent clearing was still shimmering with the sense of what they had left behind, their stink, their intruding voices and spirits. It took the rest of the day for the clearing to settle, like the mud in a pond after something heavy has stirred it up. Until it settled, he couldn't do anything. He sat on the stump by his door, the rifle over his knees, doing nothing, staring down the hill. If he was a dog, he thought, the hackles on his neck would be standing up. He'd be sitting there growling deep in his throat.

He felt the spirit of the dead deer hanging around behind the leftover sense of the two men. It had already hung around for days; Matt could sense it when he went outside. He didn't have time to mess with it. Fall was getting on and he had to get more wood. There was lots of it in the bush around the cabin. But the spirit of the deer bothered him every time he picked up the chain saw.

And now that the GreenPro guy had come, he didn't want the noise. He hated the noise anyway. He used to like it, the blue smoke, the smell of oil and grease. But now he figured one day he'd come out in the morning and forget what a chain saw was for.

It was part of the whole process of what he now called in his head "the falling away." It seemed to him his life had ascended a long hill, up through discovery after discovery, until sometime in his mid-thirties, or maybe even earlier. He couldn't pinpoint the day it had all started to descend, shedding piece after piece of what he had thought was so important, of what he had worked to build up, to acquire, to hold onto. Maybe it had started with the death of his parents. Or maybe when he broke up with Elaine instead of getting married the way they were supposed to, the way everyone expected them to. Or maybe it really started with the accident and then the long dragging hours in the hospital, watching the black hands of the clock move round and round and round. It was his first experience of being helpless and confined and stuck in the rhythm of other people's schedules and ideas.

When he was fifteen, he was taller than most of the other boys. His parents joked that he was going to turn into some kind of giant freak. He was slow and quiet and careful with what he said. He had the feeling nobody saw much future for him and nobody much cared. One day he walked out of the building where he and other bored kids stared at computer monitors, walked to the crappy restaurant where there were usually one or two crummies parked.

He came in the restaurant, stared around. Four men were sitting in a booth by the window. He sat in the booth behind them and stared out the window. When they got up to leave, he followed them out to the parking lot.

One of them pointed at him, said something to another, and they all laughed. Then they got in the truck and drove away. He began walking along the highway, going north in the direction the truck had gone. He had no idea where he was going and didn't care.

That morning at breakfast his father had been raging again. His father was convinced that someone was out to get him — if not the government or the corporations, then some vast unnamed conspiracy involving the weather, the bosses, the dog down the street. His father was always raging about something. Matt had long ago quit listening. But he watched. He watched his father and the other men he knew. He had been watching them for as long as he could remember, trying to figure out how he fit in and how he should behave.

Even when he was young he hadn't liked his father much. He liked his mother a lot better, but it was obvious she wasn't very important compared to his father.

School hadn't helped him figure anything out. To hell with it, he had decided.

He kept walking along the road. It was late spring and there were red-winged blackbirds, swallows, robins, thrushes all singing and swinging from the trees and over the fields. The wild roses were blooming.

Luke pulled up behind him, driving a quad that had been fitted with a propane tank.

"Hey, loser," Luke said. "Where you going?"

Matt shrugged.

"Hey, want a ride? I got this thing from my dad."

Matt got on and they went down the road, up a hill, to where a logging crew was cutting and decking trees.

Luke's dad was directing the crew. When he saw Luke, his face twisted.

"Matt needs a job," Luke said. "His old man kicked him out of the house."

Old Man Palmer stared at him, grunted. "Yeah, like I need another useless cunt around here wasting my time."

But he hadn't said no, so Matt stayed and worked.

He started at the bottom. At least he knew how to use a saw and chains and hooks and ropes. His dad had seen to that.

After work, he went to the bar with the crew and then snuck home, hoping his dad would be asleep and he wouldn't have to explain where he'd been.

He'd been drinking stolen or bootlegged booze in other people's basements for years. He liked drinking, but it bored him as well. Now he discovered it was work he liked. It was work he went after, hard gritty dirty work that demanded all the strength that was in him, that sent him home at the end of the day exhausted and determined to work just as hard the next day, to be a man among men, never quit, never whine, never say he was hurt or couldn't take it. His dad just grunted when he found out where Matt was spending his time. His mom whined at him.

That's what he had done until it all changed.

Even after the accident he hung around, went to the bar, drank his share, bewildered by the loss of the club of working men he had once belonged to, trying to find its substitute in the hard-drinking, storytelling club of the bar. But after a while it all let him down. These weren't real men either. They did nothing. The stories were the same every night, the same tired boasting. But he kept going anyway, and afterwards he'd go home to Darlene's house, crawl into his unmade bed, and stare into the dark.

One morning he heard voices in the kitchen. When he came out, Elaine was sitting with Darlene, exchanging gossip.

"Where'd you blow in from?" Matt asked, pouring himself a cup of Darlene's crappy coffee, which wasn't really coffee at all but some dandelion roots she had roasted and ground, and to which she had added a tiny bit of real coffee.

"Northern Saskatchewan. We came back to close down the old house. Can't sell it. We're just going to lock it up and leave it, at least until things get better."

"What the hell's in northern Saskatchewan?"

"Land," she said simply. "You can grow wheat there now if you got horses to work with. Big market. The American Midwest is having a hell of a time. No water. No crops. We're making money, Matt, not a lot, but more than we had."

Elaine had been his first real girlfriend. He had been eighteen when he met her. She came up to him one night in the bar. He was sitting by himself and she'd come in with Luke Palmer.

"Hey, you got anything you have to do tomorrow?" she said. "I need some guy to help me load my truck."

He had to look twice to be sure she was talking to him. He didn't know her, hadn't seen her before. She was older than him, in her late twenties. She had to leave, she said, because she was driving truck for a living and she had to take a load of stock somewhere early the next morning. He got up at dawn the next day, drove to the farm where she was helping load pigs into the back of an old truck that sagged on its springs and belched black diesel smoke from its exhaust. She was down in the pens, in the dust and shit, whip in one hand and her small black stock dog at her heels. She was dressed in tight blue jeans, a denim shirt, expensive tooled cowboy boots.

"What the hell you lookin' at?" she snarled when she saw him. "Come to watch a damn circus or what?" He climbed over the fence and helped turn back a pig that was trying to climb the poles. After, drinking coffee and wiping the dust off their faces, she explained that she was just cranky and hadn't meant to snarl at him.

When the pigs were loaded, she looked at him.

"Hey, big boy, you coming?" she asked. They drove the pigs out to a corral on the main road where one of the big road trains would pick them up. Then she offered him a beer and they drove back to her house.

She was all over him the minute they got in the door. She was hot and sweaty and tired and gave him shit every way she could, bit him, hit him, got on top like he was some kind of bucking steer and yelled at him. The goddamn dog sat in the corner the whole time and stared. He never had managed to make peace with that dog.

They'd had a stormy relationship where they fought and broke up and made up in bed until the day they were in the bar together and she started dancing with some visiting truck driver. The dancing got slower and slower and more hip grinding. Matt got drunker and drunker. Finally he got up and threw the guy through the window. That ended that.

So now, many years later, here was Elaine showing up at his sister's house, and he was sitting there being crippled and useless. He had no answer when she said, "So what are you doing with yourself?"

"Nothing," he had said. "I'm doing nothing and that's fine by me." He hadn't stayed to talk after that, just slammed out of the house and gone to the library. He still felt bad about that.

He shook himself. Why did he keep losing himself in the past? He got bitter if he thought too much. It was better to get on with stuff.

He needed to get started on the plans for his house. What the hell had that GreenPro guy really been up to? He supposed they could kick him out of here, but they'd probably be quiet about it. The government didn't like to take on squatters. It looked bad if it got violent and made it onto a NewsNet. Word could spread fast that the government was throwing enterprising poor people off their land.

He couldn't figure out how to build a house out of bones.

Getting bones wasn't a problem. Lots of animals got hit on the road — porcupines, coyotes, skunks, rabbits, owls, deer, moose, elk. There were more animals these days and fewer trucks, but it hadn't slowed the slaughter. To save money, trucks had gotten bigger and longer. Some of them were like small trains now. They didn't stop for anything or anyone.

Maybe he'd take some of the fruit he picked to Darlene's, talk to Luke, see what Luke knew. It was getting so he hated staying there. She disapproved of everything he was and had become, though she didn't usually say much. She didn't have to. She took his clothes immediately to the laundry, suggested he have a bath, cooked too much food and suggested he take all the leftovers. She was struggling along on the little money she made working as a clerk in a video store.

They'd grown up in a normal family, whatever that was. Sort of normal, if you didn't count the violence. Their dad worked at what was left of the sawmill, their mom stayed home, and they had a little house up the hill on the same block as the United Church, two blocks from the elementary school.

Their parents had died, one right after the other, while Matt was working as a skidder operator and his sister was happily married and it looked like everything was going to be fine. Their dad had a heart attack and then their mom went downhill after that. She got some kind of fast-growing cancer. The nurse hadn't even suggested treatment, just sent her home with painkillers. Matt sat with her while she was dying.

"I'm sorry, sweetie," she'd say, but then she'd start crying. Matt couldn't figure out what she was apologizing for. For his shit of a father? For her lousy stunted life?

Now he and Darlene had each other and the town they'd grown up in.

Matt had been thinking about the old man and what a bastard he was just before the skidder reared up into the air like a frightened mad horse and he could see the trees coming at him like spears before he jumped.

The rising of that metal edge had cut a line between what he knew and what he had never expected. He had seen clearly, in that moment of flying through the air, that he knew almost nothing about life when death was hovering so close to the edge of it. He'd seen, then, what a lot he had to learn.

5

LIA GOT A RIDE with almost the first truck that went by
after she stuck out her thumb. The driver was old, fat, grey
haired, and smoked marijuana as he drove. He offered Lia a
hit as soon as she got in the cab, but she turned it down as
politely as she could. Lately, dope made her nervous. This
trip was making her nervous. She'd left without thinking or
planning, all by herself on an October morning, carrying an
ancient brown pack with one broken zipper.

She walked down Granville and along Hastings. It took
her the whole morning to get to the freeway. She sat by the
side of the broken pavement while bus trains thundered
past. When she saw the truck coming, she stood up. She
remembered from when she was a kid, her grandmother had
pointed out the long-distance transports, with their solar
panels and the extra-sized cab to house the batteries.

The truck driver had taken her as far as Hope. Then she
got out and started walking up the long hill that led out of
town. A cold wind blowing up the hill lifted her jacket off
her back.

As she walked, she thought about her grandmother. She
had mourned her grandmother every day since the raid on
the apartment, since her life had exploded into senseless
bits. Why weren't they both where they belonged, on the

farm? The questions rolled an endless circle in her head, like a whirlpool in a river.

She was a street kid. On her police file she was listed as deceased. After her first bitter disillusionment, when she had been so excited and happy about being free, about getting out of the black hole of a room where she had been held for months — she never had figured out exactly how long — oh God, how she wanted to tell her grandmother about it, she wanted so desperately to fling herself into her grandmother's arms and tell her how horribly, how hideously she had suffered. She wanted to go back to Appleby, to her friends there. She wanted the farm and the animals and the garden and the lake, the glowing grey rocks and pink-yellow sand at the beach. Her friends. She wanted her life back.

Instead, what she got were the sullen faces of bureaucrats, the sulking incomprehension of faces that only wanted her to go away and stop bothering them.

The police were the enemy. There were stories of kids who had disappeared into police jail cells and never been seen again, stories of kids who had been tortured, stories of kids who came back out on the streets with their minds changed — zombies, they called them. People said the police planted a microchip in their heads so they could be controlled, so the police could use them to figure out everything a group was doing. People said the police would only bust someone for a crime if they were paid to do so. After they busted kids, they sold them. They used the money for their own fat selves. Those were the rumours.

She hadn't paid attention. She didn't have time for much beyond bare survival. Even after she found the squat, it took most of her time to figure out how to keep herself warm and dry. She had to learn a lot, and fast. Christy had taught her how to keep clean and healthy. A lot of kids died, usually from some combination of drugs, bad food, malnutrition, cold, and damp. Most of them had no future and didn't want one, but she did.

Then she had to figure out some way to be useful. People in the squat wouldn't just feed her for nothing. They made the rules brutally clear. She had to contribute, either drugs, money from panhandling or prostitution, or stolen items that were worth selling. She wasn't good at any of that, so for a while, in desperation, she turned herself into a semi-servant, cooking and cleaning up after people, running errands. Then she got good at finding food. She began to figure out when to hit the right dumpsters behind the stores, didn't mind standing in line for hours at the different food banks, some of which were now as large as supermarkets and had been long since taken over by one of the big charity corporations.

Doing the food banks was hard. You couldn't get food unless you could prove that you had done several hours of "community work," which usually meant cleaning the houses and yards of rich folk under the watchful eye of a guard from FosterLove. Sometimes it also meant fucking the guards. But the guards were easily fooled. All kids looked alike to them, so the squatters took turns doing this chore until they had enough credits for one really good food-bank run.

What she missed most were books. She couldn't afford the fee the one big library charged. When she could manage the time, she went to the junk stores and scrounged for old books she couldn't afford, then stood there reading until the owner or the security guard chased her out. Real books cost more than she could ever dream of affording.

Magazines and newspapers were on the internet, but she couldn't afford that either. Only the corporate NewsNets were free. They were on every corner, lying about things.

Someone told her once about how newspapers used to be delivered to people's houses every day, and whole families sat around reading them. That was when people had shelves full of books. Weird, she thought. Imagine just having books on the shelf to keep for yourself.

She kept walking. Traffic was scarce. A couple of trucks went by, but they were local. The men inside stared curiously at her. One waved and pointed sideways to indicate they weren't going far. They ignored her outstretched thumb. She went on walking. A creek foamed and boiled in the deep green gully far below the road. Ravens floated lazily in the sky. The pavement was rough and broken. In places, water had rutted the road and torn the banks away. Trees leaned out over the steep cutbank above the highway. Occasionally clumps of trees had slid down the banks and onto the road. Someone had pushed them off the pavement and back into the ditch, where they had formed a dam, trapping water and gravel behind them. There was a deep crack across the pavement. It looked ready to give way at any moment.

Lia kept walking. Finally she heard a truck grinding its way up the hill behind her. It stopped and the driver leaned over and opened the door for her. Lia climbed up into the warm cab, settled into the cracked and broken seat. As the driver started clashing through his series of gears, she looked around the cab. It looked like the guy ate and slept in the place. The dash was covered with tools, greasy rags, dead grass, clothes, hats, a thermos, indecipherable pieces of machinery. The floor under her feet was a floating mass of jetsam gone rotten with mud and age. The cab reeked of must, age, sweat, and something else, some rank smell she couldn't identify.

"So where you going?" said the guy. He was young and good-looking, but his clothes were covered with grease, sawdust, mud, and something that looked like melted plastic.

"East, maybe north," Lia said.

"Yeah, well, guess we're going the same way then." He grinned at her. She shrank into her corner. They drove the next few hills and curves in silence. She snuck glances at him out of the corner of her eye. He was concentrating on driving, and she began to relax. The truck was the most ancient thing she had ever seen. It seemed to be cobbled together out of several trucks and duct tape. The windshield was held in place by several layers of duct tape, and the window beside her was also lined with duct tape through which the wind whistled and played like a whole orchestra of manic tuneless flutes.

Lia closed her eyes. It was late afternoon and she had been walking and travelling since morning. The cab was warm. She wanted to fall asleep, but she was too guarded and tense. When she opened her eyes again, the guy was grinning at her.

"Like my truck, eh? Looks like shit but it always gets there, at least most of the time," he yelled over the noise of the motor and the manic flutes.

"Yeah, it does look like shit," she yelled back. "Smells like it too."

He laughed at that. "Yep, and that's what it runs on," he said, "shit and more shit."

So that was part of the stink — methane from a shit-eater tank in the back.

"That and water and sun and whatever else I can get for free," he continued. "Can't afford that new bio-diesel crap they got in the cities. Out here, you do it for yourself or you don't go no place, no how."

Out here. She was out here now, out where she belonged. She stared hungrily out the window. They were beside a river running a translucent crystal brown over stones, moss padding the banks, the peeling ragged trunks of alders hanging precariously over the water.

"What river is that?" she yelled.

"That there is the lovely Similkameen," he said, "and soon as we get over this goddamn mountain range, we'll be down in the equally lovely Similkameen Valley, just cruising along beside all the happy farm folks scratching out their little livings. You been this way before?"

She had, but she didn't remember it. She kept looking for something she recognized.

"Long time ago," she said. "I was just a kid."

"So, you been living in the big city for a while, eh?"

"Too fucking long," she said.

"You know, last spring when I was doing this same run, I picked up a chick about your age. Said her name was Star. Said she was looking for someplace to live."

Lia was silent. The guy was so obviously fishing now, looking for information. She had to figure out who he was and what he wanted before she told him anything.

"I dropped her off in a place called Appleby. You ever heard of it?"

She shook her head, but her heart leapt. Star. Star had come this way, had at least found the town Lia had told her about.

"My name is Magnus, by the way," he added. "I do this run a couple of times a year. I'm not licensed, so every once in a while I have to make a payment to someone. But I get by. Everything is tied up in rules and regulations. Corporations gotta keep control."

"What happened to Star? Did you ever hear anything?" Her voice was shaking.

"Nope, never heard nothing. Didn't expect to. People disappear into these hills all the time, go and do their own thing, hide out, make a life. Or not. Lots of crazy people around. She a friend of yours?"

"Sort of."

He nodded at that. "Figures," he said. "You look alike. Hey," he added, "you want to stop, get something to eat?"

"Got no money," she said.

"Yeah? Well, I can barter enough for fuel and food," he said. "Guess I can spring a bit for something for you. Star didn't have money either. You know, it's pretty stupid, heading up here with no food or money. Who the hell do you expect to look after you?"

Who the hell do you think you're lecturing? she thought, but she didn't say it. When you were receiving a favour, you didn't lip off; you just smiled and said, "Have a nice day," with the hate and the "fuck you" hidden just under the smile.

"I'll be fine," she said.

But all he did was laugh. "Hey," he said, "was I lecturing? My mom says that's what I do best. She says I probably inherited it. I come from a long line of ranters and lecturers. Pay no attention."

He held the door for her when they went inside the small restaurant. Much of the town looked boarded up. This seemed to be the only place still alive and humming with life. Several people were sitting in booths, nursing steaming cups of something. They all stared as Magnus and Lia came in.

"Hey, Jeannie," Magnus said cheerfully, "you got any real coffee? Don't give us any of that fake grain-flavoured shit. We got a long trip behind us and a longer one ahead."

Jeannie had frizzy red hair going grey at the roots, a stained apron, scarlet lipstick, and blue eyeshadow. She grinned at Magnus, poured them both coffee, glanced curiously at Lia before sauntering back behind the counter.

"Why are they all staring?" Lia hissed at Magnus.

"Huh? Oh, just to see if you're anybody they know. You're in the boonies now, kid. Relax. No one really gives a shit who you are or what you do, but they're always curious. You're a stranger. They stare 'cause they got nothing better to do."

Their food arrived — fried chicken, salad with thick-sliced tomatoes and white cheese, good coffee, pan-fried potatoes. Lia tried not to gulp it down.

"They grow it all out back," Magnus said, "their own chickens, big garden, greenhouse, local potatoes from down the road. Make their own cheese. Get electricity from the river. Not bad, eh? People come from all over to eat here."

"You from around here?" Lia asked reluctantly. She didn't want to ask questions. All she wanted from this guy was a ride, didn't need someone nosing into her life. Besides, he kept lecturing away like some know-it-all adult when he wasn't that much older than her.

Except now that she was sitting across from him, she realized how good-looking he was. He had a lean brown face, eyes that were almost grey, almost green, almost blue, changing with the light. A lock of thick, brownish black, curly hair hung over one side of his forehead. When he smiled, his teeth were even and white. He had broad bony shoulders under what looked like a woven hemp shirt.

"I'm from down the road," he grinned. "How about you?"

"The same," she said evenly.

They ate their food without more conversation and then Lia wandered outside, waited while Magnus crawled under the truck with a wrench. There was a lot of banging. Then he slid out from under the truck, climbed up in the back. It sounded like he was throwing things around.

He jumped down, yelled, "Might be good for a few more miles. Ready to go?"

She climbed back up in the cab, and with a lot of groaning and banging they moved off. This time, when sleep came to visit, she didn't resist, closed her eyes, slid back against the dusty seat, and sank into a much-needed rest.

6

LIA WOKE UP when they stopped. It was dark. The truck eased to a halt and Magnus jumped out. Then the door opened and he jumped back in again. "Sorry," he said, "the lights gave out. Can't see to drive. Can't see to fix them. We're somewhere just out of Rock Creek. God, you slept for hours. I thought you were dead. Anyway, we can sleep here for a while and get going in the morning. Probably won't be too many people along tonight. This road doesn't get a lot of traffic."

She was fuzzy headed. "Where are you going to sleep?" she asked.

"Right here."

He bunched up a jacket that had been lying on the floor and stuck it behind his head, pulled an old sweater over his shoulders.

"What about me?" she said, enraged. "What the hell am I supposed to do?"

"Whatever you want," he said, and immediately went to sleep.

She sat there listening to the motor tick as it cooled. The cab was cooling off as well. She opened the door, got out of the truck, went to pee. They had pulled onto a grassy bench beside the road. The sky was clear and clean and full of stars. The air was crisp and cold. She could feel the tiny hairs in her nose curling as she breathed. It must be well below freezing. Mist streamed off the open river far below.

She went to the edge of the pull-off, squatted to pee, and stared down as she did so, trying to see through the silver starlit dark. A steep slope of long grass dotted with black trees sheered almost straight down to the river. There were a couple of dim lights in the valley, far away. She heard a distant cow, an even more distant dog, then an indistinct yipping bark that she remembered was probably a coyote.

God, she was almost home. She took deep breaths of the chill air, laden with the smell of earth, sage, the river, pine. She was almost home. She would never leave again. She finished peeing, wiped herself on some grass, went and got back in the truck. Magnus appeared to be completely unconscious, head rolled to one side, snoring gently. She wasn't sleepy. There was nothing to read. Her legs twitched restlessly. She sat a while longer, then got back out of the truck. She began to walk along the road. Her feet crunched in the sand and gravel that had spread over the pavement. The edge of the pavement was rotted and broken. In places it was barely one lane wide.

She walked down the hill, looking at the few dim lights in the valley, trying to imagine what sort of people lived there, what sort of lives they lived. Did they lie down to sleep at night curled against each other, smiling with the knowledge that they were home and safe and secure? Did they get up each morning blessing the day, that they had each other and peace and freedom? How did they survive? What did they do?

She didn't hear the truck coming until it was almost upon her. It was creeping down the hill with no lights. The motor, probably electric, was only a gentle thrumming. She turned, startled, and the driver, seeing her shadow in the darkness, turned on a thin pencil of white light, almost blinding her.

Instinctively she dived for the edge of the road and over the side, rolling down the gravel-and-thistle-blended hillside, landing on a rock beneath some brush that knocked the wind out of her.

She lay still. She could hear men's voices above her. They had stopped the truck and were walking along the road. The beam of light probed down at her and she ran again, panicked, crashing through thick sagebrush. She fell, and her hand landed on cactus. She almost screamed then but choked it back, stumbled up, and kept on running in the direction of Magnus and his truck.

They were running along above her, staying on the road. She crouched behind a rock, the laser light sweeping in slow circles around and above her. After a while the voices and the light moved off, and she crept out of her hiding place and began to walk, step by careful step, trying to be as silent as possible, towards the bank. It was hard to see, so she climbed it by feel, scrabbling on her hands and knees, digging her feet in for purchase, grabbing on to twigs, roots, stones with her hands. She made it up the bank and flopped onto the pavement, gasping for breath.

She lay still, listening again. She could hear the truck motor and its quiet dark thrumming, so she knew they hadn't gone away. What if they found Magnus, deep in his unconscious exhausted sleep? He was the only safety she had. She began to walk up the road, coming down flat on her feet. The gravel crunched as loud as thunder. There was no way to walk quietly on it. When she got to the bench, the dark hulk of the truck looked peaceful enough. She waited. Her fingertips were aching and the palms of her hands burning from the gravel. Her legs ached. Was it really only this morning she had left Vancouver?

She loosened the chain that was wrapped around her arm,

held it ready to swing. She began to walk towards the truck, very slowly, every muscle tense and poised for running.

There was nothing. She was almost at the door, reaching for the handle, when the light caught her and she screamed. A man lunged and caught her arm. She swung the chain and felt it connect. The man swore hoarsely, then began reeling her in like a fish. She fought. She was a good fighter. She scratched, bit, kicked, but the man was huge and strong.

"Turn the light here," said another voice. They shone the light on her face, blinding her.

"This your truck?" one said. "Guess it and you belong to us now. Too bad for you, eh?"

She said nothing. Where the hell was Magnus? Why did they think it was her truck?

"Guess again," said a cool voice out of the darkness. "Unless you want to lose an arm or a leg, put her down and step away from the truck. Move slowly. Leave the light on."

Everything froze for a moment. Then Lia wrenched her arm free.

"You dumb shitheads," she snarled at them. "It didn't occur to you I had a partner? Do what he says or he'll blow your fucking heads off." She hoped she wasn't lying. She hoped he had a gun or some kind of real threat. She took the flashlight away from them, shone it on their faces. She stepped backwards, away from them, step by step towards Magnus's voice, keeping the light on them.

"I want you to walk down the road to your truck," he said, "then I want you to get in it and get the hell out of here. I'll watch until you're gone. I don't give a shit what fucking business you're up to. I never saw you and I don't care. Just get the hell out of here."

They took him at his word. Magnus followed them. Lia got in the truck and huddled against the seat. She pulled a torn green wool sweater off the seat and over her, tucked her hands into her pants to try to warm them up.

When Magnus came back, he climbed into the cab.

"I'm sorry," he said. "It's my fault. I should have warned you. It's dangerous around here these days, a lot of smuggling, a lot of people running water or pot or ethanol or illegal logs, whatever they can make a buck on. Then there's the wild dog packs, the rattlesnakes, the wild pigs, the fire ants. It's not a fun place to go for a walk. Hey, you okay?"

"I'm freezing," she said through clenched but clattering teeth. "I can't seem to get warm."

"C'mere," he said, sliding across the seat. "It's okay. I'll just hold you. I won't do anything else. I think you're in shock."

"I'm okay," she gritted, but she let him hold her. After a while she stopped shaking. "My hand feels like it's burning," she said. "Can you look at it?"

"Good thing I kept the flashlight."

"I fell on something. I think it was a cactus."

"Hold on."

He held her hand, rooted around on the dash until he found a pair of tiny pliers, began to pull out the spines.

"I got some aloe vera somewhere," he said. "Hang on." He ducked down, fished around under the seat, came out with a bottle of cloudy liquid. "Got some goldenseal in it, some other stuff. My mother made it. It'll fix anything."

She looked suspiciously at him. She could still feel his warmth on her hand. He spread the lotion on her palm, then tucked her hand, which felt much better, into her jacket.

"Think you can sleep now?"

"I don't know. I'm still shaking."

"If you don't mind, I mean, if it doesn't upset you, you can curl up against me. It'll keep you warm anyway."

"Where I come from, nobody asks if you mind anything. They take it or you fight them off. That's it."

"Does that mean it's okay?"

"I'll be fine," she said and leaned her head against the door, closed her eyes. The snarling faces of the two men rose in front of her and she opened her eyes again.

"Okay," she said, "okay," and she leaned against him. He covered them both with the warm wool sweater. He was asleep again almost immediately. She leaned against his chest, feeling it rise and fall, feeling the rhythm of his heart, smelling his rough male smell, until she also fell asleep.

The next morning, as soon as it was light, they began travelling again. They drove all day. Lia was starving and dusty and dishevelled when they pulled into a yard near nightfall.

"Food," said Magnus simply. "C'mon."

She followed him into a log house, which was a blaze of heat, light, people, children, dogs, noise. She leaned against the door, terrified, but Magnus motioned her to the table. A plate of heaped food appeared in front of her.

"Eat," said the tall smiling woman who put it down. "We'll talk later." Beside her, Magnus was shovelling in food and somehow talking at the same time. He had a kid in his lap and two more hanging on to his sleeves. The dogs were sniffing his boots and wagging their tails, and somehow he had enough hands to eat, hold the kids, and pet the dogs. She realized suddenly he was home, this was his home. He hadn't said a word. She was suddenly furious. Wasn't she allowed to know his family?

There was meat on her plate with gravy, mashed potatoes, carrots, squash, spinach, all glistening with butter. There was a glass of juice in front of her, another glass of milk. She had never seen so much food. Where did they get it? When her plate was empty, a bowl of sliced peaches and a plate of cookies appeared in front of her. She ate until she was dizzy and warm and falling over with exhaustion.

The door kept opening and closing. People were coming in. She bent her head down and stared at her plate. Everyone knew each other. People came up to Magnus, hugged him, then looked curiously at her.

The tall older woman kept touching him, ruffling his hair, putting her hand on his shoulder, leaning against him. She looked at him as if she couldn't quite believe he was there, couldn't take in enough touching and looking to be sure it was him.

Now there was coffee, real coffee, unbelievably rich smelling. This food was beyond any dreams she had ever had in Vancouver. Behind her, someone started to play a violin, and she swung around on her chair. A tall man was standing in the wide living room. She noticed that the light came from oil lanterns hanging from the ceiling, that people were spread all around the room, sitting on the floor, on chairs, on cushions, all ages, most dressed in pale-brown handwoven clothing like Magnus's shirt. There was a huge stone fireplace against one wall. The kitchen was at one end of the room, a row of windows at the other. Stairs beside the fireplace led up to a second floor.

The fiddle player kept going until someone with a drum joined him, and someone else with a flute. The little kids all immediately started dancing, laughing, the littlest ones falling down or falling into someone's lap. The music kept going, more food appeared on trays, then jugs of wine. A glass of wine appeared in front of Lia. She had lost sight of Magnus. She tried to stay in the background as much as possible. People looked at her but no one spoke. She felt miserably left out and alone. A woman got up and danced by herself, a wild whirling dance. Then a man joined her. After that, both men and women stood up to dance. Lia drank some of the wine, felt her head begin to spin, put the wine glass down on the table.

"Here's to Magnus," someone yelled, and everyone raised their glasses and cheered. Magnus had joined the musicians now, playing a guitar. He looked up when they yelled his name, grinned, and went back to playing. He looked very serious as he played.

The happier everyone looked, the more miserable Lia became. She didn't belong here. She wondered if there was a back door, if she could get her pack and be on down the road. A giant orange cat came and rubbed, purring, against her legs, then a black-and-white puppy. Despite herself, Lia felt her eyes closing.

The tall woman was beside her. "C'mon," she said, "you're exhausted. There's a room and a bed and a hot bath if you'd like it." Lia thought about it, nodded.

The woman led Lia up the stairs and into a cool dark room, lit a candle, showed Lia the bathroom, started the hot water running.

"Sleep as long as you like," she said. "I'm the mother of that wild boy you came in with. We'll have a visit in the morning or you can be on your way, whichever you prefer. My name is Amara but everyone calls me Ama. Just call or come and get me if you need anything. This party will go on for a while yet."

"Thanks," Lia muttered, got herself in and out of the bath and into the bed. Just before she fell asleep, the shock of the woman's name hit her. She knew her. Amara was someone her grandmother had known, had talked about. So she was home, or nearly home. In the morning she'd find something out. And with that thought she was asleep.

The sun woke her. The house was silent. She got dressed in her stiff dirty clothes and crept down the stairs. Despite the food of the night before, she was ravenous.

There was a plate of cold pancakes on the table, a jug of syrup, butter, milk, and apple juice. Lia ate, waiting tensely for someone to come in, but no one did. Her pack was still sitting by the door where she'd dropped it the night before. She picked it up and went hesitantly outside, wondering what to do next. Two tall figures standing in the garden saw her and waved.

"You know, you look so familiar," said Ama.

"I'm Lia," she said. "I used to live somewhere around here."

"Ohmygod, it is you. Oh, my, God." Ama came forward and wrapped her arms around Lia. She was weeping. "Oh, God, we heard about what happened. We mourned you. We couldn't believe you were lost. I always thought you would come home. Oh, my, God, I've got to tell the others. Magnus, go ring the emergency bell."

"No, wait," Lia said, "don't, not yet."

"No, you're right," said Ama. "We have to talk. We have to talk and talk and talk. Your grandma was a lovely person, a great neighbour. The police are so useless. They never told us what really happened."

"Come inside," she added. "Come and tell us what you know and we'll tell you what we know. Your being here is a miracle, just a miracle." Lia felt tears come, her legs almost crumpled, but Ama and Magnus caught her in their arms, held her up while they wept together.

7

"CLIMATE INSTABILITY," Matt muttered to himself. In the dark, lurching up the hill to his shack meant wading through a frozen broken series of snowdrifts. "Climate fucking crap." The previous winter it hadn't snowed at all. Now this winter it seemed like it would never quit snowing. Matt hadn't put up enough wood.

It was nearly impossible to get to town. Sometimes it took weeks after a heavy blizzard before the snow finally melted off the roads and local cars and the huge road trains could run again. Hitchhiking in and out of town with groceries and other supplies was hard work. His knee swelled and grew hot and sore. He limped heavily when he walked.

After he ran out of wood and food, he began spending more time with Darlene. On those nights he stayed in town, he went to the bar and sat in the corner, drinking four or five beer. Most nights, Luke Palmer came in as well. Or he was at Darlene's whenever Matt showed up. Luke and Darlene would be sitting in the kitchen, drinking coffee and talking. Darlene would be giggling like a teenager, her face pink. Luke brought her stuff. He was good at scavenging. There wasn't a dead car or a piece of scrap metal left in the countryside. Luke had found them all, hoisted them into his truck, brought them to town, and sold them to the recycling plant.

One night, when Matt was almost ready to leave the bar, he limped by Luke's table.

"What the fuck do you want with Darlene?" he said. "Why do you go around there? Why don't you leave her alone?"

"Fuck you," said Luke, standing up. He was a tall man with black hair tied in a ponytail. His face was brown and creased. He had crazy eyes, one green, one blue. "She can do what she wants. You're not her keeper. From what I hear, you can't even look after yourself. From what I hear, she's doing all the looking after, herself and you."

"You're a stupid bugger," Matt said, "and you stink. You leave a stink in the world wherever you go. Just stay the hell away from me and what's mine."

He walked on before Luke could hit him. He'd seen the look in his eyes. The only thing holding him back had been the thought of hitting a cripple, of what people would say. Matt limped out of the bar and into the snow. It was coming down thick again. The snow was already piled in huge banks along the edge of the sidewalks. There was talk of avalanches in the mountains and floods come spring.

Matt walked along the street. He passed the pile of snow that was burying the park where once, long ago, he'd met Star. Star was on his mind most of the time. He had no photo to remember her with. She hadn't left anything behind except the memory of that afternoon, the memory of her slim swift body, the hip bones jutting beneath the white skin, her small breasts under his hands and lips, how her nipples had leapt to his tongue, how she had taken his hand and placed it between her legs, showed him how to find the small bud of the clitoris, folded within sweet pink lips, and how he had put his hand and then his tongue on it, how she had made him wait, how she had played with his whole body, ran her tongue, her hands, over every inch of it until he thought he might melt from the sheer pleasure of it. When she finally let him enter her, she still controlled things, holding his ass in her hands, slow and demanding and fierce and then finally, finally, letting it go and go, out of control, the two of them bucking furiously on their heat-soaked hillside, yelling and moaning like two mad fools, until he felt his soul rush out of him and join with hers so that they were irrevocably, cosmically one, something he had never felt before and knew he would never feel again. They had lain there together, side by side, in the sun, not speaking, not moving. He had never been so content.

So now he very calmly knew that wherever she was, they were still connected and someday she would return. It didn't stop him from missing her. It didn't stop him from wondering where the hell she was, wishing he was there with her, picturing her fucking other people, a whole succession of other people, male and female and groups and whatever, which was her right, but which made him sick with fear. He should be there to protect her and he couldn't do it. The world was a dangerous sad place, no place for someone like her. But she had her own protection. She was like some kind of angel in her own right. She'd be okay. He knew that. It just didn't stop him from worrying.

He walked on through big wet snowflakes that clung to his eyelashes. He walked up the hill to his sister's house. When he went in, she was sitting in the chair.

"Luke came by," she said without preamble. "Jeezus, I wish you would stay out of my life. I don't have much fun. I've got to have something to look forward to. Luke's been good to me and the kids. What the hell has it got to do with you?"

Matt sank into a chair. He saw that snow was flaking off his boots and making puddles on the rug, but he made no move to get up or take off his boots.

"I didn't do nothing to him," he said. "He wanted to take a shot at me but he wasn't going to hit a cripple."

"I need someone," she said. "Can't you see that?"

They sat there in silence. He stared across the room at her. She was thin, tall, her black hair now peppered with flecks of grey. Her face was narrow, lined with worry. Her lips pressed tight together. She was wearing a worn sweater and a pair of torn sweatpants. He knew she worked hard. Jobs in the town had mostly disappeared. But the video store was still thriving and probably would for a while. She had talked about leaving. She put the house up for sale but there were no offers.

The hope was always that things would change. People lived on that hope, talked about the Americans coming, wealthy Americans with lots of cash looking for new places to live. Parts of the southwest were becoming uninhabitable because of the heat and lack of water. People there had given up growing lawns. The golf courses had all turned back into sand.

Water was currency now in some parts of the U.S. There was a brisk underground business in trucks going over the border, carrying water. Guys were outfitting old trucks with hidden tanks and false floors. Selling water was legal, but only if you were a corporation hack with permits. Anyone else caught carrying it south lost their truck on the spot. To get a permit, you had to bribe someone or be related to whoever was giving them away.

People did it anyway. The trouble with carrying water was its weight. You had to put in extra springs, and then there was the trouble of scrounging fuel, the difficulty of getting around rationing. But with a little ingenuity you could make a lot of money.

The other hot business was making methanol for fuel in stills hidden in the mountains. That was illegal as well, but folks had to survive. And the cops turned a blind eye to a lot of stuff these days. There were too many laws and not enough policemen. Most policemen were now ex-security guards on contract, turfed out of malls as the retail sector cut back. Or they transferred over from the military, which was now entirely made up of mercenaries. The police and the army were owned by someone, though no one was sure who it was. Since the new corporate privacy laws came in, you couldn't find out stuff like that. You could guess, but you couldn't know for sure. Not that it mattered who owned what. It was what you could get by on that mattered. So hauling water made sense. There was lots of it and it was free. If it was worth money to people, so much the better.

Matt was waiting for his sister to say something, but she was still looking at him with those calm dead eyes. He got up, got his coat, and put it on. He took his pack from the hall.

Finally Matt said stiffly, "Well, I guess I'll go then, get out of your hair," and went back out into the snow. His sister let him go without saying a damn word.

It was almost midnight and cold. It would take him three hours or more to walk to his place. He had tears in his eyes. What an idiot. What the hell. He'd be fine on his own. He could think about Star while he walked. He could think about Star and breathe free air while he swung his bent leg along the broken pavement.

8

MATT LEANED against the door of his shack, the air warm on his face. The sun filtered through a hazy pale blue sky. The mountains were such a pale blue they faded into the haze and disappeared.

There was still snow under the bushes, but mud and wet yellow grass showed through in patches in the clearing. He could see the patterns of living he had made throughout the long winter. There was the beaten icy path to the hole he used as a shitter, another path to the hole where he dumped his compost. That had a lacery of deer and elk tracks around it. A pile of ancient tin cans had leaked streaks of rust into the snow. He had thrown the hides from the road-killed animals near the shack, but the coyotes had eaten most of them and dragged them away. Tufts of hair littered a trail leading away up the slope.

He didn't have that many bones, but he had enough to make a start. Now when he walked through the trees or brush, he kept his eyes on the ground. He picked up antlers as well as old bones.

He had spent many long dark hours all winter pounding glass into sand. The sand was for the mortar to hold the bones. He had pounded and he had thought about the world. There was so much he didn't understand. He needed someone to talk to about the weird weather, about the books he kept reading, about the fact that all the NewsNets contradicted each other so you could never tell what was true. He wanted to talk to Star about Darlene, how much he worried about her and the kids. And the dying town, the dead faces he saw in the bar, the hopeless tone in everyone's voice. How people looked when they decided the time had come to leave.

He worried that the endless cold and snow and darkness would affect his thinking. He worried that his loneliness and isolation meant he was becoming too cut off from human beings.

He needed Star. He talked to her in his head, but that wasn't good enough.

He had a feeling that she would be back in the spring. He wanted to be able to show her that he had at least begun the house; he wanted to share his plans for the house with her. It wasn't only the house. He needed to talk to her about all the thoughts and ideas that had thronged his head through the winter. He wanted to share his vision with her and see her green eyes round and full of admiration.

He had never built a house before, but any idiot could build a house. His father had done it. His grandfather had done it. He had a couple of books on construction. He had helped friends of his, when life was easier and normal. He knew the basics. He had no plan. He had a vision of his house, but no plan.

He sat cross-legged on the damp ground. He lifted his face to the sun. He closed his eyes and lights danced across the inside of his eyes. After a while, he got up and began to dance. Gradually, as he warmed up, as the sun grew hotter and hotter, he began to shed his clothes. He took off layer upon layer of heavy clothes, clothes heavy and sodden with sweat, grease, sawdust, and the dirt and grime of winter. He took his heavy woollen shirt and threw it, whirling over his head, onto the branches of a young birch. He had another flannel shirt under that, then a T-shirt, then underwear. He threw them to the far corners of the clearing. Then he took off his heavy lined wool pants, his long underwear under that, and finally his heavy boots and socks. His white skin flashed in the sun. He danced awkwardly but with determination, lifting his feet with care. They hurt, they stung from the cold and small rocks and sticks and old thistles on the ground. He ignored them. His beard hung over his chest and his sweaty, greasy hair hung down in his eyes. He had grown so used to having an itchy scalp he had learned to ignore it. Now he grabbed his hair in both his hands and pulled and pulled and scratched and rubbed as he danced. Then he rubbed his hands over his body. He got an erection, thinking of Star as he danced, but he didn't want to do anything, just let it fling back and forth against his thighs.

Then the sun went behind a cloud and he stopped. For a long moment he couldn't remember where he was. He stared at the sky where the sun was disappearing. He opened his mouth and yelled at the disappearing sun, a long complicated yell full of grief and loneliness, then stood wondering what to do next, what it was he was supposed to do, why he was standing there. He had tears in his eyes. He was so goddamned lonely. He wanted Star. He wanted to be fucking Star, lying on a hill in the sun, with her skin silky and warm to his touch and the soft walls of her vagina wrapped around him. He couldn't stand to touch his penis. He wanted Star to touch it, hold it, wrap herself around it.

He wanted so much. He wanted his sister back. He wanted to kill Luke. He realized that he was freezing to death, that his clothes were lying in soggy piles around the clearing, and he picked them up, then went back into his dusty shack and built up the fire. He hung his clothes to dry and put on some others that weren't quite as filthy. He picked up his rifle and stared at it for a while, then put it down. Tomorrow, for sure, he would start the damn house. He would stop sitting and daydreaming, staring at the wall or the sky. He would go to town tomorrow and start scrounging for more parts, lumber, plumbing. He might even be able to score some old solar cells and some batteries. Everyone had solar cells on their houses now.

The next day he walked into town. He tried to hitchhike, but there were hardly any vehicles. Finally one road train thundered by. He stood aside, watching in amazement at how the road shook under its weight. It was late February and the weather had suddenly warmed up. Water was running everywhere. The creeks were high. In some places, water was running over the road. Water was cascading down off the rocks, trickling out from cracks in the granite, spraying in a fine mist from chunks of ice. Below the road, the creek growled and chewed at its banks. While he watched, part of the road slid away into the creek.

He limped to the library as soon as he got to town. The thin, grey-haired woman who volunteered as librarian let him take out as many books as he wanted and didn't bother him for a fee. The last time he went, there had been a sign saying it was closing. He wondered what they would do with the books. The paper was valuable, anyway.

He kept reading history as fast as he could. He was continually astonished at the things he hadn't known. All kinds of stuff had happened in the last few years, while he'd been working and drinking and hanging around, and he hadn't noticed any of it.

Appleby used to be a pretty town, or so he'd thought when he was a kid. He'd always been kind of proud of the place. Once it had a main street, stores on both sides for three blocks. It had what it needed, a grocery store and a drugstore and a bakery and a hardware store and a building supply store and a feed store. It didn't have anything extra, no fancy restaurants, no bookstore, no cute little gift stores for tourists to browse in. It was a basic kind of town, and the people who lived there were basic kinds of people.

The place had slowly dwindled. Things he'd once taken for granted weren't there anymore. There were no banks, although there were a couple of cash card machines. There was no post office, just a place where you could do e-mail, a machine that automatically weighed and stamped things and then took the money out of your cash card. If you wanted to use real money, which some people, like Matt, still insisted on, you had to have exactly the right number of coins. This meant going to the grocery store for change, where the one clerk who wasn't a machine grumbled about handing out change. It was a lot of what she did. There were lots of vending machines, and although people hated them — the machines broke, stuck, cheated people, took money and gave nothing back — they used them.

There weren't a lot of younger people anymore. The one restaurant that was left mainly served endless cups of weak grain coffee to old people with nothing much else to do — the ones who hadn't yet left because there was no doctor anymore.

There had been frantic meetings and committees and discussions over the years to try to figure out what to do. For a while there had been groups of people who got small grants to do studies; various reports had been issued, but now there were no more committees or grants or reports, or anyone to get money from, for that matter.

One big issue was selling water. Why not sell water? That's what people thought. But that issue had been fought over in the courts and now water was being sold, but only from a few big rivers, shipped south through a couple of huge pipelines. The GreenPros had really fought to have the exports regulated. The lawsuits and the arguments in the NewsNets had been fast and furious. Matt had spent some time reading both sides of the issue. Reluctantly he found he had to agree with the Greens. But the people in Appleby still grumbled. What the hell was wrong with selling water? So what if it meant there were a few less fish? What about the goddamn people?

The countryside had slowly cleared. Those who stuck around were either determined or nuts. A few people had enough land to be self-sufficient, but not everybody with land had stuck it out. Most of the bigger farmers had folded. Shipping costs were too high. They couldn't compete with the giant corporate farms that owned their own bio-diesel trucking lines, distributors, and grocery stores.

Now most of the people around Appleby either grew their own food or traded what they could for supplies. A lot of the old people were still depending on the stores. It was hard for them. Their pensions hadn't increased, but the price of food had shot through the roof. Most of them had family around, so that helped. If you didn't have family to help out these days, you were pretty well fucked.

Matt finally went up the hill to his sister's house. Luke was sitting at the kitchen table when Matt let himself in.

Matt went to the fridge, helped himself to a beer, sat down at the table, stared at the wall.

"So how ya keeping all by yourself out there in the woods?" Luke said. "Must get kind of lonely."

"Been good," Matt said. "Had a good winter. Thinking of building myself a real house. Tired of living in a shack."

"Not a great idea. From what I've heard that whole area is slated to be part of some new conservation project. No people let in or out. GreenPro will drag your butt out of there, burn anything you build. They don't give a shit about what you're trying to do."

"Who the hell is going to notice?" Matt said. "Nobody around out there right now except me. Lots of land and no people to live on it. Me and the animals get along all right. Hell, I'm helping the damn ecology, had critters in my compost all winter. Seen cougar, coyotes, skunks, moose, elk, even saw a pine marten the other day. Guess the animals are coming back, now the people are leaving."

"Hear they're worried about rabies this year. Saying it's too warm. All kinds of new diseases showing up. Mad deer disease or something. Mad mice. Who the fuck knows?"

"Oh hell, they're always saying something."

They said nothing for a while, just drank the beer they were holding and stared out the window, not looking at each other.

"So what kinda house you want to build?"

"Something different. Just working on the plans right now. Big enough for me and my girlfriend, lots of windows."

"What the hell you want windows for? Let out the heat. You wanta see the view, just go outside. What damn girlfriend? Never heard about this."

"Women like lots of windows."

"Yeah, they do. Always gotta think about what the women like."

Matt said cautiously, "So, you and Darlene getting along all right?"

"Yeah. She was pretty pissed off at you last time you were here. But she's over it now. She'll be glad to see you."

"She's a good kid," said Matt. "Been good to me."

He got up, went to the fridge, fished out bread and cold meat, made himself a sandwich and offered one to Luke.

"So what's this about a conservation project?"

"Ah, just another rumour," Luke said vaguely. "There's always something. They want to turn the whole goddamn country into a bloody park. I guess Canada's the last part of the world that still has trees and animals."

Matt was silent.

"Oh yeah, heard the other day they're trying to move a bunch of immigrants up here to plant trees or something, and they won't go. Nobody wants to live in a camp and plant trees for the shit wages they're offering. They've turned the whole thing over to the same corporation that owns the prisons, so now they're talking about using prisoners to plant trees. But there might be some work in it if you're interested. Heard they want to plant new kinds of trees, got some kind of genetically engineered super trees, gonna kick ass, grow faster than anything else."

"The trees we got here already look fine," Matt said. "What's the matter with them?"

"Dunno," Luke said. "Just what I heard. All this shit about the climate. Need different kinds of trees."

They finished their sandwiches.

"You guys ever talk, you know, about being cousins?" Matt said cautiously.

"What are we, third, fourth, fifth? Who knows? Who cares? Hey, I gotta go," Luke said, standing up and shoving back the chair.

Matt went down to the bar for a few more beers. After that, he figured he'd go to the dump, cruise the alleys behind the stores, see what he could find that was worth scrounging.

9

MATT WAS HIGH ON the mountain when he saw the helicopter. He was climbing naked in the hot sun, clawing his way up a steep pine-needle-slippery slope, his mouth open, panting. His hair, limp with sweat, kept getting in his eyes. Next time he'd tie it back. He stopped climbing, slid under the shadowed hollow made by a young spruce. The branches tore angrily at his skin, but there wasn't much chance the helicopter would see him if he stayed under the tree.

The helicopter went by. It was close enough that he could see several people looking out the windows. The helicopter was black, with no markings at all. It could be anything. It could be police looking for methanol stills or illegal patches of marijuana. Growing pot was legal now, but only the corporations could get licences. The wild growers trucked it to the city themselves and sold it in bars. It was far to go, and the price of fuel made it difficult, but the pot grown in vast greenhouses at the coast was reported to be garbage. There was still a market for wild pot.

The helicopter could be prospectors, wildlife people, or maybe, as Luke said, they were going to make yet another park and these were the GreenPros, checking things out. If that was the case, he should get back to his place, keep an eye on things. But the sun was hot and he didn't feel like slipping and sliding back down the long hill. He scrambled out from the tree and followed the helicopter, keeping in the shadows, then squatted on his heels at the foot of a granite wall, in a hollow shielded by a screen of brush and scrubby juniper. The sound of the helicopter finally faded and he stood up. His leg hurt too much to squat for long. He'd come up the mountain with no boots. He was trying to toughen his feet so he could go barefoot more often, but it was a miserable process. His feet were cold and ached from the rocks. They slipped on the pine needles. He wouldn't be able to run like this.

He started down the slope, but then he could hear the helicopter coming back so he began to run, slipping and sliding, crawling over downed trees. He got himself onto a narrow projecting point of rock where he could see out over the valley. The helicopter was on the far side of the valley, hovering over something. He heard distant cracks, tinny and hollow, and realized they were rifle shots. They were shooting at something on the ground.

A man slid out of the helicopter on a rope, all the way to the ground, and then the carcass of something solid and black — it was hard to see what it was — slithered out of the trees and up into the waiting belly of the helicopter. The black body of the man came right after it, into the helicopter. Then the machine tilted forward and flew away.

The silence crept back into the valley after the chop, chop, chopping faded. Matt went back down to his shack. When he got there he flopped onto the stump by the front door, exhausted. He pushed his hands through his hair to slick it back. He needed to wash it but the creek water was still frigid melted ice, and the effort of lighting a fire and heating water seemed too much just to wash his hair. He kept seeing the black body of the helicopter, the blank white faces looking out of it. What if they had seen him? He'd been behind a tree, in the shadows. It wasn't likely.

His scalp itched. He got to his feet, found a plastic pail, went and dipped a bucket from the creek. He threw some pine needles, twigs, and kindling in the stove, then stopped. What if they saw the smoke and came back? He went outside, looked up.

The clearing was still and silent under the glaring yellow sun. The sun was dangerous. Darlene was always blathering about it. No way would she let her kids go outside without hats, sunscreen, long sleeves, even face masks on bright days.

Now he stood in the sun while it beat down on his head. He closed his eyes and turned his face up to the sun so that it came in through his eyelids in brilliant red flashes. He waited, reluctant to take a step, to disturb the silence. Far away a stick cracked in the woods, then another. He leaped for the door of the hut, inside, grabbed the gun, then back to the doorway. He waited, frozen, every muscle tensed. But the clearing dreamed on in the sun. Nothing happened. A pair of ravens flew by. A squirrel stole something from his compost.

He sat back down on the stump, the rifle in his hands. After a while he forced himself to get up, to do something. The silence made it hard to move. He felt like somewhere in that silence was something, someone watching him.

He began to dream again about his house. He was going to have problems building it here. He knew that. A house was a big intrusion into space. His little hut didn't take much room and was hard to see from the air. He had even considered throwing a net over it and putting branches in the net. But a real house would change everything, change the landscape.

He started pacing, then sat down again. It was all wrong. He was going to have to move. He was going to have to pack everything up and find some other place to build his house, maybe north on the lake.

When he was a kid, staying out of the way of his dad's fists, he'd found sanctuary in the swamp at the bottom of the town. There were trails made by cows and deer through the tangles of bent-over willow and cottonwood trees. When he found it, he thought it was what a real jungle would be like. There was a bulrush-choked stretch of water that they all skated on in the winter on those rare occasions when it was free of snow.

There was lots of stuff in the swamp, red-winged blackbirds on every bulrush, mallard ducks, frogs, giant water beetles, tadpoles, lizards. He liked to crouch on his heels, staring into the water, watching the life around him. The rest of the time he practised stalking, playing war, sneaking up on invisible enemies. There was always lots of garbage, plastic bags, Coke cans, shopping carts, but that didn't bother him. It was all part of the jungle.

One day, someone built a house on a rise of land overlooking the swamp, and that was that. That refuge was lost to him. That goddamn grey stupid house, sticking up on the top of a small hill with a wall of solar panels on the roof. That had been the end of playing soldier in the jungle. He'd never gone back. Stupid fuckers. Houses ruined everything. And now here he was thinking of carrying his own brand of ruination into this quiet clearing.

He gave up. He went down to the creek, figuring he was hot enough for an actual bath in the freezing water.

It was cold under the alders and cedar that fringed the creek. It would be easy and not too much work to make a small dam, a pond to swim in, lie around in on hot days. He could make it look fairly natural, wouldn't hurt anything. He knelt and dipped his head in the creek. The water burned his scalp, but he left his head under until it was too painful to stand any longer. He didn't have any soap or shit like that, didn't want it in the creek. Water would do. He splashed around in the creek, moving rocks, until he began to shiver. Then he went back into the sun. He went carefully, stepping quietly along the path, still with the odd feeling of being watched. Just before he came into the clearing, he stopped. There were elk in the clearing, grazing on the new grass and bits of white Dutch clover springing up from seeds he had thrown around last fall. They were female, tall, brown, drifting through the clearing, sniffing at things. One saw or heard something and her head swung up. He was close enough to see the shine on her black nose, her round eyes and thin neck, the woolly winter hair sloughing off in patches.

He began to step slowly forward, watching their eyes. As long as they weren't looking at him, he could move, very slowly. They finally saw him. He stood still. Slowly, with great dignity, the elk stepped away from him. Several of them blew blasts of air through their noses, flicked their tails as they left, breaking into a trot, climbing the hill behind the hut, their feet clacking. In a few minutes they were gone.

"I'm sorry," he said out loud. He wasn't sure what he was apologizing for. Maybe because he wanted them back. He wanted them to come back, graze in his clearing, feed off his compost, hang around, keep him company. Not likely.

It was late, getting cold, getting dark. He lit the fire. He had hardly any food left. He was hungry. He needed more food than he was getting. He could have shot an elk. He could right now be frying elk meat, elk heart, elk liver.

He cooked some rice, added a few beans. It was tasteless. The rice was old, almost mouldy, but he ate it. He was still hungry. He wanted a beer, more then anything. He lit two candles, curled in his sweat-stinking sleeping bag, began to read, then fell asleep. His leg woke him several times in the night, once with cramps so bad he had to get up and walk around in the dark, limping and cursing, before he could crawl shivering back in his bag and go to sleep. It took him a long time to fall asleep. The day had been so weird, so full of omens. Something was happening, something was coming to change his life. Something mysterious. Some power he didn't understand had noticed him and was sending messages. That was all he knew for now, but he knew it for sure.

10

ONE NIGHT, when Matt went to lift a forkful of food to his mouth, his throat closed. He couldn't eat. He had been out on the mountain all day in the sun, trying to figure things out. Things were starting to worry him. They were closing in. He'd seen the helicopter twice more, cruising around as if it owned the place. It made him so goddamn mad. He'd picked up his rifle, aimed at the helicopter. "Psheoo, psheooo," he'd said under his breath. He'd taken the precaution of throwing some willow boughs over the hut. It probably looked like a heap of brush from the air.

The leaves were coming out on the trees, unfurling, bright electric green sparks on every branch. The creeks were still high, roaring down the mountain, and birds were everywhere. Bumblebees, slow and fumbling, moved in the grass, looking for the shy early spring flowers.

He had seen the herd of elk several more times; they were getting used to him. They liked the new grass in the clearing and on the slope above his cabin. They seemed to have some sort of circular pattern they wandered, ending back at his place every few days. The endless repetition of their broad feet made narrow paths that traversed the mountain slopes. Matt made use of these paths when he went hiking. He was spending time getting to know the mountainside around the clearing. It was going to be important to know his way around if anyone came after him. It was going to be important to stay tough and healthy. He spent more and more time without clothes or shoes, trying to toughen himself.

But if he couldn't eat, none of that would do any good. He stared at the food. He didn't feel sick. It was part of the falling away, a process he didn't understand and couldn't control. The last time he had gone into Appleby, he had stuck out his thumb and a truck thundered to a stop, but when he went to get in, the smell of grease and gas and oil and rusting metal hit him hard, made his head spin.

"Can't do it, man," he said sadly and waved the guy on. Matt was pissed right off. His leg hurt. The big trucks hardly ever stopped. The guy had a nice face. Matt wanted to sit in the truck, in front of the big heater blasting out warm air, with the radio on, and gossip with the guy. He wanted to hear what was going on in the rest of the world; he hardly ever heard news anymore. He watched TV and videos at his sister's house, but it was hard to tell from the TV news what was actually going on. Mostly the news was about movie stars or people he had never heard of. There was lots of news on the NewsNets, tons of it, but it was all fantastic and contradictory. Some were full of war, famine, plague, the end of the world repeated over and over. The others were all good news, soothing inanities repeated over and over. There was no way to tell what was really going on.

He'd heard the same apocalyptic shit all his life and it never amounted to anything. Things were all right. They weren't great, but they were all right. People were getting by. The climate shit was weird. But he'd been hearing that all his life too. It was true the oceans had risen. It seemed the summer got hotter every year. There was always a lot of trouble with fires. The biggest change had been in the Arctic. There was hardly any ice there anymore, hardly any polar bears, caribou, muskox. They couldn't adapt and now they were disappearing.

It used to terrify him when he was a kid. Somehow the violence of the weather and his father's violence got mixed in his head. His dad was just like the weather, unpredictable and extreme. Whatever his dad's mood was, they all caught it from him. When he was gone, it was like the sun coming out and they could all relax, bask in the sun of his absence. When he came in the door, they all instantly knew his mood. They'd learned the clues so well, the sound of his footsteps, the speed with which he opened the door, the way he said hello or didn't say hello. Everything in the house snapped to attention when he came in. The radio or TV went off. Matt and his sister vanished to their rooms or outside or to the basement. Then they listened, they listened to the tones in the voices, to the way the pots and pans clinked together as their mother made supper. When they were sure it was safe, they came out, came to dinner, ate quickly, glancing at their father.

Nights he was expansive, happy, almost explosively so, he made them do math questions, which they tried desperately to get right. Nights he was quiet, they waited for the explosion. No matter how carefully they waited, it always surprised them. It was always over something unexpected.

One night it was the cat. For some reason the cat was in the house at dinnertime, someone had forgotten to put her out. They never had the cat in the house when their father was around. He didn't mind cats, but he thought they ought to live outside and hunt mice and birds. If you fed the cat, it wouldn't hunt. It would become lazy, useless, fit for nothing. So they had it in and fed it when he wasn't around, made sure it was outside when he came home. It was a nice cat, a tabby female that dutifully produced a litter of kittens every year. The kittens ran wild, got run over. Sometimes they managed to give them away to good homes. Then they'd go visit the kittens as they were growing, keep track of them.

The cat came whining around the kitchen table, looking for food. It didn't know any better. It was used to doing this when his father wasn't around.

His father swore, looked around the table. "What's that fucking animal doing in here?" he snarled. They all flinched but sat still. It was better not to say anything.

Their mother said, "It's okay, I'll put it outside." She grabbed at the cat, lifted it in her arms.

But he was on his feet, snatched the cat away from her. Alarmed, the cat held on, ripping at Matt's mother's fleshy arms. His mother screamed, grabbed herself. Blood seeped from between her fingers.

"Fucking goddamned animal," he swore, now holding the squalling cat by the scruff of its neck, marched outside, grabbed it by its tail, swung it against the trunk of the giant willow tree in the backyard. They had all rushed to the open back door. They heard the crack as its head hit the tree, saw the squalling body go suddenly limp. Their father threw the body into the bushes at the side of the yard, marched back in, past their white faces, sat at the table, and began shovelling mashed potatoes and gravy into his mouth.

Why had his mother stayed? God, he'd hated his father. He had really, really wanted to kill him. Killing him would have been too easy. He wanted his father to die a horrible accidental death. Sliding off the road, the car engulfed in fire; crushed at work under a pile of falling logs; sliced into by a saw blade gone berserk.

But his father lived and his mother stayed and stayed and stayed. It was Matt she complained to, Matt she leaned on,

Matt she talked to endlessly, although it embarrassed him and he tried to shift the subject, tried to cheer her up, tried to talk her into leaving.

"Where could we go?" she'd moan. "What could we do? No, we'd better stay. It's not that bad, honey. He's not a bad man, you know, he just has a terrible temper. You've got to learn to stay on his good side. You've got to learn not to upset him."

Matt knew the minute he started bad-mouthing his dad, she'd defend him. It made him crazy. The cat incident replayed itself in his head for weeks. He couldn't get rid of that sound, the sudden crack, the sight of the cat's limp body swinging at the end of his dad's arm. Well, the bastard was dead now. Death was the big surprise. Ha, ha, Dad. Death swung you against a tree. Crack and you're gone.

Matt hadn't gone near the hospital when his father was dying. He wandered around town, did the usual. Got drunk. Said stupid things. People in the bar didn't say much. Not even when he threw Luke Palmer against the black curtains masking the plate glass window. They all heard the crack, unmistakable.

"Get out," everyone said, "get out before Springer hears." Springer being the owner, and Matt did. Even left town for a few days, missed the goddamn funeral, went home to find his mother, composed and cheerful, making dinner like always, the same food she always cooked, the standard meal, the old meat and potatoes thing. He sat there and ate it just like his old man, sat in the chair after, watched the news on TV, fell asleep. He moved in after that, went to work, came home, just like his old man, dusty, dirty, throwing his work clothes on the floor of the laundry room for his mother to take care of, eating the lunches she packed, the suppers she cooked, the cookies she always had waiting.

And he would probably still be living the same life —

except that it would be Darlene doing the cooking and cleaning instead of his mother — if it wasn't for the skidder, the break in his life, the sudden jolt, him hanging on and seeing, as clearly as he had ever seen anything, the moment when it came time to jump, to fling himself onto the mercy of the air, to let go of the steel turned treacherous, turned killer. It had been the most clear-headed moment of his life.

He put down the bowl of musty rice and beans. He had to get some better food. No wonder he couldn't eat.

He went outside. The evening was actually warm. He sat on the damp ground, scratching his stomach under its layer of matted hair. A few thin long red rays of evening sun reached through the trees to play on his skin. The ground exhaled cold, exhaled a smell like ripe fruit, exhaled secret sounds, worms, tiny bugs, crawling things, growing things. He held his breath, but the ground went on breathing all around him, swelling like a giant moon pumpkin, swelling under him, puffing up like a fungus — god he was hungry — and then the earth began to sink under him and he held on, terrified that it would melt and he would sink with it, melting into the mud and small stones and secret rivers and layers of granite underneath him. Jesus Christ, he thought, what the hell is happening? As the earth rose and fell with his breathing, with his heartbeat, he noticed that the golden penis buds on the alder trees were shaking, vibrating like bells being rung, shining like tiny lighted bells, that somewhere a gong had been struck and he and everything around him were part of this great sound, and even the red fingers of light stroking the trees, the clearing, his sad dusty shack, were shaking, shaking with laughter. He wanted to fall on his face and hide, but there was nowhere to fall and nothing to hide. He went on sitting there, listening to the bells and the laughter until the light died and the sound died with it, although if he listened, he could still hear it in some part of his mind beyond hearing. After a while he came to himself and realized it was cold and he had been sitting outside on the ground for a very long time. He could hear the creek now, very loud, grinding and chewing its way down the mountain. The wind came and shook his hair, shook the trees, shook him onto his feet.

He went back inside, crawled into his musty blankets. He wanted to tell Star, not that he even knew what he would tell her. He wanted to share it with her, this sense that he was changing, going somewhere new, becoming something, someone odd that he didn't know or understand. Star would take his hand, make him laugh, make it all make sense. Star would understand. In this strange place, Star would look at him, hold his hand, hold him close, and understand.

11

AS USUAL, LUKE was at his sister's house. Matt was getting used to finding him there. He had settled in. They were becoming more and more a couple. His sister looked happier, less worried, so Matt had decided he should do his damnedest to make friends with the guy at least. They could stop strutting like horny dogs when they were around each other.

"Hey man," he said cheerfully when he walked in the door.

Luke grunted. He had a rifle out and was cleaning it, squinting down the barrel and wiping off the stock and the metal with a rag.

"Saw a helicopter up my way last week," Matt said. "Looked like they were shooting elk, hauling them up into the chopper."

"Oh yeah," said Luke, "they're moving elk out of there, transplanting them. Some hunting company bought them, one of those idiot places some macho tourist pays a million bucks to shoot a tame deer."

"Oh," said Matt. Luke always seemed to know what was going on, or pretended to. What he didn't know, he made up, but what he made up, he stated with as much confidence as if it were true. Even when you caught him in a flat-out lie, he never admitted it, just changed the subject.

"You workin'?"

"Always got something going," Luke grinned. When he grinned like that, his whole face lit up. He was good-looking, Matt thought, surprised he had never noticed it before.

"Ya gotta hustle these days, but if you hustle, you stay in front, eh? Why, you looking for something? Need some money? I guess I got some wood needs bucking. You can still run a saw all right, eh? Hey, you know what I heard? All those empty summer cottages up the lake? GreenPros're gonna tear them down, recycle everything. You wanna get in on that?"

"I'm okay," Matt said. "I was just asking." Luke might be charming, but he always managed to piss Matt off.

Luke stomped to the fridge and took out a beer without offering one to Matt. It was probably beer Matt had bought last time he was here, come to think of it.

Darlene and the kids came in from work and from school. The kids looked at Matt and Luke without enthusiasm and disappeared off to their rooms. Sara was eleven, two years older than her brother David. They used to like Matt a lot when they were younger. He wondered what had happened and how the hell they had gotten so old and distant without his noticing.

Darlene made them all supper and they sat around the table, shovelling in food without speaking much. She had boiled potatoes, heated stew and gravy, made biscuits. There was even cake for dessert.

Luke shoved his plate away, leaned back. "Hey, didja hear about that body they found, up some old logging road, out by the lake? Near where those commune people hang out."

They all looked at him.

"Been dead a while, I guess. All they said was it was female, someone killed her and dumped her body up there. Guess one of them skanky commune hippies found her. You know they got trails all over the place out there, got caves, hiding places, stocked up with food. God knows how many guns they got. The cops will be happy now, give them an excuse to wander all over that mountain, looking for stuff. They been after them people for a long while. Biggest bunch of smuggle bunnies around!"

"What kind of woman?" Matt said. His gut clenched.

"Young, blond, that's all I know."

Matt stood up. "Who does know?" he asked.

Luke looked surprised. "What the hell you care?" he said, then, "Oh yeah, you had a thing with one of them roadie queens for a bit, eh? I'd forgotten. Hell, man, forget it, she's long gone. This could be anybody. It's not your girl."

But Matt was already on his way out the door.

Nobody at the bar knew much, but they had all heard something. They were glad to see Matt. They bought him beer and joked about his beard and long hair. He sat in the middle of them drinking his beer, his gut clenched and panic running through his veins like poison. He needed to get back to his cabin. He could think there. But he had to stay until he knew. It wasn't Star. It was some other woman. It couldn't be Star, but just worrying about it reminded him of how Star had been. It made his heart clench, it made him reel with loneliness and need. He could smell her, over and above the stench of the bar and the cigarette smoke and hemp smoke and stale beer, he could smell how she'd been, fresh and clean and soft. She had smelled so good. Her skin had little tiny blond hairs that he smoothed with his tongue. Her skin had tasted sweet and salty at the same time.

He looked around the room. Most of the people in it were people he knew, who knew him. He was sitting in his favourite chair, in the corner, where he could see the whole room and no one could walk behind him.

Something shifted and he realized that everyone in the

room was naked, that he could see through their clothes to their bodies, that everyone in the room, male and female, was walking around with their parts hanging out. Clothes were a polite lie, a silly fiction. He could see their pot-bellies, hunched shoulders, thin rib cages, white skinny legs, thin penis and balls, or wrinkled weary breasts. He could see even further, see the sadness, the grey lines and worries and fatigue behind the laughing faces, the jokes, the beer and cigarettes and stale jokes and repeated lines. The room stank of worry and sadness. There was a fog in the air beyond the cigarette smoke. They were all dying, standing here dying and fending it off as hard as they could, but dying nevertheless in a kind of glory and gallantry, getting what they could from these shot-through-with-smoke moments. Matt tried to breathe, felt his chest close.

"Sorry guys, gotta go," he mumbled, stood up, pushed back the chair, which fell over. A couple of people laughed. He tried to walk straight to the door, but he was conscious that his feet were coming down in places he hadn't meant to put them. When he got outside in the cool air, it was better. He leaned against the side of the building, his head whirling.

He didn't even hear the cop car pull up. Someone grabbed his arm, twisted it behind him, forced him to his knees.

"We been watching you, asshole. Don't try anything," a voice said. "Just get up, get in the car, nice and slow."

They took him to the police station, threw him in a cell where the walls squeezed shut around him. He sat on the bed, fighting for breath, while the walls squeezed him into a smaller and smaller knot. Eventually he fell asleep and woke in the morning, bewildered and groggy, feeling like he'd been somewhere far and deep and mysterious.

Just after breakfast, Darlene came to see him, her face white and terrified.

"Do they think you murdered that girl? Is that why you're here?" she hissed at him, furious. "Everybody keeps asking me. The kids didn't go out today. What the hell, Matt. I'm trying to live in this dump. I don't need this kind of shit falling in my lap."

"Was it Star?" he said. He was freezing cold. He held his arms around himself to keep from shaking. "Was it her? Do they know? Can they tell?"

"I don't know. I don't know any Star. Jeezus, we're barely keeping our head above water. We could lose the house. We could lose everything. God, how could you do this to us? How could you? What the hell has happened to you? You've turned into some kind of lunatic, hiding up in the mountains, in some kind of shack, some kind of dump. You used to work, you used to be normal. What happened?"

"Darlene, I loved Star, I never hurt her. I never hurt no one. I'm just living my life as best I can. It's not easy these days."

"Oh, for God's sake. You could help us, you could do something to get some money, you could be helping out. You could help me with the kids. They need so much. There's so much I can't give them. What's the matter with you?"

He stared at her. He couldn't think of anything to say. She shook her head and walked away down the hall, crying, her shoulders hunched.

He sat back down on the bed. Nothing happened all afternoon. People came and went in the hall. The sun shone outside. He stared at his rotting boots and thought about sunlight on the clearing, on the red coats of the doe elk, on the white bones of his shining castle house that he had yet to build. If Star was dead, she would never see it. If Star was dead, and they thought he'd done it, what the hell was he going to do? Would they railroad him into going to jail? He couldn't live in jail. He knew that. He'd go crazy fast. He'd kill himself before he'd live in here. If Star was dead, he'd have nothing to live for anyway.

They brought him some dry and tasteless food, and after he ate it, they let him go.

"You're a troublemaker. We got our eye on you. Now, get the hell out of town," said the cop. He grinned. His teeth were broken and stained. He was short and skinny, with thin greasy hair. The rumour was that the police were recruited from desperate people, street kids, drug addicts. They were sent somewhere for heavy duty programming, hooked on weird drugs, and turned loose on the population. That way, the cops were loyal to each other and vicious to the local people.

Matt walked down the street, his head whirling, trying to think. He wasn't going back to jail, he knew that for certain. And just because he was in trouble, Darlene had turned on him.

He went down the alley behind the grocery store, but there was nothing to see there. He headed down the hill out of town. He'd left some stuff at Darlene's but what the hell. Let it stay there. Then he stopped, irresolute. It was late afternoon. If he left now, he wouldn't make it home until it was dark. He needed to get food, supplies. He went down the bank, sat down just off the road, perched on a low rotten log full of ants, painfully stretching his game leg in front of him so he'd be able to get up again. He was in a clearing, surrounded by wild roses in blooming pink masses. The air reeked with roses, the hot sunny spring smell of roses and other flowers coming into bloom. There was a dark pool of water trapped in the rocks that he had never noticed before; something moved in the water and he realized it was a turtle, pulling itself up to sun on the rocks. The water was full of things buzzing, moving, sliding over its surface. The wild rose bushes hung down to touch the water. He slid down on the ground, lowered himself until he was lying face down, his head on his arms. The glint off the water shook and shimmered inside his half-closed eyes.

If Star were really dead, what would he do? He lay still while the dry agony of that thought twisted his muscles.

And what were the police after? Maybe they'd picked him up just as a warning. Would they come after him if he disappeared? He was pretty good in the mountains, but he was still a cripple. Besides, the police had helicopters, electronic sniffers, heat sensors, robots. He'd heard on the NewsNets that they put electronic chips in criminals to track them. Maybe he should find some new place to live that no one knew about, no GreenPros, no helicopters.

He turned over on his back. A small brown speckled bird was hopping from branch to branch in the tangle of brush above his head. The sun burned his eyes.

He must have fallen asleep. He wasn't sure if he was asleep or dreaming or awake in some place that didn't make any sense. There were voices in his head, a whole collection of voices, and he was listening, trying to make sense of what they were saying. He was drifting in and out of the dream, watching what was happening, watching people coming towards him in a rage, their faces changing as they came, their faces distorted and savage with rage, and then just for a moment he saw Star, going away from him. She turned and her face was full of both sorrow and light.

He woke and his eyes were full of tears. "Stay true," said the voice of the small bird above his head. "Stay true." The voice rang clear and soft, like a small thin bell.

Then he finished waking up and realized it couldn't have been the bird. But the voice still rang in his head. What the hell did that mean? Stay true. Shit. He got up, went and peed in the brush, came back, drank some water from the pool in his cupped hands. It was cold but tasted of algae and swamp.

He had some decisions to make. That much he knew.

12

LIA LOOKED UP from the corn she was hoeing and grinned at Magnus. They interplanted the corn with green beans and hemp. The hemp grew faster than the corn and smelled wonderfully rank and skunky. Sometimes Lia rubbed her hair on the leaves, just to say hello.

"Hey, you," she said softly.

"Hey yourself," he said, and laughed. "Look at you, all hot and sweaty and stinking. You look like a damn farmer."

"I was born to be a damn farmer," she said. "All those years in that shit-stinking city made sure of that."

"Yeah, but were you born to fuck a farmer now? That's the question." He came closer. The heat between them rose up and shimmered like pollen in the sun-laden air. So now she loved two people, Star and Magnus.

It had been different, sex with a man she actually cared about. The rhythm was different somehow. It was hard to connect, hard to find the pulsing going back and forth that let her know what she wanted, what he wanted. At first she panicked, not sure.

"I can't do this," she said. "Wait," she said, but he was sure, said he'd been sure from the moment he saw her standing on the road, thumb out, looking so serious and worried and determined as hell. No matter that she wasn't sure, he went on stroking and licking and sucking until she started to get excited. He spent lots of time, waiting to put his penis in, which wasn't what she'd been used to. Men always wanted to stick it in first thing, that was all they cared about, but Magnus waited, and even then he didn't come until she did first, and he waited until she was coming again so they came together, both of them furious and thrashing and moaning. It was pretty funny, really, what people did in bed. Only now she wanted very much to do it again and again, maybe just lie right down here in the corn rows and fuck in the dirt and the mud and the worms and the microbes. Fertilize everything. Wasn't there some olden day thing where people did just that?

"I know a place we can go," Magnus said. But they didn't move for a while, just stood there, teasing each other with their lips and their hands, enjoying the nearness of their bodies and the rush of heat and lust like adrenaline thrilling along every nerve.

"Yaysoo christer, you two, go find a bed or maybe some cold water," someone called. "Just watching you be making me crazy." It was Mairi, one of the older women, coming with a bucket to pick greens for lunch. She was ancient, round like a barrel, clothes tied haphazardly around her squat torso, hair so short she was almost bald, but her face was red and beaming with delight. "It's so hot again. Seems like every year is hotter than the next, but then they be saying that all my life and they be right. They're always right, whoever the hell they might be." She cackled and went down through the garden.

Lia and Magnus looked at each other. It seemed to Lia at that moment that the garden, her body, Magnus's body, the corn, the weeds, the ground itself, were laughing in contentment and delight, that life was only, in truth, about growth and fertility and birth and death, a truth she knew already and had only just discovered. Her body was so full and round with delight. It might already have a child in it. She giggled. The dope they had smoked that morning in bed was still with her. It had been delightful, a gold smoky resonance.

"Gotta finish the corn," she whispered, "gotta be real farmers, hoe the corn, plough the ground."

"I already know the ground I want to plough," he said. "Come here."

"No, you come," she said, "show me the place you want to show me. We just might be late for lunch."

He took her hand. She loved the feel of his hand. It was huge and warm. It swallowed her smaller hand and kept it safe at the same time. He was so tall, leaning against the sun like a tree might lean, his hair lit with bits of flame.

They went along the corn rows to the end of the garden, and in behind a wall of spruce that had been planted on waste ground they found a bed of moss in a tiny clearing among the spruce. The spruce trees pricked her skin going in. Magnus spread his shirt and the cloth he had tied around his lean hips that morning and smoothed it into a bed. Then he lay down, brown and naked, his prick up in the air so that Lia couldn't stop giggling. They began to kiss each other and kiss again and again, very very softly and slowly, but she still giggled. It was the trees and the moss and the sun warming her bum, and then Magnus got her to lie on top of him, and when his penis slid inside her again, she began to cry instead. She had no idea why she was crying. Then she stopped and closed her eyes while they rocked together — there were waves of bright blue playing behind her eyes and she went on dreaming and waiting until it began to build again for both of them. This time she knew when it was right and they rolled off the blanket and up against the sticky trees with the ferocity of fucking and crying out, and then they were both crying and laughing because Magnus had bits of moss all over his hair and Lia had pitch on her bum.

"God, this is sure better than with Jane," he said.

"Jane! Who is Jane?" She stopped feeling warm very abruptly. It was funny how quickly she went cold.

"My friend," he said. "We've been playing at sex since we were little kids, but it never meant anything, it was for learning."

"You had sex when you were a little kid?"

"Yeah, doesn't everyone?"

"I don't know," she said. "I didn't. I sort of had sex with Christy, when I was kidnapped, but it wasn't much fun, just her fucking me. Sometimes she'd touch me nice, but it was more for comfort for her than anything. And Star."

"Oh," he said. "Star. That's the girl that disappeared."

"She's okay. She's just gone — somewhere. She heard this story, we all heard it, about this place you could go where they'd take you in, no questions asked. It was a story that everyone believed, even if they didn't believe it. You know? There's different versions of the story. In some it's run by a group of old women. One guy even knew the name of it. He said it was called Kind House, or Kind Place, something like that. He said all you had to do was tell them your story, and if they believed you, they'd take you in and look after you and they'd give you whatever you needed most. Star said even if it wasn't exactly true, there had to be someplace like it. That's what she was looking for."

"Lots of places will take you in," Magnus said, slightly scornful. "You just gotta do your share. Feeding people is a lot of work. You can always use help. We took you in, didn't we?"

"You brought me here."

"Yeah, that was my lucky day."

He leaned over, began to lick her shoulder, moved down her arm. But she was suddenly cold.

"Magnus, why did you say Star had disappeared? She's just travelling. I'll find her or she'll find me. Somehow."

"Yeah, sure," he said, now tonguing the salty lines on her flat brown stomach.

"I'm really hungry," she said. "Let's go eat."

Lia could smell the garlic-tomato smells and rich baking-bread smells from the house. It was hard to get used to sitting down to three meals a day. She was never quite sure who lived in the house with her, Magnus, and Magnus's mother, Ama. There were a number of houses on the commune, and other buildings that were more like sheds, some of which were kept locked. She had gradually gotten to know most of the people. It was hard to trust people, hard to relax and stop worrying about starving or being ripped off or raped.

Everyone on the commune went in and out of the main house at least once or twice a day. There was always someone in there, cooking and cleaning, always the smell of food being prepared or canned or stored away somehow. She couldn't believe how much food the earth gave out and with so little effort. It made her dizzy. Some days she couldn't eat anything. She just sat and stared at people stuffing food away inside themselves without thinking.

When she first arrived, she had wanted immediately to load a truck with food and take it to the people at her high-rise. But Magnus pointed out that wouldn't work. It wasn't the right time. They couldn't afford to make the long trip for nothing. He said in the fall, when work was done, he'd have to make another trip, and she could go back then, see everybody.

"They'll be gone," she said sadly. "Nobody stays for long, people move on, find someplace else."

"God," he said softly, contemplating that. "Most of the people here I've known my whole life. I was born here. I'll probably die here."

"Don't you ever get bored?"

"Sure, that's why I go on the truck runs." He was boasting a little. "But what the hell, I figure I deserve a break now and again. And look what happened. I got you."

Now she found herself staring at him, wanting to keep touching his velvety, tanned skin. Instead she said, as severely as she could, "I mean it. I'm hungry."

He grinned and fell over backwards, laughing. She loved his grin, she loved his laugh. What the hell. She loved him. She fell back onto the scratchy moss with him.

"What am I going to do?" she murmured.

"What about it?" he said, still laughing. She looked at him. The sun lit his hair so it looked like it was on fire.

The sun scarred her eyes like tiny knives. She closed them as tightly as she could.

13

LIA CAME INTO THE HOUSE, rubbing her arms. She had been working in the garden, cutting the raspberry canes and stacking them into a pile. Now her arms were covered with scratches, like a rash. She had to grub out the grass and weeds stubbornly attached to the ground around the canes. When she was sweating and thirsty, she trudged up the hill to the house for a drink and a rest.

Ama was alone in the kitchen, which hardly ever happened. There were always people around.

Lia got a glass of water, sat at the long wooden table where so many people ate so much food every day, and watched Ama, who was chopping vegetables for soup.

"Hot, eh?"

"We always get a hot spell in late spring."

"My grandmother always said she loved spring best. Said it was the most exciting season because everything was new again."

Ama paused, looked at her. "Your grandma loved a lot of things. That was one of the things that made her so special."

"Do you think she's still alive?"

Ama sat very still for a moment, then went back to chopping onions. "She could be."

"But why wouldn't she find some way to send a message? How could they have disappeared so easily? I've been thinking about it for five years now and it still doesn't make sense."

"No, it doesn't." Ama's face was grim. "Things happen."

"What do you mean? What kind of things?"

"The world's a scary place these days. Like those guys that chased you when you were coming here. There's just too much weirdness. Nowhere is safe. You know what I mean."

"But you said you looked. Did you?"

"Sure," Ama said. But she wasn't looking at Lia.

"Looked where? Asked who?"

"I looked," Ama said. "Your grandma was my friend too."

"You mean you didn't find anything? I don't believe you."

"Just leave it," Ama said. "There's nothing you can do."

"What do you mean?"

"I mean when someone disappears like that, it's not a good thing to get mixed up in."

Ama sighed deeply. She wiped her hands on a towel. "Lia, those of us who stayed here and didn't move to the cities, we've had to figure out ways to survive. People do all kinds of things. They hunt, they cut trees, they grow dope, they smuggle water, you know all that. Mostly it's petty stuff and there's no real law to bother us. But sometimes it gets bigger and uglier. We just keep our heads down, try not to draw any attention to ourselves."

"I've been thinking about her place. I want to go to our old house," Lia said. "Maybe there's something of her still there. Besides, it's kind of mine now, isn't it? I've been wondering if I could live there."

"We'll take you, look around," Ama said. "But you can't live there. Don't be silly, it wouldn't be safe. There's nothing there. It's a wreck."

"It's my home. It's mine. It's the only real thing I've got

left." Lia stood up. "I can't believe I've waited this long."
She heard her voice get louder without her willing it to.

"Don't go back there by yourself," Ama said. "Wait for
us. Wait for Magnus."

"I have to," Lia said. "I'd rather go by myself."

She went upstairs, stuffed her things into her ancient
pack, and walked out of the warm soup-smelling house into
the lazy sunlit spring afternoon. Ama stood in the doorway,
arms folded, and watched her go. Magnus wasn't around.
He hadn't told her where he was going, just left early that
morning before she was awake.

She couldn't believe she had been here for a whole long
winter and she still hadn't made it all the way home, still
hadn't seen the place she had dreamed of for so long. She
knew why. She knew she was afraid to walk in a door where
her grandmother should be waiting for her and be greeted
only by silence.

She hadn't forgotten the hard-learned lessons of the
squat. Don't trust anyone. Do it yourself. Depend on yourself. Don't be weak. Don't show weakness. Keep your feelings to yourself. She had been careful not to be sucked in by
it all, Magnus, his mother, the commune, all the food and
warmth and comradely bullshit.

Her grandmother's house was three miles down a sunlit
silent highway. She walked and walked, the straps from the
pack rubbing sores into her back. She walked with the lake
on one side and the treed slope of the mountain on the
other. She walked by Boulder Creek, the place where the
crazy old man used to live up the mountain in a shack on
stilts, and shoot at what he claimed were bears. She walked
by the Rat Slough, with its acres of bulrushes and small
ponds in between. The ponds were full of ducks, the slough
was full of noise. An eagle sat in one of the cottonwood
trees that lined the bit of high ground between the swamp

and the lake. She used to walk down there, used to go along a path beside the swamp that went out to the creek. There were beaver, osprey, kingfishers, and muskrats. There was always something to see.

She came to the road leading up the mountain to their farmhouse. The apple trees in the field near the bottom of the driveway were tangled with too much growth. They hadn't been pruned for a long time, but they were heavy with tiny green apples. She used to help her grandmother prune those trees, every spring. She loved pruning, loved climbing around in the trees, hanging out on a tree limb, giving the trees what her grandmother called "haircuts."

"A healthy apple tree just wants to grow itself to death," she had told Lia. "They're mighty relieved when we come along and open them up, give them light and air and room to breathe." She had believed everything her grandmother told her.

The branches of the plum trees on the hill above the rock wall along the slanting driveway drooped almost to the ground. New emerald grass on the hillside grew through the yellow dead grass. Dried stalks of knapweed and sweet clover stuck up above the shining green. She went on up the hill, over the creek that fell into a concrete tank. The tank, which always used to be full of still brown water, had cracked and the water had drained away, leaving a green scum at the bottom. That made her feel worse than anything, even worse than the unpruned trees, seeing that. That water was the irrigation system for the orchard.

The house was up even higher, the road switchbacked through a fringe of trees into an upper field, which had once been pasture for the milk cows, and a flatter section that had been garden. The pasture was bisected by a gully carved by the creek. They used to toboggan there in the winter, down the frozen flume the creek made. She went on up the hill to the house.

As she got closer, she could see that the windows were broken, the front door hanging by its hinges. There was a verandah along the front of the house, and a grapevine growing over it. There were two wooden chairs and a table, dusty and grey but normal looking. The wooden door from the verandah into the house was open. Lia went through it, into the house.

It was like walking through a corpse. It was like being inside a body that had been ripped apart and allowed to die with no one to care for it. The house stank of pack rat and skunk. The furniture was mostly intact under a layer of dust. The floor was a mat of broken glass, mouse shit, and dead flies. She went from room to room, looking at things.

There was wood standing beside the wood stove. The familiar rolltop desk stood in the corner of the living room. The papers it had once contained were scattered on the floor, but the few precious books were still on their shelves, behind the glass doors of the cabinet.

She went back out on the porch, which faced northwest, towards the evening sun.

"I want my own life," she said out loud to the red sun. "That's all. That's what I want. That's what I'm going to have."

She spent the next few hours until darkness shovelling and clearing out the mess. She built a fire in the wood stove and unrolled her sleeping bag on the floor beside its warmth. She couldn't quite bring herself to sleep on the musty mattress on the floor of the bedroom.

The house folded itself around her, murmured its complaints and sadness in squeaks and crackles. It was completely familiar. She had never left. The city, the squat, the terror, the stupidity all fell away. This was where she belonged and where she would stay. In the morning she'd start digging a garden, start thinking about storing food and wood for winter. There was a lot to do. She fell asleep and slept deeply with no dreams.

14

MATT DIDN'T COME BACK to town for a couple of
weeks. When he did, he sat nervously in the bar in the late
afternoon. The door was open and a streak of bright sunlight hit the floor, bounced upwards, dazzled the dust motes
floating in the dim air.

The place hadn't changed in years except to get dustier
and dingier. The sun lit up a patch of linoleum on the floor,
pitted and scarred, black with a mixture of grease, mud, and
age.

He wanted a smoke, but good tobacco was hard to find.
People grew that too, but it was hard to grow much of it.
The bar imported tobacco, but it was expensive and not
many people could afford it. People smoked other things —
dried lettuce, kinnikinnick, mixed tobacco and cheap marijuana — but everybody mourned the loss of tailor-mades.
People made money bringing them in from the coast or
across the border, but no one could bring in enough to meet
the demand.

Joe came in. He worked as the janitor at the police station. Matt bought him a jug of the sour dark beer and a
plate of fried potatoes with almost the last of his cash
money.

"Yeah, I heard them talking," Joe said. "It might have

been up Sheep Creek somewhere. That's what I heard, anyway. Sorry, can't tell you much more, Matt."

It was all gossip and rumours, Matt thought. Maybe none of it was true. Maybe there hadn't even been a body. Maybe it had just been an excuse to pull him, give him a scare.

But he had to go look.

"Hey, Joe," he said just before he left, "you know anything about some kind of chip? So they can tell where you are?"

"Sure," said Joe. "No big secret. They've had them for years. All the cops have them. In the city, they put them in all the little rich kids in case someone kidnaps them. Then if the kid grows up and decides to run away from home and have a life, they have to find some jerk in an alley who'll take it out for them. Costs a lot 'cause they all have an alarm in them. You got to take it out then run like hell. That's what I hear, anyway."

"They do that to prisoners?"

"Only after you're convicted. It's illegal, otherwise. Then they make them so if they get taken out, something happens, you get sick and die, something like that, I dunno."

There was a feeling of something going on. He couldn't quite figure what it was or put his finger on what felt different, but something was strange. The streets were very quiet, too quiet, when he walked through them. Darlene wasn't home. It was evening and he couldn't figure where she and the kids might be.

It was late and he was asleep in the back room when Darlene and the kids came in. She came into his room and turned on the light. He closed his eyes, turned over, said, "Jeezus, Darlene, what's with the light?"

"I have to talk to you."

"Yeah, well, talk," he said. He hated being woken out of

a sound sleep. He had been sleeping a lot lately, deep hungry sleep, and was always tired when he woke up. His sore leg made him cranky.

Darlene was silent for a while, fiddling with a fold in the blanket he had wrapped around himself.

"You're my brother," she said, "and I want to hold to that. I got to hold on to that in the best way I know."

He waited. Darlene never was one to spit things out.

"I went to a rally tonight. There's a new group of people in town. They've got a preacher with them, he's stirring things up. I think he's right, though."

"Why, what'd he say?"

"Well, it's kind of complicated. I didn't understand all of it. He's got some new system for figuring things out, but he says, far as I can tell, that the end of civilization is coming, we got to get ready. He says there's going to be a last war, a really big one. We've got to store food, prepare ourselves, and that means cleaning up our communities. That means living right, obeying the laws. We gotta quit all this smuggling and shit."

His heart sank. "Oh, for God's sake, Darlene, not another one of those religious shysters. They been coming through town since we were kids, one after another, the same message, repent, boohoo, the goddamn world is ending."

"This one's different," she said. She wouldn't meet his eyes, just kept fiddling with the blanket, pleating it up like a skirt, then dropping the whole thing and starting over. "These people are different. You oughta go listen. Practically everyone in town was there tonight."

"Nope," he said. "No way."

"You oughta. Might do you good, Might change your ways."

"Change my ways. What's wrong with my ways?"

"The way you live."

He sat up. "Darlene, if you got some wild hair up your ass about how I live, you'd better tell me."

"You live like a wild animal," she said tonelessly. It sounded like she was rehearsing a speech, "like some kind of caveman. It's bad enough with everything falling apart and everybody moving away. There's nothing to hold onto anymore. Everything is changed. Even you. You've changed so much. I don't know you anymore. I hardly recognize you. People think you're crazy. They're scared of you, do you know that? They think you're wacko."

"What do you think?"

"I think I got kids to raise. I think I got to give them something decent to hold onto. I think I got to teach them to keep themselves clean and decent and live right. I want them to hold on to what's right, to live within the law."

"How do you know what's right?"

"The way things are supposed to be. The way they've always been, normal. I want things to be normal. The way society used to be. No wonder we got no schools, no hospital. It's our fault, all of us, trying to live our own way and not obey."

Her face was white. She was sitting bolt upright on the bed. He moved to touch her hand but she jerked it away.

"Do you want me to leave again?"

"Yes," she said, frowning with effort. "Yes, I think I do."

The words hung there in the air between them. The words flashed like knives coming at him, little tiny knives, moving very slow but sure and deadly. He knew once they entered him, some part of him would die. He pulled the blanket tighter around him, fell asleep for just a second, crawled back into a place of warm restful sleep, of peace, and tried to stay there. But he couldn't.

"Can I stay tonight? Leave in the morning?"

"Okay," she said, "but go before the kids get up."

"Where's Luke?"

"He's gone off again. I never know where he is anymore. He comes around but he don't say nothing. I told him the same thing, he's gotta change his ways. We gotta get ourselves back living in the right way. Then we'll get stuff."

"Stuff," Matt said. Then he stopped.

They sat together in silence. He opened his mouth several more times but nothing came out.

She got up without a word and left. He could hear her in the kitchen, putting things away. He heard her bedroom door close and then the soft shuffling movements as she undressed, the creak of the bedsprings when she lay down.

Stuff, she wanted more stuff. Christ almighty, he thought, so that was her new dream, that being meek and law-abiding would bring all the old stuff back.

He figured he ought to be angry, but he couldn't raise any sense of anger inside himself. He could see the logic in her thinking. She needed something to hang onto, to give her the strength to raise her two lonely kids and keep herself going, get her out of bed every morning. He wasn't much help and now Luke was a washout as well.

He should do something for her. The problem was, at the moment he couldn't think of a single damned thing to do about any of it. Not a thing. She was like some relic left over after a battle had been fought. She was still standing, still making her way along, but he couldn't see how it was ever going to do her much good.

The kids would leave for the city as soon as they got big enough and smart enough to figure it out. These days the smart kids went as soon as they were teenagers if they had ambition and wanted more school.

Maybe Darlene would go then as well, but he doubted it. She'd stay on, get older and more wizened up. Maybe there'd be other guys like Luke, maybe not. She'd make a life out of the crumbs of what she could get. It was crap, but it was up to Darlene. He didn't figure she was going to change much now.

In the morning he got up early, took his pack, and left. He didn't take food from Darlene's kitchen. There wasn't much there to take. Instead he walked downtown. It was just after six o'clock. The town was stirring. A few people were going by on bikes, mopeds, diesel- or solar- or methane-powered cars. There was even a couple teams of horses. It was slow and peaceful. The town was still in shadow, but the light was on the mountains on the other side of the valley.

He sat on the dried grass that used to be a lawn in front of the building that used to be a bakery. Now it was a junk shop that sold a little bit of everything, scavenged parts for machines, old dishes, threadbare clothes, ancient worn editions of magazines, computer parts for obsolete computers, junky solar stills, worn-out batteries.

He sat on the concrete bench beside the sidewalk. The morning was already hot, even without the sun.

There were lines of dry sticks around the edge of the lawn. A few years before, someone had gotten keen on planting more trees as a belated response to climatic instability, but the trees had withered and died in the summer heat. Now their bare dry stubs stuck through the tangled brown grass.

It was just another symptom of the way things were being let go. Christ, they could have at least mowed the grass. It didn't take that much effort. But it was more effort than anyone cared to make.

Some people did. The video store where Darlene worked had a green mowed lawn in front of it. The town hall did as well, though what anyone did inside there anymore was a mystery to Matt and everybody else. But people showed up to work there because cheques kept coming from the government. He supposed there was still a government. You never heard much about it these days, unless you screwed up somehow. Or maybe this new group Darlene was on about was the government rearing its head again.

He sat there with his eyes half closed, dozing in the heat, wondering what he was going to do next.

Someone plopped onto the seat beside him. Matt looked up, grinned at his friend Sky, who, as far as he knew, had left for the coast a year or two ago.

"Hey, man, good to see you," Matt said.

"I heard you got in trouble over some girl," Sky said. "That's bad, Matt, a bad thing. We don't hold with such anymore. You got to change your ways or it's gonna mean trouble. It's your kind that is ruining this town."

Matt smacked his hand on the bench. "Sky, I haven't seen you in a year or maybe two, and that's all you got to say to me?"

"I got the word, Matt, and the word is out. We got to change. You got to change."

"What the hell are you talking about?"

"Folks are fired up. Haven't you heard this new preacher? They're not gonna stand for wrong ways anymore. We want our town back, we want the old ways back."

"What wrong ways? What are you talking about?"

"Messing with girls. Messing around. Not being true. Not walking your numbers."

"What numbers?"

"You gotta find out yourself. Okay, so I told you, eh? Now I gotta go."

Sky got up and hurried away. His shoulders were hunched around his ears. His hands were in his pockets. God, had those been tears in his eyes?

Matt went on sitting. He had nothing better to do. People went by, most people he knew by sight if not personally.

People glanced at him, turned their faces away, and hurried on. He went on sitting. He liked sitting here in the sun with nothing he had to do. After all, it was his goddamn town. He'd been born and raised here. He had no reason to leave or even be afraid of anyone.

Still, he felt kind of sick from the conversation with Darlene. It kept replaying in his head. "You're my brother and I want to hold to that." That's what she had said. So why ask him to leave? And why had he agreed so easily? Now, thinking about it again, it finally made him mad. It was a shitty thing to do, and the only reason she had done it was fear. Someone had made her scared. Normal, she said. She wanted to be normal. She wanted her kids to have normal lives. Christ, what a word.

When the hell had things last been normal? When he was a kid they seemed normal enough. It seemed to him now that things had been so much easier then. Normal. Sure, if life in a small town was ever normal. There were movies and parties and other kids to hang out with, and then you tried to figure out what to do with your life and how to get along, and then you either got married or you didn't.

When had life gone off the rails? There had been all those warnings about climate change in the early years, but no one paid much attention. Things got bad so gradually, no one had noticed. Yeah, it got a little hotter every year, but nothing dramatic, nothing exciting. Most people still hoped it was some kind of fluctuation, it would clear up eventually. And when had the corporations taken over everything?

There had been that big world trade agreement. That had happened when he was a kid, but he remembered people talking about it. No one was too happy about it, but no one really understood it. Lots of people thought it sounded good.

He remembered his dad complaining. Then it all happened really fast that things like schools and the police and the library, which everyone had taken for granted, were sold and that was that, there wasn't much said about it and at first it was kind of exciting. The new corporations promised all sorts of things, but of course they all cost too much for most people.

Matt realized he was thumping his fist hard, hard against the bench. He wanted to hit someone, fight with someone. He should have smacked Sky, just to make himself feel better. Instead he went on sitting there, his thoughts spinning around so hard it made him dizzy.

15

HE SPENT HIS LAST bit of money on a load of food, which he hauled on his back up the hill after Luke drove him to the bottom of the old logging road. Luke had offered him a ride out of town after he passed Matt walking. Matt figured Luke just wanted to make sure he was leaving.

"Don't come up," he said to Luke. "I'll carry the stuff."

"Your call," said Luke. Matt knew he didn't give a shit.

"Keep your head down," Luke said as he was leaving. "If I hear anything about that chick, I'll let you know."

Matt didn't watch as Luke drove away. He was desperate to get back to the shack, to rest his leg, to sit in the silence. He had been away too long, so he hid most of the food under the trees, covered it with a tarp, and limped up the hill.

The shack lay dreaming in the sun, just as he'd left it. The leaves on the brush shone like they'd been polished. The grass was developing iridescent red-purple tops that rippled like waves.

He sat in the sun and dreamed. He sat in the sun with no clothes on and listened for something he could barely hear. He sat in the sun waiting and trying to decide what to do. He had to find out if Star was okay. He had to decide to move. But he didn't know where to start.

That night he was still sitting outside on the ground when the sky shifted and began to fall. That was what it looked like. He thought it was meteors, flashing against northern lights. But there were so many of them. Some of them were so close they flamed across the sky and lit up the ground.

He fell onto his back, lay there with his mouth open like a man catching rain. His prick rose. He wanted Star. He wanted her. He held his penis for comfort, tried to imagine her there with him and convulsed, instead, into a loneliness so acute it was sharp enough to cut him in half.

The lights fell like broken souls, a brief flame into darkness, while green and yellow ribbons writhed behind them. He fell asleep on the ground, and when he awoke his clothes and the ground around him were wet with dew. The dawn was grey. Birds were already talking from tree to tree. He got up, went inside, lit the fire, made himself tea from the mint he had gathered by the creek.

It wasn't enough to stay here hiding, waiting for a vision, a sign, something to propel him back into the world. He had to know. He had to find Star. If she were alive he would find her. If not, he would mourn her and then avenge her death. He would find out what happened and he'd exact justice somehow.

The sun was coming up full of warmth and promise. It was time to move to a new future, one where anything was possible and stars fell like promises, burning messages from Star.

It took him all day to pack. He couldn't decide what to take. He kept putting things in his ancient duffel bag and taking them out again.

He got increasingly nervous as the day wore on. He kept thinking he heard a far distant truck, or a helicopter lifting its way up the valley towards him, and went running outside to look. A couple of times the sound seemed so strong he almost grabbed his rifle and headed up the hill. Then it faded again.

He decided to take the rifle and shells, despite the bulk and weight. He had to hide them down inside the rotten ragged canvas bag he was using to carry everything. Finally, in addition to the rifle, he took only a little food, his sleeping bag, matches, and a change of clothes. And he took the book Star had given him.

What the hell. He'd be fine. It was warm enough to live outside. He didn't even know where he was headed, but he figured he'd start at the beginning. Star had to have gotten a ride out of the valley with someone. Therefore, someone had to know something. The rest he'd trust to blind luck and intuition.

There was that commune bunch just down the road from where that girl's body had been found. He'd go there. They might know something if they'd talk to him.

He curled up in his nest of dusty mildew-smelling blankets and tried to sleep, but loneliness shook him awake again. He lay there and thought about the world and its sadness. He couldn't bear to be alone any longer and yet he had to bear it. Perhaps he should get a dog, something, anything to get him through these moments. The weight of it all bore down on him, crushing him into the sagging mattress. Everyone lived such sad and desperate lives, or so it seemed. The world was sliding into a hellhole, and it was hard to say how it would emerge. He could feel the sadness coming up from the dirt floor of his shack. The earth was sad and it was communicating that sadness to him.

There was always a note of such cheery desperation in the voices of the announcers on the NewsNets. Even when they put the best face on things, it was hard not to notice that things had gone to hell. Now that the Arctic ice cap was almost gone, whole herds of caribou had drowned trying to cross what used to be safe patches of ice. Scientists were trying to save the last of the polar bears and muskox. The Arctic had become a giant swamp. Most of the people had been moved out and settled in camps in the south, where they up and died at alarming rates.

People were restless all over the globe, moving, looking for places to go. There was always some group of pathetic people being rescued off a sinking derelict boat or being sent back to sea at gunpoint after they'd made it to land.

The Middle East was having a war over water. Half of Russia was uninhabitable due to nuclear pollution from melted-down reactors. Asia was usually having a drought or floods or a cyclone.

It felt like everything was speeding up. The planet was plunging further and further into some doom-laden catastrophic future, and yet even when the stars burned and fell out of the sky, the birds woke up in the grey dawn and went on singing. Somewhere in Africa, elephants were dying of thirst. Somewhere in the U.S. Midwest, farmers were abandoning farmland to the creeping edges of desert sand. Somewhere in China, a giant dam had collapsed, sweeping millions of people away. It was all too much to take in. It was too much to hold inside himself. He had to let it go, get back to the immediate and insoluble problem of Star, her life, her laughing mouth, her singing eyes, her thin body, taut against his, his need to find her and make her really see him at last.

16

MATT WALKED UP the drive to the log house sitting on a rocky bluff. He stared around him. He hadn't seen anything like this place for a while, a long while. A couple of dogs came to meet him, barking an alarm. There was a ratty old truck in the driveway, with tanks and solar panels wired on the back. It looked like some kind of homemade nightmare contraption. A huge garden stretched away south of the house, the young corn just beginning to reach upwards.

There was an orchard below the house, a gully with a creek, and beyond that a meadow with cows grazing. Past that was the lake, bright blue in the afternoon light. There were flowers all around the house. He had to admit, it was a hell of a pretty place.

Two men stepped out on the porch above him. They wore overalls. Their hair was long, tied back. The scowling one was heavy-set, with a black beard. The other man was younger, with brown hair and a friendlier expression. A wide set of stairs led to the deck.

"Howdy," one of the men said.

"Hey, how's it goin'?" Matt said, squinting. He had to look up into the sun to see them. He wanted to sound jovial, at ease, but he was doing a lousy job of it.

"Something you wanted?" said the bearded one.

"I'm looking for someone, thought you might have heard something. I'm from Appleby, been around here all my life, thought I'd come pay you guys a visit."

They didn't smile.

"Yeah?" said the other guy. "You don't look familiar."

Matt tried to move forward, go up the stairs, but the damn dogs blocked his way.

Someone else came out on the porch. A woman with long brown braids.

"What's going on?" she said. "Who are you?"

"Name's Matt," he said. "I'm looking for a friend of mine, thought you might have heard something."

"Who are you looking for?"

"A kid named Star, young chick, might have been through here sometime, maybe a year ago."

She went very still, looked at the guy with the black beard.

"Come in," she said.

One of the men whistled to the dogs, and they ran up the stairs ahead of him.

"Come inside," the woman repeated. She looked kind. She was wearing heavy overalls woven from brownish-gray cloth.

When he went in there were a few other people sitting around a table, obviously finishing lunch.

"Had your lunch yet?" the woman asked. "Come and sit with us. There's lots left."

They made room at the table and someone brought him a plate. There was new peas, fried potatoes, salad, biscuits, bacon. Someone poured him a cup of real coffee. He loaded it with cream and honey, settled in to eat.

"Came from Appleby, eh?" said the heavy-set man next to him. "We don't get down that way much. What's the news?"

"Not much," he said, with his mouth full. "Heard the

GreenPro guys are at it again, talking about turning the lake into some kind of protected area. They want to burn all the houses, move the people out, that kind of shit. Probably don't mean nothing."

"Yeah, we heard that," the woman said. "We don't believe it. We've heard too many rumours of that kind over the years. No one really knows."

"Heard the cops found a body, young girl, somewhere out your way," Matt said. "That's why I come looking. Have to be sure it isn't Star."

They all looked at each other.

"Didn't hear nothing," the heavy-set man grunted. "Hey, I got to get back to work. Take it easy, man. Good luck with whatever you're after."

The rest of them left as well. Matt went on sitting at the table, eating, while the woman watched.

After a while she said, "I know who you are. Your sister works at the video store, right?"

"Yeah."

"Yeah, figures. You're the one squatting up on the mountain."

"How do you know about that?"

"Oh, word travels. We're interested. We're squatting here too, technically. This place was my great-grandfather's. He sold it. We took it back after the dope wars, when everyone got cleared out. No one's complained so far. Guess if they do try to chase us out, they'll have a fight on their hands." She laughed softly. "Got nowhere else to go. We'd have to fight."

Matt finished eating and pushed his plate away. "So nobody knows nothing about Star."

"Guess not," she said. "Guess you'll just have to keep looking. Didn't hear nothing about a body. Maybe it wasn't around here."

"People said it was."

"You talked to the cops?"

"They talked to me. Picked me up, gave me a night in their free hotel."

"You check yourself after? Did they put a chip in you?"

"How would I know?"

"Check your wrist. See a scar?"

He turned it over. She picked it up, held it, turning it various ways so it caught the light. Her hands were warm, strong. He looked at her hands instead of her face. Her breasts were too close. Her hands were brown, with thick blue veins running over the sinews. There were several small burns, nicks, old scars.

"Don't see anything," she said. "Better check yourself over. They might have put it someplace else."

She went to put the dishes in the sink and he went on sitting. His body sagged into the chair. He stretched his sore leg out in front of him.

"Hey, you okay?" she said. She had turned, was looking at him, her face full of kindly concern, wiping her hands on a dishcloth.

"Just tired," he said. "Guess I haven't been eating much lately."

"Well," she said, "I guess you could stay a couple of days, get yourself together. I have to ask, but it should be okay. There's a tipi outside that no one is using at the moment. Put your pack in there, have a nap, then come back to the house around four. We'll have tea and see what everyone thinks."

The inside of the tipi was cool, dark. There was a wood frame in one corner with an old foamie on it. He threw his pack in the corner, shook out his ratty sleeping bag over the foamie, and lay down. His leg hurt so much for a moment he thought he was going to be sick. He turned and stretched to ease it, pillowed his head on his coat. Star was near, he had that sense, he didn't care how. Star was near, he could almost feel her presence.

He woke from a dream of drowning. The last thing he remembered was the burning rush of water in his lungs, the effort to not breathe, and then opening his mouth and breathing it in. He had stopped breathing because he was dead, and then there was a blank space until a voice just beside him said, "It's all right, you can breathe now." He had taken a deep whooping breath, woken, gasping.

He lay still, wondering who had spoken. What had the dream meant? It had some kind of message. Sunlight slanted into the tipi through the hole in the top, long slanting bars in which dust motes swam and curled in lazy arcs. The dream still swam inside him, like the water he thought he had breathed. He wondered if he was really alive or if he was dreaming a dream of being alive.

A bell rang. He could hear footsteps, voices. He didn't want to go to the house, face a whole bunch of strange faces, bodies pressing in, looking at him, staring, asking questions. He curled on the bed, holding loneliness to him like a pillow. He wanted to weep, but his throat closed like a trap until he could barely breathe.

He had nowhere in the world now that he had left the mountain. He had nowhere he belonged or could lay his head down and think of as his, as a place to stay for a while. He had this bed, this space, this body. He wrapped his arms around his own warmth to keep himself from floating away, from detaching entirely from the earth and spreading out into molecules, particles of dust with nothing to adhere to and nothing but air between them. Finally he took out his book and began to read.

17

HE STUCK AROUND for three days, but it was obvious they didn't trust him. Some of the women wouldn't even look at him. Only the girl had stared at him, curious. She started forward to talk to him. She opened her mouth to ask something, but the guy to whose arm she seemed to be surgically attached stopped her.

He'd keep looking anyway. Nothing would stop him.

This afternoon he'd brought the conversation to a standstill by asking if they had heard of the Kind Place.

"It's a place Star talked about," he said. "It was the place she was looking for. She said you could go there and tell them what you needed, and they'd give it to you if they believed you. Didn't matter what it was. I don't know what she was going to ask for, but that's where she was headed."

The girl, Lia, said, "I heard of it."

"Nothing like that around here." This from Sam, the man with the black woolly beard.

"It's just a legend," the woman said. "It's a legend from the city. There's no such place. It's just a dream some kids buy into to keep themselves going. I've heard it a few times."

"Star believed it," Matt said, "so I got to believe it too, for her sake."

"You're about half crazy, mountain man," said Sam, disgust in his voice. "I don't know why the hell we're listening to you and your crazy stories."

They were all sitting in the big kitchen in the log house. There were two tin kettles of tea on the wood stove, and they'd all helped themselves when they came in. There was real cake to go with the tea. The cake was made with dried fruit and honey. Matt helped himself several times. He noticed Sam watching him eat too much cake.

Matt looked at the guy.

"I know what I got to do," he said. "That's not crazy."

"You'd better get on with it then," Sam said.

"I just want to know if anyone heard anything," he said. "If you seen the cops sniffing around, or helicopters. It was out your way. You must have seen something."

"I saw a helicopter, up Ash Creek," Lia said. "You remember, Magnus, you saw it too."

"Yeah," he said, "but it was just sniffing for dope. Those guys come around here every once in a while with their sniffers and heat sensors. They never find nothing, but they keep hoping. They're idiots. Got nothing better to do with their time."

So then he left because he could see there was no use talking to them. He could see in their faces the shadow of hidden things. It was strange to him, this new thing of seeing behind people's faces. Like in the bar, when he saw everybody naked.

Yesterday he had sat in their kitchen and watched their faces shifting like water under clouds, the light coming and going like that. It was as if something was shining out from behind their faces, making them transparent so he could see inside.

He'd noticed this happening for a while. He'd seen it in Darlene's face when she told him to leave. He could see her face when she was little and he could see their parents' faces and her children's faces all coming and going behind her thin white worn face. He could see that she wanted him to go, just go away, stop being this crazy man, and behind that was this desperate pleading person going, Help me help me, so he knew she didn't love Luke at all and was just hanging on and using him to get by. Only she didn't want to believe it so she covered it up with food and smiles and the nicest clothes she could find in the dingy second-hand stores still left in Appleby.

At first when he saw Luke's truck stop beside him, his heart leapt. He thought, Darlene's sent him, but he saw Luke's face and realized soon enough that Luke was only there to make sure he was going, to make sure he'd get the hell out of their lives, stop trespassing on what Luke had claimed as his territory.

Luke was shining and sweaty with danger, the anger in him leaking out from all around his closed tight face. It was like looking through the glass in a stove door at a bright fire. Matt was afraid of that fire, afraid of the moment he knew was coming when the fire would leap at him, try to burn him up. He knew now something he hadn't known before: that there was a greedy fire in other people that wanted to devour things, that didn't see what it hurt in its path towards things, that didn't care what it rolled over, didn't care what squeaked and squawked as it was crushed or brushed aside. Maybe it was what people called evil. He didn't know.

There was lots of talk about evil these days, but it was vague talk. People had been ranting about evil since he was a kid, and mostly it always seemed to be the same shit — anything that was fun was evil. As far as he could tell, it had always been that way. Hell, a little sex, a bit of pot, a few beer, those could hardly be evil. But with his new vision he could see something else, something he barely understood. People were always doing things they didn't really like to do or want to do, hiding these things from themselves and each other, doing things for reasons which sounded good but, in the end, served themselves and no other.

Like these commune people. Looking at him with mistrust. Hiding behind their safe walls. Dismissing him as some kind of crazy because he was from outside their safe little group. He had seen the dismissal in their eyes.

He was thinking about it while his feet placed themselves, one after the other, in a steady procession down this road, once paved, but now falling away in places, grass and dandelions growing through the cracks. It wasn't so much the being outside and alone he minded. That was easier than living with people. It was easier than bothering to explain himself.

It was the closing down in people's eyes, the doors shutting, that hurt. It meant they couldn't see him, or had decided not to. There might as well be a thick veil covering him. But he could see them. It was a puzzle. He could see those lights in their faces; it was the lights that made him feel sorry for them. It was the flickering, changing nature of their faces that made them look so helpless. He wanted to tell them something, reassure them. But he didn't know what to tell them. He was helpless too.

He began to sing. It was better than thinking. He didn't know how to sing, but there were old songs stuck in his head so he sang them. He swung along the road with his bad leg lifting and falling, coming down with a definitive thunk in time to his singing.

The sun blazed down on the deep blue lake. A wind was coming out of the north, and the lake was scattered with furry wave tips. At this point the road lifted high above the lake, but he knew if he kept walking it would drop down again, to a place that once had been a thriving resort but was now just a collection of rotting, dusty cabins full of pack rats and squirrels. It was amazing how fast things came apart. He knew about this place because his parents brought him here a few times when he was a kid. Then there had been lots of people around, lots of cars, parties on the beach at night.

When it was truly ferociously hot in town, his mom would sigh and say something like, "It might be cooler out at the lake."

It always took an argument to get his dad to do anything. His dad thought the idea of a picnic was stupid. Why eat outside with bugs and ants when you had a perfectly good table and chairs at home? But the heat would eventually even get to him and he'd say, "All right, let's go to the god-damn lake."

Then it would take hours for his mother, flushed and sweating in the kitchen, to make a proper picnic, which for some reason was always the same menu: fried chicken, dev-illed eggs, biscuits, potato salad, and chocolate cake. If she started first thing in the morning, by late afternoon they'd be ready to go.

The drive to the lake was a combination of bliss and hell, stuck in the back seat of the car with Darlene, both of them pushing and shoving at each other in acute stupid irritation. But the windows were open, the breeze blew over their sweaty bodies, gradually they'd all start to relax, and by the time they got to the beach, even their father would be in a little better mood.

When they finally got the car parked and got themselves and the food carted to the beach, Matt's father would start by rearranging everything. They couldn't just have a fire, they'd have to have a whole goddamn fireplace, with rocks piled up and a grill on top. Then he'd go rummaging among the driftwood and logs to find enough flat boards and stumps to make benches and a sort of table. He'd yell at Matt to help. Matt would drag a few boards, then escape as soon as he could to the water and the rocks, grottoes, and caves beside it.

After his dad had the fire lit and his mother had spread out the food, he'd come reluctantly to eat, then head back to the water. He stayed in until he was blue and shaking with cold. When it was finally dark, he'd come and stand by the fire, a damp towel wrapped around his shoulders. He'd stand there, watch the fire, listen to the waves and the wind coming down the mountains behind him. He never wanted to go home.

Finally they'd have to pack up and stumble up the black steep trail to the car. Matt and Darlene would fall asleep almost instantly, curled against each other like puppies. He was always disappointed when he woke up in his own bed the next morning.

He was sweaty by the time he got to the beach. It was late afternoon. The sand felt like a stovetop on his bare feet when he undressed. He ran into the water, swam, and then floated like a lazy whale. Afterwards, he didn't bother getting dressed but went up to scrounge among the dusty cabins.

Once there'd been a restaurant here, a motel, cabins, concrete pads for trailers. The grass under the giant fir trees was tall, full of brushy seedlings sprouting through its fringed golden aura. It had matted over the concrete trailer pads until they had almost disappeared. He could still find them with his bare feet. He looked in the motel and the cabins. Most of the windows were broken and there were leaves and dirt on the floor. There were mattresses standing against the walls in most of the rooms, but no blankets, nothing he could use. The private cabins were better. Here people had obviously intended to come back. They had nailed plywood sheets over their windows and had left all kinds of things in the cabins — furniture and blankets, matches, wood stacked beside stoves, dried food and canned good in the cupboards.

He had to knock padlocks off some of the cabins. Others had already been broken into. It took him most of the rest of the afternoon, but by evening he had a substantial pile of usable stuff gathered on the beach. He found rocks, made a fireplace, even put a grill on it, then lit a wonderful fire, a roaring pyramid of driftwood that crackled and snapped and sent a cheerful shower of sparks racing out towards the lake water.

He opened several of the cans, dumped them into a saucepan, and set it to heat near the fire. He scooped another pan of clear lake water, set it on the grill, and threw in a couple of ancient tea bags. He had even found some soap and thickly congealed shampoo, and he went to wash in the lake, luxuriating in soapsuds, in being clean. He soaped himself several times, dived under the inky black water and swam around, trying to see anything, coming through the surface with a swoosh, shaking his head, his long hair sticking to his shoulders and curly beard.

When he came out of the water, his skin was burning from the cold. His food was hot, his tea steeped. He flopped cross-legged on the sand, scooped in the food in huge steaming spoonfuls, juice dribbling down his chin and onto his chest. Then he drank the tea, still naked, sitting in the warm dry sand by the fire, loving the silky feel of his own clean dry skin, his lean body, the thin ropy muscles. After a while his bad leg began to ache and he stretched it out. It was still crooked, a little shorter than the other leg, with a thick white scar running down the thigh. He rubbed it to ease the ache.

The next morning was hot, but by the time the sun was up, Matt had already left. He found the place where an old logging road left the highway and climbed the steep hillside. Someone had been here all right, driving something that must have been like a tank. The road was full of two- and three-foot-tall trees, and these they had simply mowed down. He followed the road for a while, then stopped.

Many things puzzled him. Why would Star have come here? There was no reason, and it would have taken someone with the agility of a mountain goat to scramble across those washouts where there had once been bridges.

There was nothing up here, just forests, mountain peak after mountain peak, and far below him a creek running in its valley.

It seemed more likely that someone had come up here and wanted an excuse to look around. The tracks ended and he could see the place where they'd turned around. He tramped through the willow, the thick brush and seedlings at the edge of the road. Someone had been here, but apart from that he learned nothing.

When he got back to the beach, it was almost evening. He cooked some food and sat by the fire, rubbing his leg, exhausted.

A stick cracked in the brush behind him and he froze. In one quick movement he rolled to his feet and moved away from the fire into the shadow of a giant boulder. He waited but nothing came. He began to shiver, away from the fire, which shrank from yellow flames to glowing coals, twinkling and creaking.

"Hey, mountain man," a voice behind him said softly. He whirled around and at first could see nothing. Then the boy from the commune slid down from the top of the rock and landed in the sand beside him. Lia followed a few moments later.

"Hey, man, we're gonna go for a swim, then we gotta talk. Okay?"

Without waiting for an answer, they pulled off their few clothes, ran into the water, and swam away. He went back to the fire, pulled on some clothes, and added a pile of wood until the fire was blazing, casting weird lights and shadows on the surrounding granite.

They came back out of the water, shaking themselves like dogs, standing naked by the fire, giggling at something. Then they went serious all of a sudden.

"We want to talk to you about Star," the guy said.

"I have to find out what's going on," the girl said, "what happened to her."

"I'm Magnus," he said, "she's Lia, and you're Matt, right? My mom knows you. We're from the commune."

"Yeah, I seen you there," Matt said. "What about Star?"

"We're looking for her too. She's a friend of ours. But first we want to know what you want with her."

Matt was silent. He was about to tell them both to go to hell, but bit the words back. "I'm her friend," he finally said. "We spent some good time together. She means a lot to me."

Magnus nodded. He sat staring at the fire. Then he said, "My mom wanted to talk to you too, but then you took off."

"No one was talking to me."

"Tell me about Star," Lia interrupted. "She was my best friend. Tell me every single thing you remember about her. Don't leave out any details."

Matt turned on her. "I don't have to tell you shit. Who the fuck are you people? What are you doing sneaking up on me like this? I'm the one with the questions. When I showed up at your place, no one would talk to me. So what are you doing here?"

"Hey, calm down," Magnus said. "Slow down." He pulled his pants towards him, fished a joint out of the pocket, lit it with a twig from the fire. "New crop," he said, taking a deep pull and then passing it to Lia. She took it, smoked, passed it to Matt.

Matt looked at it, then put it to his lips. The smoke was sweet and resinous. It sank deep into his lungs, went out of his lungs into his muscles, into his bones, into his ass sitting on the cold sand, coiled back up into his head.

"Okay," he said. "Okay. Sorry I blew off. I met Star once. We spent a few days together. It was ..." he hesitated. "It was special. She taught me something. She showed me something I needed. It changed me. I don't know how to explain it. I knew we were connected. After she left I started to see things, figure stuff out. I kept thinking she'd come back. I kept thinking that she must have felt it too. She'd come back when she got through looking. I don't know what she was looking for, but whatever it was, I was willing to give it to her. I was gonna do whatever it took. I was going to build us a house. Had this place, up on the mountain."

Now that he had started talking, the words flowed out of him without his volition or control. Some dam had broken inside, some restraint that he hadn't known existed.

"I was going to build this amazing house. I seen it, you know, in my head, like a vision, and I knew what was needed. I knew that's what Star needed, a place, a home. A real home."

He stopped. Now he was scared. He'd said too much.

"Star was my lover too," Lia said. She was fiddling in the sand with a stick, drawing circles. "I've got to find out what happened to her."

A silence fell after that. Thoughts whirled in Matt's head. He shouldn't have smoked that pot. It was too strong. He shouldn't have said anything. He didn't even know these people. Star might be hurt. Something might have happened. She wasn't dead. Star had other lovers. Of course she had other lovers. Well, so what?

He began rearranging the wood in the fire. It took a long time. He wanted to arrange it so every part was burning, not smoking, nothing sticking out or protruding into the air so it wouldn't burn. Magnus and Lia watched him. They were all fascinated by the fire.

"So talk," he growled finally. "That's what you came for, what you said."

Now Magnus was poking at the fire. Pretty soon they'd all be doing it.

"What did the police tell you?" Magnus asked.

"Not much. Everyone in the bar had heard something. Someone, don't know who, no one seemed to know, found a body, up Sheep Creek. Guess it had been there a while. They could tell it was female, blond hair, not much more. Coyotes had messed it up pretty bad. Fucking cops grabbed me coming out of the bar. Threw me in jail overnight, told me not to go too far. What the hell did they figure I'd do, eh? I got out of there as soon as I could. But I didn't figure it was Star. I'd know that, wouldn't I? I'd feel it somehow."

"We been looking for her too," Magnus said, "but we don't want any cops around. That's why nobody was happy to see you. Mom figured maybe they were tracking you. But it's been quiet. We sort of came to apologize." He looked at Lia.

"I want to find out what happened," she said. "That's all. I just want to know. Then I can decide what to do."

"So who the hell are you?" Matt said. "You from the city?"

For some reason, this young woman was getting on his nerves. Something about the way she was hanging on to Magnus, something about her little perky tits, now turning pink in the heat from the fire, something about the suspicion and anger in her voice when she talked about Star. He shook his head. It was clearing a bit now. The dope had muddled him, interfered with his thinking, but it also made everything bigger, clearer, sharper. He could see terrible pain and sadness behind Lia's eyes, but it didn't make him feel sorry for her. It made him mad. All she saw, looking at him, was some crippled guy who'd fucked her friend and then abandoned her. He could tell everything she was thinking. It made him terribly sad, the way people misjudged each other, the way their thoughts went right by each other with the best of intentions and they made a mess of their lives.

She hadn't answered his question, just sat there shaking her head.

"Fine," he said. "So what do we do now?"

"You have to talk to my mother," Magnus said. "She's the one Star talked to. Stay here tonight. We gotta get home. It'll take us a while. But we'll come in the morning, bring you some food. That shit," he gestured towards the cans, "that'll kill you in a hurry, man. There's no life in it. You got to eat live food, you want to keep going. My mom could give you a treatment for your leg, too. She can do some amazing shit."

He stood up in one swift movement, pulled on his clothes. Lia dressed as well, but slowly and out of the light of the campfire.

"Hey, man," she said, coming back, "take it easy. We'll figure it out. We're all on the same side here, okay? Some things I just don't want to talk about, okay?"

"Hey, did you know there's another war on?" Magnus

said suddenly. "We got a short-wave radio broadcast last night. Someone came in real clear from Africa or some place like that. I guess they got this new policy — places where everything's fucked up, dying of AIDS or whatever, they go in, drop some biocide, kill everybody off, re-colonize it later when it's been cleaned up. We got some African guy who was asking for help. Claimed everybody but him was dead."

"Jeezus," Matt said. "I never thought they'd go that far."

"Probably what they'd like to do to us," Magnus said cheerfully. He took Lia's hand and they disappeared into the darkness.

Matt sat down by the fire, his head spinning and full of too many thoughts. After a while he got up, built up the fire, made a bed between the fire and the slab of granite behind him, and lay on his back watching the stars until he fell asleep.

He woke at first light. The sun was just catching the peaks on the opposite side of the valley. Trout circles dappled the flat silver surface of the bay and he thought about fishing, thought about going back up to the cabins, hunting for a rod, finding some bait. It all seemed like a lot of work. He watched while several sleek mink dove from the rocks. He hadn't seen those for a while. They got up early, then disappeared during the heat of the day. Their shining brown bodies stitched holes in and out of the water.

He unrolled his blankets, trotted naked down to the water, ran in, dove under, and came up fast, shaking his head in shock. His skin felt like it had shrunk a couple of sizes. He ran back out, got some dried grass and wood, got a fire lit fast, stood by it, shivering, still unwilling to get back into clothes. He took some pleasure in carefully, leisurely, toasting his backside, then his front, then turning around to do it all over again.

He was incredibly hungry. Fucking pot. Man, he should know better than to smoke that stuff. But Magnus had said they'd be here early with food. He could wait.

The edge of sunlight toddled down the far mountains, slid across the lake, crept up the beach, warmed his skin, blanched the flames of the fire, lit the mica flecks in the granite rocks, and went on climbing up the mountain behind him, lighting up each yellow-green branch tip.

They didn't come until the sun was almost overhead. By then he had given up waiting, had tackled the job of sorting the pile of stuff he had brought down to the beach. At second glance, it wasn't all that usable. There were old musty blankets, tin cans of food with the labels rotted off, some dishes and aluminum cooking pots, a couple of knives, an axe and a saw, a hammer, rusty shovels, rakes, pruning shears.

He was still going to build the house, the monument, even if Star was dead. It made it seem even more important. A man had to have something to build his life around. He'd build his love for Star into the house. But he had to find a place, he had to do both things: find out about Star and find a place for his house.

They didn't seem very compatible at the moment.

"Fucking idiot," he muttered. What the hell had he been thinking? Had he been thinking? No, he had been dreaming about his house, dreaming about finding Star, dreaming all sorts of things, of being able to rescue his sister from Luke's sweaty clutches, of going back and confronting the police with his innocence. He rubbed his butt where the skin kept itching. He had a rash there, maybe too much sun.

But he didn't want to give up the stuff. He needed it. Maybe he could make a bundle, get some wheels under it, old bike wheels or cart wheels, tow it along. Maybe Magnus could help him.

He was still staring in puzzlement at the pile, trying to figure out what to do next, when Magnus, Ama, and Lia came trudging through the trees. Magnus had a pack full of food, which he proceeded to unload.

They made coffee over the fire.

"How the hell do you get real coffee?" Matt asked. Not that he really cared. The smell alone was enough to set his mind twitching.

"Smuggling," Ama said. "We pay a ridiculous price for it. Magnus found us a supplier, couple of years back."

"You grow dope?" Matt said.

Ama just looked at him. "We grow lots of things," she said. "We're farmers, that's what we do."

They drank the coffee, flavoured with cream and honey.

"We live good for now," Ama said, "but something's going on. I wanted to talk to you, see what you knew, see if you had picked up anything new from talking to folks in town."

He waited, a hunk of fresh bread and butter in one hand, the mug of coffee in the other. God, food was a great thing.

"We've been here thirty years now. We were here all through the dope wars. God, that was a bad time, but we survived it. Our family used to own the land. We don't really know who owns it now. As people moved out, we took over their places. We took in a lot of abandoned animals, abandoned people too, for that matter. We've done all right. Nobody bothers us. We don't bother anyone. We make a run to the coast to trade twice a year, and everything else we need we produce for ourselves."

"Sounds great."

"Except now something's up. We've had helicopters buzzing our place, we've had animals shot, a couple of people have left and wouldn't say why. We feel like we're being watched, but we can't figure out how or why. And what's worse, there's someone, maybe a few people in the group, who are up to something. Some kind of power grab maybe."

She paused again, poked at the fire. Her fine, thin features were twisted. She chewed on her lips, rubbed her face.

"I thought I knew everyone so well. I thought we had finally achieved something, some kind of harmony. Sometimes I think we're the people the legends are about. Maybe we're the Kind Place. Your friend Star found us a year ago, she came by, stayed for a while." Ama looked at Lia, who nodded. "She seemed happy enough. But then something happened, I don't know what. And she left. She wouldn't say why. Someone had said something, or done something. She just left. And after that, things really started to go wrong."

She looked like she was going to cry. Magnus looked uncomfortable, moved to sit by her, rubbed her shoulders.

"Hey, it's not that bad," he said. "We're still together, we still got the land, we're fine. Don't get all wired now."

"What have you heard?" Ama said. "Right now, I just need information, any information. Any little bits. Tell me what you've heard."

"Well, not much," Matt said. He scratched his shaggy head, grimaced. "Just what I told you. The GreenPros been snooping around. There's talk about some big water project going down, them maybe wanting to turn this valley into a park, move everyone out, maybe take some water out of the lake, ship it south. I guess the south is getting pretty dry. I heard the whole Midwest is just one big desert. But why the hell do they care about you guys? A few people living here don't upset the ecosystem. I don't get it. I just want to find out what the hell has happened to Star."

"We're looking into that," Ama said. "But really, we don't know anymore than you do."

"I got another favour to ask," Matt said. "It's a big one." He hesitated, glanced around the circle of faces. "I need a place. I got this idea for a house. I mean, I got nothing now, since the accident. Darlene, she's got our parents' house. It's both of ours, but she needs it. I been collecting stuff to use. You guys have a truck. I need tools to build, lumber. Can you think of a place, somewhere I can build?"

Ama looked at him, at the pitiful pile he had collected from the old motel buildings.

"Sure," she said, "we'll do that. Not right away. We'll help you, but you gotta help us. We gotta figure this out. Our lives might depend on it."

18

MATT PAUSED in his work and looked out over the valley. His new place was past the commune on the side of the mountain. He loved being up so high. He looked again and the scene in front of him shimmered and shook as if flames were dancing over the far green misty places below him. He shook his head and the flames danced with the shaking.

He put down his shovel, sat on the ground, buried his head in his knees. When he looked again, the flames were gone.

He sat there for a long time. The silence folded around him. He could hear a very tiny breeze coming down the mountain. A raven called and was answered. Several ravens rose from a pine tree and went winging south.

The breeze arrived and blew through his wet sweaty shirt. He got to his feet. He had been thinking that maybe he should ask Ama about these visions or whatever it was he was seeing.

One morning he looked out of his tent and saw an angel perched in the top of the huge ponderosa pine that leaned out over the cliff below the clearing to which he had finally relocated. He saw things out of the corner of his eyes. One morning he saw a monstrous cat bound out of his tent; he had seen a bat with enormous wings soar over his campsite.

He wondered if these were signs that he had chosen wrongly, that his house was in the wrong place.

Ama had brought him here. It was an old clearing, flat, full of tiny bushy trees. His first job was to reluctantly cut the trees on the road and in the clearing. He felt sorry for these baby trees, so energetically trying to re-colonize the ground. His second was to borrow the truck and, with Magnus's help, bring his collection of building materials from the other place to this new one.

When they got to the other clearing with the truck, the shack had been burned. The pitiful stack of lumber he had hauled up there on his back was also burned. But the bones were there, the cans of nails, the buckets of white sand, the stacks of rusting junk and bent solar panels.

Magnus had laughed at him. "What kind of house are you building?" he said.

So Matt told him, reluctantly, about Star and the bones and his vision, his idea of making a house that was a monument, a shrine. He told him about the accident, how he had known then that up until that moment his life had been empty, but he had seen that he had to do something, that he had to figure out what was important.

Magnus laughed some more, but not unkindly. He didn't laugh when Matt insisted on loading all the junk on the truck. "Man, you are one whacked-out fucker. You've taken on a hell of a task," he said. "But it might work. You could get Sam, Mom's boyfriend, to help you. He knows more about building than any of us. He built the log house at the commune."

So Sam and some of the other commune people had come over to the new site and spent a day with a team of horses, cutting logs and hauling them to his house site.

That night, at dinner in the big log house at the commune, they were more relaxed and friendly than they had been. Ama even apologized.

"We didn't know who you were. Some people got the idea that you were accusing us of murdering Star."

He drank too much wine and boasted about his house. He heard his voice going on and on and couldn't seem to make it stop.

But they were all taken with the idea of the monument.

"Even you guys," he said, "even you guys, you kill things all the time, you never think about it. Every goddamn thing is somebody's home. Every tree, every bush. Look around you."

They stared at him.

"We got to eat," Sam said. "What do you want to do, keep all these animals for pets? Get over it."

Matt subsided. He wasn't sure what he was talking about. These days everything puzzled him.

"You know what used to get to me," he said into the middle of the discussion, which had reverted back to gardening while he was thinking.

The heads around the table turned to him. His voice had been too loud. He realized that. But it had been so long since he'd had people to talk to. All the thoughts that had been clanging around in his head for months had gathered into a mob, were rushing to come out, demanding to be expressed.

"I used to sit at the breakfast table. The old man always had the news on, radio, remember that? And some days the news would be so bad, plagues, disasters, floods, and then someone would always come on and say something vague about climate change. I used to feel like running out of the house, I was so scared, but you know, no one ever said anything. The old man went off to work and Mom did the dishes and Darlene and I went to school and everybody just carried on. I thought for sure sooner or later we'd have one of those disasters, but we never did. So I stopped listening too. But now I realize I never stopped thinking about it and trying to figure it out. How come nobody noticed how bad it was getting?"

"They did," Ama said patiently. "People were always yelling, fighting about it. But you got to remember, people were making money out of all that. It's still the same way. Nothing much has changed. Why do you think we got these Greens running around up here protecting everything? You think they're protecting us? No fucking way. They're protecting resources, they get their money from the corporations, just like everybody else does."

"But we're not hurting anything."

"No," Ama said slowly. "It's not that. We're just irrelevant. They figure we'll leave sooner or later. We'll get tired of the isolation and the harassment, or our kids will get sucked into the bright lights and the rest of us will stay here and get old and die. I don't think they care. They just want a place with clean water they can export and trees they can cut down and wild animals that people will pay to shoot."

"They want people they can control," Sam said.

"Yeah, that's true. As long as we're here, people will find us. People like Star."

"But why kill her?"

"We don't know that they did."

"Somebody did."

"We don't know what happened. Maybe she stumbled over something she wasn't supposed to know, maybe somebody's drug deal, maybe something bigger."

Matt sat back in his chair while the conversation flowed around him. He had eaten a lot of food and drunk a lot of homemade elderflower wine, which made him sleepy. Now that he'd had his say, he was tired of talking and wanted to go home. He looked around the room. There was a golden glow from the honey-coloured log walls, the oil lamps, the fireplace.

"Excuse me," he said and pushed himself away from the table, collapsed onto the fur rug by the fireplace. The flames were licking around a pile of applewood. One of the dogs came and collapsed beside him, rolled on its back, asking for attention. Matt scratched idly through its golden fur.

Behind him, other people were getting up, leaving the table, clearing dishes. It was so nice, being here. It felt solid, more solid and real than anything he could remember.

Magnus sat down next to him. "Lia's been crying for Star," he said.

Matt thought about this. Was he supposed to be crying for Star? There was Star, there was his house. Somehow they had become interchangeable in his mind.

"We're still not even sure she's dead," Magnus went on.

"We could talk to the police, they might tell us something. They might throw us in jail for bothering them."

"They might not. Besides, they're the only ones who know anything."

"I got to get the foundation started for the house. Maybe I could take a few days."

"I'll pick you up tomorrow," Magnus said. "We can go on a scrounging trip for your house on the way. Maybe Lia will come."

19

MATT FINALLY FOUND Luke. It had taken a while. No one had seen him, or no one would admit to it. Then Matt saw his truck coming into town, covered with dust.

Luke was in the bar, drinking beer, when Matt came in. His hair, face, and clothes were covered with dust. He drank a glass of beer in one long swallow, crooked his finger to order another one.

"I been looking for you," Matt said.

"You and a whole lot of other people. Sit down, have a beer. Jeezus, you're always so damn serious. Lighten up, fer chrissakes."

"Where were you?"

"What the hell is it to you?"

"I'm just trying to figure what's going on. I got some stake in it. There's just too much shit around. Maybe a dead body, maybe not, maybe me being charged, maybe not, maybe Star has disappeared, maybe not, maybe Americans coming in, maybe not. Now we got this new preacher in town, stirring things up. Darlene thinks it's all our own fault we got no town left. Says we got to obey the laws. Now when I come to town I got to sleep in Stan's basement. He don't care who comes and goes, long as you bring him some beer now and then."

Luke looked at him, amused. "Yeah, you sure get your ass in some shit."

"People are saying all kinds of things," Matt went on. "Nobody looks at me."

"Well, folks'll do that." Luke laughed. "The goddamn folk are so goddamned spooky they'll say anything. People are jumpy. Or maybe you ain't noticed, living up there on the mountaintop like a goddamned bear. Maybe you ain't noticed that the rest of us aren't having such a good time. Maybe you ain't noticed that we're caught in a squeeze. We got the goddamned GreenPros on our back, screaming about saving every tree because we all gonna burn up if we don't. We got a government way to hell off beyond the mountains that don't care shit what happens to us. They'd be happy if we all moved out or starved to death or the mountains fell on our heads. Then they could close the doors and let the goddamn animals have the place. Well, they got a few things wrong. We ain't dying and we ain't leaving. We got a chance to get some good stuff back. So the government can go fuck itself along with those stupid flat-landers squatting in the cities. They think they're so much better than us. I'd like to see them pick up a gun and figure out how to survive up here."

It was a long speech for Luke. He picked up another beer and drank half the glass in one swallow, put it down and glared at Matt.

"So you'd better figure out where the hell you belong — up in the mountains like a fucking hermit or down here with us. The time is coming, boy. Something new, gonna change things around." He finished his beer, pushed back his chair, stood up, and went out.

Matt stared at the filthy red terry towel tablecloth for a while. Finally he got up and sat next to a guy named Soapy.

"You still working for Luke?" he asked.

"Now and again," Soapy said.

"So what the hell game is he playing at? I can't figure it. And now he's got my sister involved somehow. What's going on?"

"Jeez," said Soapy. "I dunno what I can tell you, just a few things I heard." He held up his glass, signalled for another round. "But I think he's caught between a rock and a hard place. Word is he's involved in something big, really big, got all kinds of strange people coming around — you see that Hummer up the street earlier?"

"No, never saw nothing."

"Built like a tank, that fucker. Runs on nuclear. Man, you should keep your eyes open. Big things happening, big things. New people moving in." Soapy was getting excited. White spittle flakes appeared at the corners of his mouth.

"Man, something big is coming," he said again, softly, after a long silence.

"Soap, this is Appleby. Nothing big has happened here since the last ice age. What the hell are you talking about?"

Soapy's voice dropped to a whisper. "Corporations, man, corporation money, got their own militia. Bible thumpers mixed up in it. I don't know who they are. Got money though, setting up some kind of enclave, whatever that is, bringing in some new money, that's for sure."

"So what's Luke got to do with it?"

"He's looking for land, looking for the right place. Word is they want land up where that commune is located, want to take it all over, maybe blow up the road or put up gates, keep everyone else out. It works, you see. There's just the one road, just goes north and stops. They want some place they can defend."

"What's this preacher got to do with it? What are these numbers people are talking about?"

"Dunno," Soapy said. He took another long drink of

beer. "Something weird. Numbers got to do with laws. Hey, man."

Bodies thumped heavily into chairs on either side of Matt.

"Heard you were in jail," someone said. They were men Matt had seen but couldn't say he knew. Suddenly he felt crowded, stifled. More men were drifting over.

"Gotta go," he said, thumping down his glass. There was silence behind him. He fled the bar without looking at anyone, without bothering to say a thing to anyone.

He was suddenly desperate for the clean air of his house site, the quiet, the deer stepping delicately around it with their eyes flicking past him in suspicion. He thought of how one day he could be sitting by the stove with the fire going, the doors open and heat blasting out, a cup of tea and a new book and supper cooking and nothing but the peaceful darkness hovering past his door.

He crossed the street and went down the hill across the rusty disused railroad tracks that had grass and weeds and patches of moss growing over them. Even trees and brush were starting up, he noticed. It didn't take long for the forest to start reclaiming its own. What the hell were the Green people so worried about? He supposed they all lived in glass-and-concrete palaces on a hill somewhere, looking over a city. This growth was exuberant, a bright startling acid green. Matt looked more closely. It was a thick vine, something tropical-looking that he had never seen before. It was growing up walls, trees. In one place he could see it had completely enclosed an ancient rusting car.

He went on down the street past abandoned houses that were crumbling and falling in on themselves. God, there were a lot of vacant houses. He hadn't been in this part of town for a while, and the last time he'd come down he'd been too pissed at Darlene and the world in general to notice anything. The vacant houses were disappearing, hidden behind grass and tangles of that same weird vine and brush. Nature was a greedy bitch. People had been fighting back the goddamn jungle for a million years, and the minute people stopped digging and hacking and mowing and cutting, here it came, sneaking back like a hungry alley cat. Well, good for it. He felt like cheering it on.

He went in the back at Stan's. Stan was asleep half the time and drunk the rest. Matt went upstairs to scrounge for food, but the state of the kitchen defeated his hunger. He found an ancient packet of dried soup in one of the cupboards and ate it dry. He drank some water from the tap from his cupped hands, threw the soup package on the floor where he didn't figure it would be noticed amid the general wreckage, went back downstairs. Somehow the dried soup only exacerbated his hunger. He'd been eating too well at the commune, had gotten out of the habit of starving. His stomach jumped and growled. He tried to think. He'd had a sandwich sometime earlier, then the beer in the bar, now this shrivelled shit. Not much food for a man, he thought. Christ, he couldn't think, he had to get some food.

He had no money, hadn't had any for a while, but he was going to need stuff for his house. He supposed he could hit up Luke for a job, but that was about the last thing he wanted to do. Christ, everything he could think of was disgusting or stupid. Steal food, scrounge from the town dump, what the hell. He hadn't sunk that low yet. He went back upstairs, went through the cupboards a little more thoroughly this time, found nothing, drank some more water.

Finally he went back out on the street, wandered his way uptown. It was late afternoon. He found the patched-together, scabbed-over, rusting junkheap that was the commune truck. No one was around, but if he waited, Magnus should show up. He could hit Magnus up for some food and then persuade him to get the hell out of town.

He lowered himself heavily to the running board of the truck. His leg ached like someone was twisting a knife deep in the muscles. He stretched it out, trying to relieve it, but that only made it cramp, so then he had to hoist himself up and limp around in circles, cursing, until the leg eased and he could sit back down.

When Magnus came, he was bent over carrying a huge sack of something on his back. He dropped it into the back of the truck. "Wheat," he said. "Get in, I been looking for you."

Matt got in the truck and they started north towards the commune. The light outside was somewhere between dusk and dark. The window was rolled down and warm air rushed by his face. There were birds calling somewhere in the darkening overgrown fields. Magnus slowed to avoid a herd of elk standing placidly in the middle of the road.

He rolled a joint with one hand while he was driving, lit it, and handed it to Matt, who took a deep long drag and held it. He felt his nerves begin to settle. He'd been tenser than he knew.

"Lia's mad at me about something," Magnus said. He was laughing softly. "She's pissed about something, but I figure she'll get over it. Won't say much. Women, eh?"

"Yeah, I guess so," Matt said. "I wouldn't know."

"What happened with you and Star, anyhow? I've always been curious."

"We only spent three days together but, man, it was the most amazing three days of my life."

"Oh yeah?"

"It had to mean something to her, right?"

"I guess so. Hard to say with women."

"Christ," Matt muttered. He turned to stare out the window, took another long drag off the joint. Maybe it would clear his head. He needed it.

"We're going to Lia's house," Magnus said. "She's moved to her grandma's old place. Says she's going to stay there. I been trying to talk her out of it, but she's stubborn. Says it's her home and she's not moving, so I guess I'll have to go there. My mom doesn't want me to."

"Well it's home for her now, I guess."

"Yeah, she lived there until she was twelve. Then she went off to Vancouver with her grandmother to get an education. She was kidnapped by some apartment invaders, one of those gangs you hear about. Her grandmother disappeared. It was weird. Just vanished. The place has been sitting empty ever since. But it's not in bad shape, considering. I been helping her fix it up, but she won't let me stay there. It's hard. Mom needs me too, says Lia can make her own choices. Right now they're both mad at me."

"That's the way it goes," Matt said. "My sister is pissed at me. I used to stay there sometimes, but she's got this boyfriend, this Luke Palmer."

"Yeah, we've run into him a few times."

"Yeah, after Darlene threw me out, I found I didn't have a thing to say to her. Jeezus. I'm her brother, she's all the family I got left. Now we don't talk."

"Rough," Magnus said.

The truck banged and rumbled along the road. Magnus had to wrestle with the steering wheel, weaving between holes in the pavement. Matt closed his eyes. Colours and patterns wove dancing designs behind his eyes. Shit, stoned again. And now he was hungrier than he could ever remember being. His thoughts danced and jangled in black-and-white patterns. They hurt his head.

"You got any food in this rig?"

"We'll get food at Lia's. Mom's bringing stuff. Her and some friends, the people she trusts. We don't really know who to trust anymore. God, some of these people I've known my whole life, and now maybe they're enemies. Weird, eh?"

They turned off the highway and began to climb a hill through the darkness. The lights made a tunnel under the trees through which they climbed, the truck body banging even harder and noisier around them. Matt hung on to the dash. He could feel his teeth rattling.

Finally, they drove into a yard and stopped. Matt followed Magnus into the house, which was lit only by a couple of candles and the light from a wood fire in the fireplace. But at least it was warm.

Lia hugged Magnus for a long time, then poured tea and filled bowls of stew for them both. Matt gulped his down and held out his bowl in a mute plea for more. Lia laughed but filled it up. She poured Matt a mug of wine, which he gulped down as well. While they were eating, the door opened and Ama, Sam, Mairi, and another couple, Carrie and Phil, came in. Ama and the women spread more food on the table and Matt just went on eating and drinking wine. He figured, the way he was feeling, he could eat pretty near forever. But after a while they all stopped and settled on the floor and the dusty-smelling furniture with more tea.

"Here's what's happening," Ama said. "Luke Palmer came with some guys, we don't know who they are or who they represent, but they want to make us an offer for our land. They say they own the land on either side of us, which is news to us. They say they own this place too. What they didn't say, they just implied it, was that we had better take their offer if we know what's good for us."

"What was the offer?" Matt asked.

"Not much. A few thousand American and their help finding a place to resettle."

They were all silent at this.

"Stupid fuckers," Magnus growled and leaned forward to poke at the fire.

"It's ridiculous," Mairi said. "What makes them think we'd do such a thing?"

"Do we know anything about them? Can we find out anything? Does this Palmer guy know anything and will he tell us?" asked Sam.

"Luke is working for them," Matt said impatiently. "Why would he tell you anything? All I heard is they're some corporation, maybe religious, got their own militia. We're gonna have to fight."

"I was down south last fall," said Phil, a thin dark man who sat in the corner, out of the light. "Lots of that country is going through hard times. The climate change thing is really starting to hit. They're fighting over water pretty bad. Them rich folks who built houses and golf courses out in the desert — the government is making them leave and paying them shit for compensation. The coastal towns are over-crowded. The coasts are eroding. The trees on the West Coast are dying back 'cause it's not a rainforest climate any-more. It's getting more like the Mediterranean. Britain is freezing 'cause the goddamn Gulf Stream has gone off somewhere. All kinds of environmental crap going on. Apparently Nebraska is one big sand dune. People are mov-ing into cities, making shanty towns on the outskirts, get-ting government food if they can, doing whatever they have to to stay alive. People claim the government is warehousing food, starving poor people. Everyone is blaming everyone else for the mess. There's shit coming, anyone can see that. People with enough sense and enough money are looking for a place to go."

"I heard there's a hell of a land boom going on in Saskatchewan," said Matt. "You can make a fortune there growing grain. It's like the Old West all over again, people moving in, fighting with each other, homesteading."

"Maybe they're onto something," Ama said unexpectedly. "Maybe we should look at this as an opportunity. Maybe we're too close to the border, and if trouble comes, maybe we should be a lot farther away."

"What are you saying, Ama?" Sam rumbled. He kept his eyes fixed on Ama. Matt had noticed the guy never went too far from her side, never stopped looking at her.

"I don't really know. Maybe before we all start yelling at one another, trying to make a decision, we should know we got an alternative if things do get ugly."

"What do you mean, ugly?" Carrie said. "This is still our country. We still got laws, police, government. We're still a democracy, aren't we? You think they'll try to run us off?"

Ama snorted. "When was the last time you voted, Carrie, and who did you vote for? Do you remember? Can you tell me who's in power right now and what they stand for?"

"It's that guy from the Ecology Alliance or something like that. Isn't it?"

People shrugged. Matt tried to remember the last time he'd thought about the government.

"They still run the cities, but we're too far away and there's too few of us. Nobody wants to live out here. No services, no schools, no doctors. They're talking about pulling the police out of Appleby next. Pretty soon there won't be anybody left for the police to worry about anyway. Who cares about a few outlaw pot growers anymore?"

"What about the people who smuggle water and logs?"

"What about them? Nobody's busting them either. The Americans don't care because they need the stuff. The Canadians don't care because the trade is too small to bother anyone. Unless the GreenPros start bitching about it. Look, we've had our heads stuck in the sand for too long. We've been living here thinking we could escape, that we could just have our happy little idyll in the woods forever, away from politics and bullshit. But we were wrong. The world has caught up to us and now we have to try and figure out what's going on and we don't have a whole lot of information."

"Do you want us to just give in and move, is that what you're saying?" one of the women asked.

"No," Ama said. "I just think we should look at all sides of what's going on so we have some options. There's someone I need to talk to," she added, "someone who might know what we should do. I think we need help, or at least we need to know where we can go for help. I brought you here to talk about that, about going somewhere to look for answers."

Matt was sitting as close to the fire as he could, but he kept shivering with cold. He was having a hard time following the conversation. His head was fuzzy with exhaustion. He didn't want to be here. He wanted to be home, even if home was only a tent up a mountain somewhere. He wanted to be home with Star or at least with his memories of her. He was half asleep and the words seemed to spill out of him without his volition.

"What did they do with her?" he said. "Where did she go? She should be here with us. We got to find out." He tried to get up, but his legs were asleep from sitting on the floor for so long.

"We're not talking about Star," Ama said.

"You said you're going somewhere, going to get answers. Well, get some answers about her."

"We haven't made any decisions about anything yet," Ama said. "We need to finish talking things over."

"Well, I'm gonna find her," he said. "I'm gonna find Star.

I'm gonna bring her back, build her a house, look after her memory, better than you people ever could. All you do is talk, talk, talk, talk. Jeezus, I'm sick of talking."

There was silence after this, then Ama said, not unkindly, "You'd better get some sleep, Matt. We'll fill you in in the morning."

He had finally made it to his feet. He stood there swaying, while the fire glinted off his beard and long hair. "God-dammit, people are always telling me what to do. Nobody tells me what to do. I'm gonna build my own place, my own fucking life, my own way of doing things. I'm looking for Star, she's mine, that's all there is to it. I gotta find her. I don't care what you people do."

He lurched sideways and would have fallen except Magnus was there and caught him.

"You can sleep in the other room," Lia said. "C'mon." She and Magnus half hoisted, half carried Matt into the next room, lowered him onto a mattress on the floor, covered him up, and left him. He was aware of all this. He didn't resist. He fell into a dreaming sleep where he was aware of everything, aware of the endless murmuring of voices in the other room, of the stirrings of tiny lives in the walls around him, of the world outside and the stars. He lay there, entranced, while the universe whirled around him in a mighty and sonorous dance and he whirled with it, ecstatically, majestically alive.

20

IT TOOK THEM a day to get ready to leave, and Matt fretted like a giant bear on a leash the whole time. He wanted to go look for Star, or at least talk to people who might know something. But at the same time he was fretting about getting started on his house.

They took the rusty truck. Magnus, Ama, Lia, and Sam packed it with food, blankets, water buckets, bits and pieces of tools, rope, spare parts, anything they could think of they might need.

They brought two dogs as watchers. Magnus, Lia, and Ama sat up front, while Matt, Sam, and the dogs sat in the back. The truck groaned, farted, and rattled more than usual under its accumulated load. They figured it would take them two days to make it to Trout Lake, which was a small lake at the end of the big lake that stretched from south to north through the long narrow valley.

By the end of the first hour, Matt hated the truck, hated riding in the back, hated the noise and the stink and the dust that boiled through the floorboards and the wind that blew grit in his eyes. He decided he also hated the sound of the motor. Motors were the enemy. There was something wrong in the noise they made, something that hurt his head and his teeth and his ears. When they stopped for lunch, he announced that he'd rather walk.

"Fine," Ama said. "Before that, why don't you do us all a favour — go for a swim in your clothes and take some soap with you."

"Maybe I'll just go around naked from now on," he said, glaring at her from under his shaggy hair.

"You do that," she said. "Do what you want. But if you don't clean up and ride in this truck, you won't make it to Trout Lake with us."

She sat there in the sun, shining with calm. She was always calm. She was a tall tanned-brown woman, brown hair, brown face, big brown hands, usually wearing something dark and soft. She sat on the ground, carefully feeding bits of sticks into the small cooking fire. Pots bubbled on a rack over the fire.

Matt blinked. Just for a moment the sun glared off Ama's shining brown hair, and lines of light shot out from her head in all directions, glancing off and passing through each person, each thing, the people, the dogs, the rusty burnt yellow brush, the sagging heat-laden trees. It was so fast he almost missed it.

He backed down the bank, headed for the lake. The place where they had stopped had once been a provincial campground. A river ran into the lake, and a long shelf of gravel beach curved in a semicircle on both sides of the river.

He took off his clothes, threw them in the water to soak, dove, and stayed under for a long time. When he came up, he turned on his back and floated. He tried to think about this new perception. He'd have to be careful. Ama was someone who had a kind of power. She seemed so kind, but there was a secret aura about her that was terrifying. He'd have to watch himself around her.

It also made him wonder about everyone else. Magnus obviously was just a tool of his mother. Lia was another mystery; crazy about Magnus, that was obvious, but with her own secret protective watchfulness.

Sam shambled after Ama like a protective dog. In fact, he was a lot like a dog. He even spent most of his time with the dogs, all three of them ranged around Ama like some kind of guard. The two dogs, one of them an enormous black thing with yellow eyes and the other a little black-and-white collie bitch, didn't much like Matt. He'd tried to make up to them; he liked dogs, but they weren't having it.

The sun slanted through a few fat clouds lingering above the mountains. The mountains were a series of flat blue profiles, shading from light to dark in the far northern distance. The lake was still; only a few fish made rings in its dark green surface. He turned over, dove down beneath the surface, down as far as he could go, farther, his eyes open, searching the dark depths, until his ears hurt and his lungs were screaming. When he burst back through the surface, gasping for air, he shook his head and the water from his hair made rainbowed arcs flying through the air.

He frowned. What the hell had he seen while he was down there? A shadow of some kind. He went back to the sand, trotted naked up through the trees to the fire.

"Food is ready," Ama said from her place by the fire. Sam sprawled at her side.

"Where's Magnus?"

"He and Lia went up the creek, fishing."

"I need him to help me. I saw something out there, just at the edge of the deep water."

Her head came up, wary. "What?"

"I think it was a car. It was so black, hard to see. Christ, it was spooky."

"Eat," said Ama calmly. "We'll go look after lunch. Whatever it is will stay there."

He was shaking from the cold water, from something. He gulped hot tea and beet soup.

Magnus and Lia came back.

"Let's go," he said.

"Wait, you can't go diving so soon after eating. Wait."

"Christ, woman, quit telling me what to do."

She stared at him, impassive. "There's some soap in the truck. Go wash your clothes while you're waiting. They'll dry fast in this heat."

He turned on his heel, went back down to the water, swished his clothes around, hung them over a willow bush, sat on the gravel. Magnus came and sat beside him.

"Mom said you saw something."

"Christ, I don't know. Sometimes I see things."

"Let's go see."

Magnus could go down deeper and longer than Matt. He surfaced beside him, gasping.

"You're right," he said. "It's an old Jeep truck, covered in mud. Tried to get inside. Looked like someone was in there. Couldn't get the door open. Couldn't see in. Could be nothing."

Ama frowned when they told her. "The guy who used to own the place north of us had a truck like that. He pulled out last year. They came down on him for illegal logging. He finally gave up and left."

They were all silent. The truck was in too deep. They had no way to get it out.

"Let's get going," Ama said. "We'll have to come back when we've got more time."

It was a long, hot, bone-rattling, jarring afternoon. They came to the end of the pavement and began climbing up a washed-out, rutted, gravel road. They lurched and crawled over washouts, fallen trees, gravel falls. By the end of the afternoon they were creeping along a narrow slash of road, a cut in the face of the mountain, with a thousand-foot drop to the lake.

Towards the end of the afternoon, bright jagged flashes of light were stabbing from Matt's eyes deep into his brain. The truck finally stopped at an old logging landing, where a creek boiled under a half-crumpled log bridge and fell down the mountain.

Matt jumped off the truck, sat on the ground, his head in his hands. His whole body was buzzing. "Them fucking motor-things are evil," he said, waving his hand at the truck.

"You're just full of complaints, aren't you," snapped Ama. "We need wood, we need a fire, we need the truck unpacked. You can do your share."

He leapt to his feet, full of fury, prepared to snap back, but she swung her head at him and he stopped, blinded by the lights coming out of her eyes. He stood with his head down.

"Help Magnus get the tents," she said and stalked off to gather wood.

He stumbled to the truck, began to untie ropes and pull off the tarps that covered everything. Magnus came to help.

"Your mother is one scary broad," Matt said.

"Mom? She's a pushover. She just has her own ideas of right and wrong is all. Right is her way. Wrong is any other way." He laughed. "Naw, she sounds tougher than she is."

Matt shook his head. He wanted to ask Magnus about the lights, but he couldn't think how to put it.

Lia came and helped them. They got the tents set up and sleeping bags unrolled. By that time, supper was ready and they sat around on old logs, eating fried potatoes and bacon and drinking cup after cup of smoky sweet tea.

"What the hell was all that stuff about the Kind Place?" Matt finally asked.

"It's a story," Ama said. "It's been going around for years. It's mostly the kids who pass it on to one another. No one really seems to know much about it."

"But Star was looking for it. She must have known something."

"She was following a dream, chasing rumours. Maybe this place we're going will know something. People come and go at the commune. We all pass along news because there's things we need to know and we'd never hear otherwise. Someone was talking about some blond chick they'd given a ride to. They'd taken her as far as Trout Lake, dropped her off. She told them that's where it was, the Kind Place, the place where they give you whatever you want most. She was going there to ask them for something but she didn't say what it was."

"What the hell does that mean?" Lia interrupted. "I used to hear that shit on the street, but what does it mean?"

"I don't know, maybe some religious nut promising things he can't deliver. Maybe some rich nut hiding out, promising things he can deliver. Maybe it's really Mecca, or utopia. I don't know. But if we got to move — and God knows I hate the thought, but it's better than getting killed — if we got to move, we should know what we're heading into. We got to find people we can talk to, who will tell us the truth, no bullshit. People we know we can neighbour with. A place we can defend. A place we can stay forever. If we have to. I don't even know if that's true. We're living in a crazy world full of shadows and half-truths. No one really knows what's going on anymore or what to expect."

She shifted around on the log, poked at the fire.

"I didn't grow up here. I grew up in a gated community in West Vancouver. We had a perfect, beautiful, calm, serene life. Everyone I knew lived like us. We never saw anything unpleasant. We had a nanny, a cook. Our parents were kind in their own way. They'd grown up with money, but they were still grateful for what they had. It used to puzzle me, what they were so afraid of. Why the gates, the security? They never explained, just said it was to keep us all safe.

"I never saw the real city until I was a teenager. We used to drive through it, but we never looked. We were usually watching videos or playing on the internet while we drove. There was nothing much to see outside the windows, so we never looked.

"Then one day there was a riot. It never came as far as our part of the city. But we got caught in it, driving across town. That was when the first food riots started. Really scary stuff about global warming was coming out. The weather got worse and worse, floods, droughts, blizzards that lasted for weeks. The price of gas and heating oil shot through the roof. People started freezing to death. The corporations and the government started throwing money into developing solar and other kinds of power, but it was too little, too late. People who could afford it bought it, but most people couldn't.

"People blamed the corporations of course, but corporations are faceless. Who do you fight? Sometimes people in big cars were attacked. But no one could actually do anything. The cars were armoured. We couldn't be hurt. But other people got hurt in the riots. They turned on each other in frustration, burned down their own houses and neighbourhoods. Everyone was just so scared about the future.

"Anyways, this particular day, we drove through a neighbourhood that was burning. Someone ran in front of the car. Our driver just kept going. I felt the bump. I heard the guy scream. I couldn't believe we had just killed someone. I yelled at the driver to stop, but of course he knew better. It was a rough time. God knows what it's like now. Maybe it's better, but I've been gone a long time and I don't know."

"It's the same," Lia said. "There's lots of poor people and a few rich people. It's two different worlds. I saw inside the gated places. We went there to work for the food bank. We were supposed to be volunteers, there to help them with their gardens and their housework. Jeezus. A lot of them were really old. It was sad in a way, all that money and they were still old and sick and dying and lonely. A lot of them got shots to keep them . . . if you can call that living. One of them gave me money once, just to sit with her for a while."

They were all silent after that.

"Was it always like this?" Magnus said. "I read all that history you gave me, Ma. Seems to me things used to be pretty good."

"Yeah, there was a time when it was. But there's always been poor people, that doesn't change."

"What did change?"

"Lots of little things. The price of gas. The weather scaring everyone. The corporations buying everything scared people. They felt they had no control over anything. So no one trusted anyone anymore. No one knew what was true anymore. The NewsNets said all kinds of things. Everyone had their own theory about who was behind the mess. That's what was scary. Everyone hated the corporations, but no one knew who to fight. There was no real war, just a few riots. Just a few little things changed and life began to fall apart. Maybe that's what always happens in history. Little things change and people lose their balance. Little things that change everything."

"Didn't they try and fix it?" Lia asked.

"Of course they did. But there's a momentum when things start to fall apart. It's hard to turn around. There was always groups, movements, lots of people trying to change things, make things better. But they slid anyway. It was like trying to hold back a mountain with your bare hands. I tried. We all tried."

"What did you do?"

"Oh, after the riot I left home. For a long time I joined things, wrote letters, marched, petitioned. Stuff people have been doing for centuries. The worst time was the food riots about twenty years ago. When gasoline really started getting tight, the price of food shot through the roof. The whole agricultural industry was dependent on oil and gas. People were demanding the government do something, but the corporations wouldn't let them. There was all kinds of trade rules against it or something. By then the economy had really fallen apart. People were actually starving to death before they broke the trade rules and got the price of food down."

"It's still too high," Lia said. "We could never afford to shop in the stores. We either stole or went to food banks."

"That's when we left," Ama said. "When people were starving. By then I'd met Magnus's dad. We knew about this land and so we left the city. But my parents stayed. I haven't seen them for a long time now. They might have died for all I know."

"Why didn't more people leave?"

"They did, but farming's a hard life. People couldn't take the isolation. They needed to be somewhere they could get help, get education, still get NewsNets, TV, all that stuff. People were afraid to be alone."

A log exploded in the fire and they all jumped.

"Spirits walking," Ama said softly.

A wind snarled itself in the tops of the fir trees around them, and the fire flattened, then shot up into a yellow tulip of flame.

"Bed," Ama said, but none of them moved.

"What will happen?" Lia said. "What's going to happen to the world?"

"It'll survive," said Ama, "somehow. It's what's going to happen to us that concerns me. Right now I don't have the time or energy to worry about the whole rest of the god-damn world. Just us, here."

21

TROUT LAKE didn't look like much — a few buildings, some ancient trailers and RVs gone green with mould, sitting on a flat gravel fan where the creek ran into the lake. The lake was long and narrow, deep deep blue in the middle, grey-green along the sides.

They came over the top of the rutted narrow road they'd been bouncing along for two hours since their last pit stop. Magnus stopped the truck again, and they all got out to stretch their cramped legs.

"Looks like nothing," Sam grunted. "No smoke, no vehicles, no sign. You sure there's people here?"

"Used to be," Ama said, frowning.

They loaded up again and rattled down the hill. Surely anyone around would hear them coming. The truck backfired. The brakes screeched like a wounded animal whenever Magnus let the revs get too high.

Finally they drove into the middle of the cluster of shacks, old trailers, and ramshackle unpainted houses that had once constituted a town.

When Magnus stopped the truck, Ama jumped down immediately and went across the street, into a sagging building that had once been painted white but was now a bleached and faded grey. The rest of them sat silently watching the doorway. The street was a dusty empty strip. Bits of pavement showed forlornly through the layer of sand, weeds, and old leaves that covered the road. The building next to the one Ama had entered was boarded up, but the one next to that was a small white-trimmed house with a wire fence around a mowed lawn, flowers, blinds drawn down over the windows.

At the end of the street, a cluster of poplar trees drooped over a strip of reedy mud before the lake water began. Matt wanted to go fling himself into the water, but he figured he might as well sit still and watch. It was the hottest part of the day. Had to be late afternoon, but none of them had a watch. He couldn't actually remember the last time he had seen a clock. The slanting sun burned his face and chest like someone had opened an oven door over his head.

"Christ, it's too fucking hot to just sit here," he muttered.

Sam looked at him but didn't answer. Magnus and Lia were in the front of the truck, their heads together.

"What the hell is taking so long?" Matt said again. "At least we could have parked in the goddamn shade."

"Ama knows what she's doing," Sam said. "Whyn't you quit your bitching for five minutes? She'll get here when she gets here."

"Whyn't you go fuck yourself?" Matt said, but he said it without heat and turned his head away. He didn't have the energy to fight with Sam, who wasn't worth fighting with anyway.

The heat beat at him like a hammer, but he could stand up to it. He could stand up to anything.

Ama came out of the building with a man. "This is Tom," she said. "He owns the only thing that passes for a store in these parts. We can camp down by the water, come up later, get some food. There's no electricity or solar here, but he's got a root cellar that keeps things cold enough. Let's get settled, get camped."

Tom wouldn't look at any of them, just showed them a circle within the trees where a dribble of water ran out of a rusty faucet and soaked into a patch of green mossy ground. There was a blackened ring of stones for a fire and a pile of logs that someone had dragged up from the beach.

"Replace the wood when you're done," he grunted and turned back to the store.

"Friendly guy," Matt said.

"He's a good guy," Ama said. "Don't be so negative."

They set up camp, went for a swim, made dinner. Ama was plainly waiting for something. She kept staring down the road, startling at every noise. It was strange to see her nervous.

Matt and Magnus cleaned up. Lia and Ama came back from the lake and sat on a rock, side by side. Lia combed and braided Ama's hair as they talked and laughed in low voices, occasionally looking at the men.

"Women," Matt muttered to Magnus. "They sure know how to make you feel self-conscious."

Magnus nodded and laughed, but he seemed nervously self-conscious as well.

Nothing happened all evening. They went up to the store, found some flour, beans, and lentils, some old canned stuff. Matt wondered how it got here. It was doubtful if a delivery truck had come over that hill in a long long time. Maybe the guy went out for it. Obviously people still lived around here. What the hell, there might even be beer. Beer was easy to make but you needed grain. The country here was too steep and high to grow grain.

They went to bed but no one slept much, and they woke up stiff and crabby, bitching at each other.

The group came just after the sun rose, three men on horseback. It was like being in an old western movie. They came up the road from the east with the sun rising red and gold behind them, got off their horses, tied them to trees, and came over to the fire. They were dressed in an odd and nondescript collection of clothes, patched and re-patched so many times it was impossible to tell what the original colour had been. But they all wore high leather boots, polished to a shine, and leather vests. And they had guns holstered on their hips. Matt stared at that. Even having handguns was illegal. Wearing them openly — that meant there was no law here at all anymore.

One of them came to Ama and put his arms around her. They held on to each other for a long time. They came to the fire holding hands. Ama didn't introduce him.

The men squatted rather than sat, nodded to everybody. Nobody said anything until Ama poured cups of tea and passed the almost empty jar of honey. The men accepted the tea without saying anything, put far too much honey in it, slurped it rather than drank it. They were clean-shaven and looked to be in their late twenties, maybe younger. It was hard to tell.

They finished their tea, poured the leaves into the fire.

"Well, let's go," the one who had hugged Ama said. "No point in trying to bring the truck. The trail is too steep."

They walked, while one of the men on horseback went ahead and two followed behind. It was still hot. Matt shuffled his feet in the dust, stopped often to drink water from the jar in his pack. He slowed them all down, and twice Ama turned and snapped at him. He didn't care. He was beginning to think this was a fool's errand and he was a fool to be on it.

They went uphill, past ancient dried logging slash overgrown with dusty ropes of bittersweet, new trees thick and skinny as quills between the piles of slash. The road became two wheel-tracks; the trees got taller, met overhead. A creek came to meet the road, tumbled down beside it. At least it was cooler. Birds sang and whistled in the trees beside them.

After a last steep climb they came out on a flat piece of meadowland with a log house that looked like a fortress at the other end. It had a palisaded wall made of upright logs guarding it, and log towers at either end. Cows and horses were grazing on the meadow.

There was a barn and several other buildings clustered around the house, a fenced orchard and garden, a herd of goats in one pen, several mules in another.

They went in through the wall and the men tied the horses. Then they went up a steep and treacherous stairway made of notches in a log. There were no handholds, but they made it and went inside through a wide double doorway.

They entered a huge room with a high ceiling. A long table surrounded by chairs ran half the length of the room. At one end of the table sat an old woman. She rose when they came in, waved them to chairs. One of the young men came with glasses and poured a golden liquid into each, passed the glasses to them. Matt took a sip. It was chilled mint tea mixed with apple juice. He drank the rest of it in one gulp.

The woman at the end of the table sat down and said nothing until they had finished drinking and settled themselves. The men they had come with sat near the windows and doors.

There was a quality of stillness about this woman that silenced them all. She was wearing the same ragged clothes as the rest of them, and her head was shaved, but the light in the room seemed to coalesce around her. Light came through the window and lit up her face. Matt wondered if it was some sort of trick, a skylight that shone light just on her. She seemed very old to Matt. She came forward, shook their hands. She seemed delighted to see them.

"Welcome, welcome. It's so good to have visitors," she said. "We get tired of just seeing each other. You have come so far. Are you hungry?"

But Ama wasn't so easily won over. "Hang on," she said. "Let's get a few things out on the table before we eat. I think we need to know a little bit about each other first, who we are, who you are."

"I know who you are," she said smiling. "Your friend has told us about you."

"He hasn't told me enough about you," Ama said.

"My name is Maeve," the woman explained patiently. "I came here thirty years ago. I saw what was happening, what was going to happen. I brought people with me, some friends, some followers — I thought here we could live in peace and survive well. And on the whole, we have. But we have also been prepared to defend ourselves.

"Now we have heard disturbing stories. We decided a long time ago to send people out to watch what was happening and bring back information. We watch the News-Nets and record them. We decided we had another duty: to record, as much as possible, what we saw happening and to store it here."

"So what do you think is going on?" Matt asked.

"We're not sure, but we think what we have long predicted is coming. We have known the end times are coming. What we must do is watch, wait, and prepare. Right now, all we have heard is rumours. Part of what we try to do is sort out rumours from facts."

"What do you mean, prepare?" Ama asked. "We know we're under some kind of threat. We've got people trying to buy our land. We don't know who they are or how far they're prepared to go. We've got to decide what to do, and we need information. We were hoping you could help us."

Maeve closed her eyes as if in pain. "Maybe you're about to be invaded," she said.

Ama bristled. "Someone can't just waltz in and start saying they own a place. Surely living somewhere, taking care of it, surely that means something."

"You're partly right," Maeve said. "We own this place because we live here, because we care for it, we protect it, and because we can defend it. That is what ownership means."

"So if someone told you to go because they wanted to turn this place into a theme park, you'd what? Fight them with knives?"

"With whatever we have," Maeve said. "And what we have is considerable. Although, on the whole, we don't believe in fighting, we do believe in being ready. We keep talking and meditating about it, but we also have what we need to defend ourselves."

She was so calm.

"Yeah, right," Matt said. "A few rifles against an army?"

"There's never been an army that could defeat guerrilla soldiers on their own territory," Maeve said calmly.

Matt was suddenly terribly tired. He didn't care about the people around him in this room. He didn't want to think about fighting, about war.

Maeve said abruptly, "There are some things you need to understand. First of all, I am the leader here and the decisions I make, go, not because they are the best decisions but because every group must have a leader. Democracy has been tried and has failed. Corporate rule has been tried and has failed. The corporations have destroyed everything because they have no leaders, because they are mindless. Look at the sky. Look at the earth. They have ripped them to shreds, mindless and without control, because a corporation has only one mandate: To look after itself. No, there is only one answer in all of history. There must be a clan, there must be a leader. There is no other way."

Matt could see that Ama had gone very still, her lips pressed together. Right, he thought, like she would sit still and take orders from this woman.

"And what are these other rules?" she asked.

"You get the land I give you, you farm it, you give a portion for the defence and maintenance of the clan and for the welfare of the young and old. Ten days a year you give to the whole clan to work on whatever needs doing — water, trails, buildings, fences. One day a week any man or woman under fifty gives to training for defence. We have group meditation and community get-togethers once a week and everyone comes to those."

"We smuggle things," Ama said, "dope, whatever anyone wants. That's our business. It's how we make cash, buy things, tools, coffee, good things."

"No," Maeve said, "nothing to bring attention here. We live quietly. We're not going to provoke a war, just be ready to fight if we have to. We want to be the ghost people, the myth people. That way the only people who come here will be the people who really need us."

"You're not making this easy," Ama said.

"No, I'm not," Maeve agreed. A very thin smile creased her cheeks.

Matt could see the anger building in Ama. The skin had tightened over her cheekbones, around her lips. He looked around the table. Lia had her head on her arms. Matt couldn't see her face. Magnus was looking at his mother.

"Can we meet some of the other people, look around?"

"Yes," Maeve said. "You'll meet them all at dinner. They

are just as eager to meet you. We should have done this a long time ago. We need to talk, form bonds. We're very glad you came. We have much to learn from each other."

Ama stopped. She looked around the table at all of them, then back at Maeve. "Fine," she said. "You've made your position clear. Now we need to talk among ourselves."

"Sure," Maeve said. "Look around, go walk around the land, meet everyone, then come back for dinner. We'll talk further then."

The young men brought in more tea, bits of goat cheese on rounds of bread, pickles, vegetables, bowls of spiced yogurt. They served Maeve with great respect, backing away from her when they were done. Finally she got up and left.

The rest of them ate and drank and talked. But Matt was silent. These new people scared him. He couldn't see through them. He couldn't see what they were thinking.

"I'm sorry," Ama said. "I apologize for bringing you all this way for nothing. I thought these people would help us. But this isn't the place I thought it was."

"Maybe they're right," Magnus said. "Maybe being ready to fight is what we have to do. Maybe you have to have a leader, be organized."

Matt thought of his house site, of the sun on the giant fir, the smell of hot pine, the deer and elk picking their delicate way along the mountain. He wanted to be there, he wanted to be there and alone. Away from there he felt skinless, exposed to everyone.

He could hear their voices, far away, arguing. He could see them, voices billowing from their faces like smoke, roiling and confused.

Finally he stood up and went out into the garden beside the house. There was a bench placed so it looked out over the rolling land below the house. From here, Matt could see there was a series of flat areas, several other houses, gardens, fruit trees. He realized the house was placed so that from this garden you could see most of the countryside.

He put his head in his hands until a soft voice said in his ear, "Are you okay?"

He looked up. It was Star but it wasn't Star. It was a young woman with long blond hair.

"Can I get you anything, help you some way?" she asked. She slid onto the bench beside him. "You look so sad."

That was what Star had said, "big sad man" she'd called him.

"Would you like to come for a walk?" she said. She held out her hand and he took it. They went down a steep rocky path, through flowers and shrubs, past a creek that shot foaming into a small pond. They went down a lane between fences and fields where placid animals grazed in the bright sun.

"I was born here," the woman said. "I've never been anywhere else. Sometimes I think I'd like to see the outside."

"Not much to see," Matt said. "You're lucky you got this place."

They wandered along the path, looked at the barn, the garden, leaned over the fence to pet the goats. Finally she sat on a bench outside a small cabin.

"Tell me about where you're from," she said.

"It's like here," he said, "but with more people."

"But the city — have you seen the city?"

"Sure," he said. "I was there for a while. But I hated it. It's a mean place."

She was silent. Matt looked around. She made him uneasy. He was about to stand up, make excuses, walk away, when she grabbed his hand.

"I want to show you something," she said.

She opened the door of the cabin, led him inside. He caught his breath. The interior glowed with light from the panelled cedar walls, light that bounced off the stained glass windows, the pillows and quilts on the bed.

"Do you want to have sex?" the girl said simply.

He wasn't sure what to say or do. She closed the door.

"Sit down," she said, smiling. "I'm sorry to surprise you like that. I will try to explain."

"I want a child," she continued, "but I want a child that isn't related to anyone here. It's one of the dangers we face, that we'll all end up being related. When I saw you in the garden, I thought how beautiful you were, how strong and tall. I thought you might like to make a child with me."

"You don't even know me," Matt said. He felt like an idiot. He could barely talk. His words gibbered together like frightened birds. His prick was rising in the air in spite of himself and he almost groaned.

The girl laughed. "It's just sex," she said, almost impatiently. "You don't have to do it. I just thought I'd ask."

Matt still stood there, like a tall stupid blond bear, unable to move.

"I'm sorry," he managed to get out. "I think I should go." But he didn't move.

She laughed again, took his hand, led him to the bed, and pulled him down.

"Wait," he said in agony. "Wait. What's your name?"

"Bird," she said. "My name is Bird. It's all right," she added. "You don't have to do anything."

"Wait," he said again stupidly. "I have a girlfriend."

She lay back on the quilt, watching him. The cover was silk; the pillows were soft, puffed with feathers; the light shattered in the stained glass and spread bits of red, blue, purple, green around the room.

She sat up, leaned over to kiss him, and her breath smelled of mint, of meadows and sweet soft mornings and fresh mountain air. He kissed her back. Then he began to kiss her and kiss her in a ferocious agony of need and sadness and lust, still thinking it was wrong, he should leave, he should run out of this place, find Ama and Sam, and get the hell out. He put his hands on her small breasts and she gasped in delight and surprise.

"Oh, that's good," she said.

He meant to tell her he was leaving, he was going to find the others and get out of here.

"Now," she said, "now" and rolled over on her back, taking him with her, and somehow slid his penis into her all in one smooth motion. Now he was lost. He knew it. They rocked together, and he knew he was lost, unfaithful and impure, and when she let him go and lay beside him, he rolled on his belly and lay in the multicoloured silken room and wept. She lay beside him, stroked his back, murmured her thanks. He got up, pulled on his clothes without looking at her, ducked out of the cabin, and sat in the garden until someone came to call him for dinner.

Matt ate dinner with his head down, chewed his food without tasting it. The room was crowded, glowing with candlelight, full of people, conversation, young men, young women. Bird didn't reappear.

Ama sat with the man who had escorted them here. She kept putting her hand on his arm. Sam glowered at them both. Magnus and Lia were sitting with Maeve, talking hard, surrounded by people who hung on Maeve's every word.

After dinner, Matt got a chance to get close to Ama.

"Let's get out of here," he muttered.

She looked at him, surprised. "We'll go tomorrow," she said. "We can't leave tonight."

"These people are crazy," he said. "We can't stay here."

"They might be crazy," she said slowly. "They might also be our only hope."

Matt gave up and went to sit with Sam. He poured each of them a glass of apple cider and they sat in the corner, watching and drinking, until finally they were shown beds in which to sleep.

22

LIA WOKE one morning and something in her belly turned over. She put her hand on the warm flat round of her belly, listening. She lay perfectly still while nothing happened but her breathing. Then it came again, a movement so tiny it might have been a butterfly wing, a tadpole tail.

"Little frog," she thought, "little frogman." She knew she was being silly, curled her hand over her belly, wanting to lie as still as possible, wanting to not wake up, wanting to not tell anyone ever about this moment when her belly turned over and she was no longer alone.

Lia stretched in the big double bed, wrapped the blankets higher around her shoulders. Around her, the house ticked, hummed. She'd spent most of what was left of the summer after they got back from Trout Lake working on the house. Magnus had helped. She had discovered an unexpected talent for building and fixing, and now the house had a stove, a patched roof, windows, and two solar panels that powered a hot-water heater.

She dozed some more. Outside, the sun dripped off yellowing leaves and silver tree trunks. When she woke again in the late afternoon and went outside, the air had a chill under the sun's warmth. Magnus came swinging up the drive.

"Winter's coming," he said, squinting at the sky. "You're sure you're ready for this?"

"I just have to get more wood."

"Winters here can be weird. Sometimes they're long, sometimes it doesn't get cold at all. We never know what we're in for."

"I don't know much," said Lia, "but I guess if I'm going to go on living here, I'll have to keep learning, won't I?"

"At least you've got lots of apples."

"Can't live just on apples."

"No, that's what I been trying to tell you. You need a lot of stuff, like flour, rice, maybe some honey. You need a lot of things."

"Sometimes I miss the city," Lia said. "I knew how to get stuff there. I knew what to do, how to behave. I miss some stuff."

"Like what?"

"Oh, videos, booze, drugs, stealing, hanging out."

"We could have a party. We could make apple cider, invite everyone over."

"I'm lying about the city. I hated it." Her voice shook. "I hated everything about it."

Magnus put his arms around her and they stood together for a long time. She wouldn't let him live with her, which he hated, and she wouldn't stay at the commune, which scared him. He came by every other day, but Ama was putting more and more pressure on him to help her. Things were falling apart. People were fighting, talking about moving. It was driving Ama crazy and she passed it on to Magnus.

They spent the waning afternoon wandering the farm, looking at things, making plans, talking about gardens and fruit trees. They held hands as they walked and ate the apples that had fallen off the trees. Juice ran down their chins and they licked it off each other. Finally they wandered back into the house, made tea, curled up on the bed.

Lia said, "It's been so quiet. Maybe they'll leave us alone. Do you think they'll just let us live here? Do you think we can really do it, have a life of our own?"

"I don't know," Magnus said. All the talk coming back from Trout Lake had been about what to do, whether the threat was real, whether this shadow group, whoever it was, would make good its threat or whether it would fade away if met with some kind of determined resistance. Magnus wanted to make a trip to the city, get guns, but Ama was against it.

Over and around the conversation had gone until Lia was sick of it. Why were they so fucking concerned with security? All her life she'd lived with disaster — not just hovering disaster, but real disaster, her grandmother, her family, the precarious life of streets and squats. Nothing was ever for sure, nothing lasted. Why worry about it?

But after she returned, walking around on land that might finally belong to her, she began to understand. Now, lying beside Magnus, she took his hand and laid it on her belly.

"Feel," she said. "Someone new is here." He laughed, delighted. He wanted to stay for the night, but she wouldn't let him. She needed to be alone with her house and her land and her thoughts. She could stay here with her child. Her child could grow up here, as she had grown up, at least for a while. Her child. It would have her and Magnus to look out for it and a place to live and stay, a place to which it belonged.

After Magnus finally left, she sat by the window, staring into the darkness. Her thoughts were full of pictures of herself walking behind a little girl with blond hair who was running through the tall grass and dandelions under the blooming apple trees. Her thoughts were only pictures, and her belly, breasts, heart, and guts were seized and twisted by a longing she had previously not known existed.

"My grandma," she had said to Magnus, agony in her voice. "I wish I knew. I can't have a baby and not ever know what happened. And Star."

Magnus nodded. "I've been thinking about something Star said once. She told me she was going up on the mountain to fast and take drugs until she saw God and talked to him or her or someone and told them what a mess everything is. She thought it was time God finally took a hand. I just said good luck. I figured what the hell, it's her life. Not a bad way to go, considering."

"I was always going to just go swimming," Lia said. "Except the ocean was so fucking dirty I never had the nerve."

"Can't kill yourself if you're going to have a kid. Got to stick around, get old."

"Old."

"Like everyone else," Magnus said vaguely. "Like old, like normal people. Wrinkles, old age, grandchildren."

"So you think that was Star, on the mountain? You think she killed herself?"

"I think it could have been," Magnus said carefully. "That's all I'm saying."

"Don't tell Matt," she said.

The next morning she got up, determined to show Magnus, Ama, and anyone else who might wonder that she could manage on her own.

From then on, Magnus divided his time between the commune and her farm, helping with wood, bringing food, trying to make the house more livable. He knew about things she wouldn't have thought of, like cleaning the accumulated sludge and sand from the water storage tank. They spent a day at that, got thoroughly muddy and cold, cleaned off, made supper, and went to bed together, but it wasn't a success. They were too tired, got cranky, eventually gave up and fell asleep, and got up in the morning without looking at each other.

23

MATT SAT BY HIS FIRE outside the tent, head hanging. His stomach twisted itself around and around in knots. For days after they came back from the trip, he hadn't been able to eat. He knew his clothes were hanging off him. He had to punch another hole in his belt to keep his pants on. He couldn't think straight.

He was sitting here on the ground by his fire while a cold wind whistled up the creek gully, bringing clouds and probably, soon enough, rain. He'd had to spend time cleaning the mess rats and mice had made of his tent and camp while he'd been away, but since then he hadn't worked on his house. He knew he had to get organized to face the coming winter. He was a man, wasn't he? A man who had stood up to everything that life had thrown at him so far. Then some woman had thrown herself at him and now he was undone.

Sitting here on the ground wouldn't solve anything. He had to act. He had to do something. He got up and put more wood on the fire and sat down again. While he'd been sitting, the clouds and mist had come creeping up through the ravine, past the alders and birches with their rattling yellow leaves, and now the mist tried to get inside his clothes, paste his hair and clothes with silver. He began to shiver but he couldn't move. He was glued to the ground, weighted down with the thing he'd done.

It was the inevitability of it all that frightened him, the way things felt wrong. The sense of wrongness was so strong he could smell it. Wrongness came up out of the earth like rot. And somehow he was involved in it. He was part of a pattern.

He could see it now. He only wondered why he hadn't seen it before. The accident had broken more than his leg. He was supposed to have died. In effect, he *had* died. His life had been cut cleanly apart, and he had flown through the air into a whole new reality. The problem was, he kept trying to act in the same old way, as if he was the same old Matt. He had gone on doing the same dull things, trying to stay alive, keep his shit together, go see Darlene, go see his friends, buy food, eat, sleep, like a dull mindless robot.

The lesson of the skidder had been so clear. Everything had changed. There had been other signs: his dreams, his falling for Star. Everything fit together like an intricate puzzle that he couldn't yet quite see. It was up to him to tease the meaning from the puzzle. But what it seemed to mean, sitting here in the rain with the fire beginning to splutter, was that he had something important, something extraordinary to do. He just had to figure out what it was and go do it.

Rain began dripping off his hair, running down his nose, his chin, plastering his clothes to his body.

Finally he got up, went inside the tent, lit the lantern. He began carrying things outside and throwing them on the fire. What a lot of crap he'd managed to accumulate. The fire outside got larger and larger, began to reach licking tongues for the sky. He dragged out old clothes and blankets, flung them on the fire, boxes of useless junk he'd dragged here. What the hell was this stuff? What the hell had he been thinking? Or not thinking.

There was more junk piled in heaps around the tent. He

began to sort through it, threw more stuff on the fire and piled other things under tarps.

Eventually he stopped and looked around. The fire had died down. The inside of the tent was almost empty. It must be close to the middle of the night. It had stopped raining and cleared off. The stars were brilliant, so bright and clear they might have been dancing. Maybe they were dancing. Maybe it was a sign of approval that what he was doing was right. He knew he should stop, eat something, get some rest, but he felt neither hungry nor tired. He unrolled his sleeping bag and lay down, but his mind was still dancing like the stars.

The sleeping bag smelled. He should wash it. He got up, still naked, took the sleeping bag to the creek, threw it in, and stomped on it, jumping up and down, splashing water over himself. The freezing water felt warm when it hit his skin.

He went back to the fire and began to throw more branches on it. The flames jumped out at him, tried to lick him up, but he was too smart and jumped back, laughing. He began to dance around the fire. Eventually he threw back his head and began to yell. He yelled and whooped and howled until his throat was hoarse.

Now he began to feel tired. He lay back down on the ground, pulled a ragged blanket over himself. Tomorrow, he'd go see Ama, he'd tell her what had happened, see what she thought. Then he'd go to town, see Darlene. He'd tell her she had no right to throw him out of her house. He'd find Luke, see if he could get the truth out of him even if he had to beat it out of the guy. He'd put things right.

He began to dream again about his house. He could see it so clearly, tall, clean, and full of light, full of faces, full of dreams.

When he woke the next morning, grey curtains of mist cloaked the notches between the hills, but the sky was blue behind the mist. The wind was sharp and bit at his flesh through the holes in his clothes. Hunger hit him like a blow in his belly. He cooked some oats and ate them plain, drank hot water to wash them down. His sleeping bag hung soaking wet and still stinking from the tree where he'd flung it last night.

He remembered that he had decided to go see Luke. He had to confront him, find out what was really going on. He pulled on his coat, almost ran down the hill, dragging his leg behind him.

He was limping along the hill leading up into town when he heard the noise. It was someone yelling through a microphone and a lot of voices, a low roaring, a bit like the wind in the yellowing trees beside the road.

It had cleared off and he had been walking with his head thrown back, drinking the air like wine. The hills around the town were a pale blue with gold threads trickling from every ridgeline. The grass was shot through with red and purple. On the way here there'd been a birch tree full of red-winged blackbirds, all yelling together like a demon chorus. As he walked by they lifted out of the tree in a single cloud and circled higher into the sky. He got dizzy, standing with his head back to watch.

"Have a good time," he had yelled after them. He hated every sign of the coming winter, the dying leaves and whistling grass and stupid squirrels madly leaping from tree to tree and chasing each other in pursuit of the very best nuts. He hated every clacking goose and swallow slipping away. There were a lot of geese lately. The other day it had taken one flock half an hour to go over.

He liked the walk into town. The hay and grain fields had

mostly gone to pasture, with a few moony placid cows standing in the middle of the yellowing fields. It was hard to put up enough hay for feed without mowers and balers. He'd seen people over the summer stacking hay with horses and wagons and men with pitchforks. It was good, the old ways coming back. He approved of that. Life was quieter without all those shrieking, querulous machines demanding endless time and attention. He walked along feeling happier than he'd been in a long time.

He felt like he was waking up from a long nightmare. He was almost dizzy with the shock of it, of knowing what he could do, what he had to do.

As he came up the hill, the noise got louder. He walked a bit faster, still lighthearted, feeling like he was going to a party and it had already started without him. The main street was deserted, so he went towards the noise.

People had gathered on the school grounds, or what had once been the school grounds. There was a sort of a platform where people were standing, next to a gas generator purring softly to itself. There was a microphone and amplifiers, but no one was talking into the mic. Instead people were talking to each other.

He edged his way into the crowd.

"What's going on?" he said to someone, but she turned her head away and didn't answer.

He hadn't seen this many people gathered together in one spot in years. There were more than he would have guessed still lived around here, several hundred anyway, all standing around in the late autumn sun, gabbling away like a bunch of birds.

Different groups of people stood clumped together, some dressed all in black, the men standing separate from the women and kids. There were lots and lots of women and kids, fewer men. They'd come in on horseback and in wagons. Their horses stood together, heads down, tails swishing, tied to trees or the backs of the wagons.

The ordinary people stood in the middle, ordinary looking old people, people with kids, people Matt had never seen before.

Matt saw Darlene and the kids in the crowd and began working his way towards them. People moved away from him. Even Darlene turned her face away when she saw him.

"Hey, kids! Hey, Darlene!" he said. "What's going on? I just got into town. You got any food? I'm starving." The kids stared at him but didn't answer.

Someone had set up a stall at the edge of the crowd and was frying something in a pot of hot oil set over a charcoal grill. The reek of it made Matt's stomach jump, made his throat suddenly close up. It reminded him of when he was a kid, when there used to be travelling carnivals with rides and booths selling tacky toys.

"Hey, when did the carnivals stop coming? Remember them? Cotton candy and hot dogs and all that shit. Hey, kids, you ever tasted cotton candy? Whoo, that's amazing stuff. Or those crappy bags of popcorn. What the hell happened to all that?

"We should go travelling sometime," he continued, filling the silence. "You guys never even been out of this valley. We should go look at stuff someday, go to the city, see the bright lights."

They were all staring at him. Finally Darlene said, tight-lipped, "Keep your voice down, please." The kids looked scared.

"Hey, I'm just being friendly. What the hell's the matter with you?"

"Oh, for God's sake, Matt. Why can't you, for once, behave? At least you could try, for my sake."

"Who is that?" he gestured towards the people standing on the platform.

Darlene looked even more frightened. "It's their army," she said.

"What army? Whose army?"

"The people I told you about. That new corporation. Luke knows them. They've got stuff you can look at. You can go through all the trucks. It's kind of a display. They've got these little tiny atomic bombs. Miniatures. They're built to burrow into the ground and then blow up. They've got robots. All kinds of guns. Lasers. All kinds of stuff. Everyone's going in to look. They've got people to show you around. They're giving away food, candy and pop, junk."

"Did you look?" he asked.

"I tried," she said. "I got too upset. All that money just to kill people."

"It's always been that way. Don't be so goddamn wimpy."

"Don't swear at me," she said. "Matt, I'm scared. I thought these people would help us. Now I don't know."

"Where's Luke?" he asked.

"Somewhere. He's been showing them around."

"Yeah, he would."

"Shut up," she hissed. She looked around to see who was listening. "Just shut up. You don't know what you're talking about. Luke looks after us. You don't. You don't even care."

He turned away. He was tired of fighting with Darlene. He turned and pushed through the crowd towards the platform. He could see what he had missed before, the long line of white trucks standing behind the school buildings. Two armed guards stood by each truck, beside a set of stairs leading into the trucks. Lines of people stood in front of each set of stairs.

The people were babbling away, full of smiles and excitement. No wonder the damn place reminded him of a carnival. It was a carnival, with this tinpot army providing the entertainment, and the people eagerly swallowing it up. He tried to push forward to see if there was any insignia on the trucks, but they were plain white.

The guards were talking to the people going into the trucks, kneeling down to give the kids candy.

Matt turned away, sickened. He was pushing back through the crowd to find Darlene again when he saw Luke. He ducked his head and turned away, almost running. The crowd parted for him. He headed for Darlene's house. His stomach churned.

Halfway up the hill, he stopped and flopped onto the grass to catch his breath. He had to go back. He had to find out what was going on.

He turned around, went back down the hill. By the time he got to the school grounds, the crowd was starting to disperse. A wagon passed him, driven by a dour-looking man whose fat bum overloaded and overflowed the wagon seat, while behind him a group of women and children in bright flounced flowery dresses sat on the bed of the wagon, looking like a heap of crumpled laundry. Magnus was standing at the edge of the crowd.

"Hey, Magnus," Matt said. "Keep your head down. That's a weird-looking bunch."

Magnus turned. "I got to get closer," he said. "I've got to see if they're for real or just a bunch of dressed-up clowns."

Matt stood frozen, watched him walk across the ground. He saw what he hadn't seen before: men with guns, their black round holes pointed at him. He stopped and began to walk rapidly in the other direction. Crawly things slithered up and down his spine. He left the school grounds and retraced his steps, back up the hill towards Darlene's house, in an awkward limping run.

He came in the back door as always, then stopped. Dar-

lene and Luke were sitting at the kitchen table with two soldiers. But these weren't men with guns. These were smiling
men, beer-drinking men, their rifles propped in a corner.

He heard the words "resettle you, of course," as he came
barging in the door, just before they all stopped, fell silent,
staring at him. Darlene's face jumped out at him, white, her
eyes staring. He saw everything he needed to know in her
face.

One of the soldiers stood up, but Matt was already gone.
He heard them come out of the house behind him, heard a
yell, but he was through the overgrown hedge, into the
neighbour's yard, into the overgrown lane, and then into the
brushy, vine-covered jungle that had once been a vacant lot
on the corner. He crouched there in the centre beside the
remains of many old campfires, bottles, garbage, burnt tin
cans, syringes.

He sat with his head in his hands and closed his eyes.
When he closed his eyes, inside his head there was another
man walking around. Matt could see him standing under
some apple trees somewhere, the sun shining, standing there
feeling young and capable, full of himself, full of his own
strength. Matt tried to go there too, tried to imagine himself
under those same trees, the emerald grass full of dandelion
blossoms and contented bees. The man was so easy there,
relaxed and at home. But it was no good. The image faded,
became colours, became nothing.

He tried to make a tent of his hands and arms around his
head, to shut out the light, to hold onto the dream. He
wanted desperately to fall asleep, but terror ran along his
muscles like a whip, like an electric current, making him
jerk and shiver.

After a few seconds he jerked his head up. He heard
voices a long way off, but it was only a bunch of kids coming along the road, talking excitedly about the things they'd

seen in the trucks at the old school grounds. He waited until they passed, then tried to get up. But something was wrong with his muscles. They didn't move, didn't do anything, when he wanted to stand up. He realized he was shaking too hard and that he hadn't noticed. Fuck, he thought, maybe he really was going crazy. All this shit with Luke and Darlene had been going on under his nose and he hadn't noticed.

He had to figure out what to do, he needed a plan. He was desperately hungry, weak with it. He tried to remember what he had been eating. He tried to think, but all that came to his mind were images of food. The food had been so good on that trip to Trout Lake. Ama, whatever else she was, was a great cook. It had become a joke, how much he ate on that trip.

He thought of coffee, how much he'd like a cup of coffee with cream and birch syrup in it, the hint of bitter tree perfume from the syrup. He thought of how good it would smell. He could smell it now. Someone must be making coffee somewhere in town. Somewhere else, someone was frying meat. People were home, in their houses, settling down, watching TV or talking to one another, playing with their kids. Probably talking about how wonderful the army was, how great it was that the army was here to protect them, how wonderful all their new toys had been. What a bunch of idiots. But then he'd been like that once, he couldn't blame them. He wasn't even angry at them.

But he was the only one in possession of the truth. Which meant he had to do something. He just wished he knew what it was. He had been selected for some special purpose, singled out. Nothing that had happened had been an accident, it all fit a pattern.

He'd never thought about the idea of God much. In fact,

from the time he was a little kid he'd hated the idea of a God, a big boss moving people around, telling them what to do. He didn't know much about it, actually. He remembered his mother weakly trying to convince them to go to church. His father scorned the idea, so she rarely brought it up. For some reason, though, she insisted they go at Christmas and Easter. Matt found the whole thing embarrassing. He sat next to his parents and Darlene with his head down. He had the vague idea that churches had strict rules and he'd get in trouble if he drew attention to himself. He stood up and sat down when everyone else did, and in between he covertly studied the people around him for clues as to how he was doing.

When the service was over, they all escaped out the door with a sense of immense relief, his father jocular and silly, making stupid jokes with the few other men; his mother tense and serious until they got home and she could take off her good clothes and make a cup of tea.

Matt always went to roam around the neighbourhood after one of these sessions with a sense that he had been through a narrow escape, that he had been under surveillance and made it out alive.

But now he wasn't so sure. Maybe there was some plan going on, something larger than he could imagine taking a hand in everything. He was suddenly overwhelmed by the idea. He stood up and began to pace around the black charred rocks of the fire space, then sat down again. He couldn't understand why they hadn't come looking for him unless it was because he was under some special protection.

He was overwhelmed by it all, by the knowledge and the loneliness of that knowledge. He rocked back and forth with the terror of it, clutching his stomach. What was he going to do?

No matter how bad things got, he had had that vision of

peace and silence, of birds and elk and coyotes, the vision of his house, his mirrored shining house, rising in the middle of it all. What could he do without it? Where could he go?

Maybe he could go to the city, lose himself there among the streets and the buildings. But he had no idea how to survive there, no idea what the rules were, no idea what people meant when they talked, what the meanings were behind their words. He only knew this place. It was his home. He couldn't leave it.

He stayed crouched in the clearing while the town settled down around him. More people strolled by, talking, laughing. As evening came on, soldiers on four-wheeled motorbikes began to patrol the streets. The motors on the bikes gave a high-pitched, almost silent whine, like a squeal. He could hear them moving around the town, up and down the streets, going slowly. People who saw them smiled and waved, and the soldiers waved back. But they never got off the bikes, so Matt began to feel somewhat safer. He studied them as they went by. They seemed huge, bulky. He thought either they were larger than normal people, or they were wearing some kind of armour that made them look enormous.

As it got dark, they kept going, up and down, whining like sad dogs, the lights on their handlebars flashing through the trees and shrubs of the town yards.

When it got dark enough, he left the thicket and walked rapidly through the lanes and alleys to Stan's house. Thank God there were no streetlights anymore.

He pushed his way into Stan's black basement and felt for the overhead light. When it flashed on, he felt only a tired recognition when he saw Luke sitting on a chair in the middle of the floor.

"Figured you'd show up here," Luke said. "Got no place else to go, eh, you sad bastard?"

"Fuck you," said Matt. "I gotta get some food before I

pass out. Then you can turn me in to those bastards you work for."

"I don't think they're a real army," Luke said. "They're like a bunch of dressed-up kids playing pretend. I don't think they're good people anymore."

"Well, what a goddamn surprise. When did that light go on in your thick head? I got to eat." Matt stomped up the stairs, went rummaging through Stan's kitchen. There had to be something to eat. The place was looking better, cleaner. Someone had washed the dishes, swept the litter off the floor, even washed the table. He found some ancient packets of dried food, tasteless gunk but what the hell, dumped them in a saucepan, and put it on the electric stove. It took him a few minutes to realize the stove wasn't working. There was a propane stove in the corner with a propane tank on the floor. Matt pawed through a drawer for matches until Luke stepped forward, held out his. Matt lit the stove, put the pan on it, looked in the empty fridge, slammed the fridge door, and turned to face Luke.

"What the hell are you doing here then, if you're not going to turn me in?"

"I think I've done something stupid," Luke said.

Matt stared at him. Luke actually looked scared. The soup started to sputter and Matt turned to stir it. He looked through the cupboards and found some dusty noodles, dumped them in the soup and stirred it again.

"I think they're just some jumped-up corporate militia," Luke said. "I thought they were the good guys. They promised us so much. Now I'm not so sure. It looks flashy, those trucks and uniforms. But everything has to be their way, not ours. It's sounding more and more like they get everything and we get shit."

"What the hell do they want with us? We're nobody. We got nothing."

"We got land, trees, water. That's what they want."

"So, call somebody."

"Call who?"

"We got police, we got government, away over the hills somewhere. Not that they give a shit about us, but we're theirs, or they're ours, something like that."

"Christ," said Luke, turning away. "Remember when we were kids, things seemed to make sense. They weren't great but, you know, we had a life, we had a community, people worked together, helped one another. You remember. This used to be a great little place to live. We even used to have a hockey team. We used to all play together, remember? You and me always got along, right?"

"Except for Elaine."

"Oh yeah, her. What happened to her anyhow?"

"She married some cowboy trucker, went to Saskatchewan, got out of here."

"Man, she was a great fuck."

"The best."

"So what the hell do I do now?"

"I got to find Magnus, that's what, then get the hell out of here."

"Who the hell is Magnus?"

"That kid from the commune up the lake."

"Hope he didn't run into those guys. They're mean fuckers."

"I heard them say something about resettling you guys."

"Yeah, that's what Darlene wants. That's what they promised us. Seemed like a good deal, get out of here, get a new life, some money to get started."

"In return for what?"

"Oh, Christ," Luke said. "I should get going."

"What? What did you promise them?"

"I didn't promise them nothing. I just showed them around, is all. I didn't do nothing, just showed them stuff."

"You brought them out to my place. And out to the commune. You drove them around."

"Didn't see no harm in it. I thought they were legit. They were talking good things, bringing in new people, development, money. Stuff we need. This community is dying. Even you can see that. I thought we could get going again, maybe get a doctor back, schools."

"Fat chance."

Matt took the soup off the stove, found a spoon in a drawer, sat, and began slopping the soup into his mouth. The warmth went all the way down his throat, burning as it went.

"Look," said Luke, "I got to get going. Stay here tonight. Tomorrow I'll bring you some food, blankets, stuff."

"No," said Matt. "I'm going. I've got to find out about Magnus. These guys think you're their buddy. Find out where he is and get a message out if they've taken him. Tell them something. I don't know. Say you're worried that people might hear rumours, get upset."

Luke shrugged. "I'll see what I can do," he said, "but I ain't promising anything."

After Luke left, Matt couldn't think, couldn't settle. The soup hadn't done anything about his hunger except make it worse. He went through all the cupboards and drawers in Stan's house but found nothing useful, no money, no more food. There was one unopened beer that had escaped detection, and he drank that down, immediately wanted another. When he opened the beer, he noticed how hard his hands were shaking. He held one hand with the other, tried to hold them still, but then his whole body started to shake again. He was freezing. He went back downstairs, wrapped himself in a blanket, closed his eyes, tried to think, but his mind flickered like a really bad video: images of Star, Magnus, images of Lia and Magnus together. Darlene's face turned towards him, the desperate hope in her eyes. Luke's face, the lying bastard. Matt still wasn't sure what Luke had wanted, why he had come.

He shook harder now. He had to get warm. He had to get somewhere with people. He couldn't go on sitting here in this damp freezing basement, alone, starving, still wondering what the hell it was he was supposed to do about everything.

He lay down on the thin mattress. There was another man in his head, the dreaming man, walking through the woods in the sunshine. He was singing now as he walked, going towards his house. Matt tried to imagine himself into that other body, that strong young body with two whole legs, that one who didn't know defeat, who still believed that his strength and courage would overcome everything. But he couldn't stop shaking.

He had to do something about Magnus, but he had no idea what. His mind wouldn't stay under control. It kept jumping around, flickering back and forth. He tried hard. He thought he should concentrate on one thing, and that one thing should be Magnus.

He could hear a bike go by outside the house, whining like a sick puppy, and he held his breath until the sound faded into the distance. He curled up again. The food he had eaten burned in his stomach. Maybe there had been something wrong with it. It was so old.

The house made noises. He kept thinking someone was walking around upstairs, but then it would be quiet again and he'd change his mind. Maybe something else was going on. Star had believed in spirits, in omens, in dreams. He had listened to her, but maybe the problem was he hadn't truly believed. He hadn't truly paid attention. Maybe that was why things hadn't worked out with Star. He hadn't truly earned the right to be with her.

That bird had talked to him. There were messages all around him that he couldn't hear.

His mind slipped. For an instant of time it was like looking at a void, a blackness with no beginning and no end. If he slipped, or lost the threads that bound him to the world, that's where he would go. That was what lay underneath everything, and no one knew. They just walked around pretending everything was normal and okay, and underneath was this blackness, this void, this terrifying nothing.

He had to hold on to the mattress underneath him. He put his arm to his mouth and bit down hard, hard, then let go. Gradually, he felt the parts of himself that had fled in terror creeping back. The world righted itself and started to make small bits of sense again.

It was quiet outside. He hadn't heard one of those damn bikes for a while. It must be late. When they were kids, they used to sneak around outside at night. It was what they did every weekend. He'd wait until his parents were asleep, then sneak out. Sometimes he'd meet up with some other kids, but mostly he'd just prowl around by himself, in and out of yards. He knew all the dogs, the ones that barked, the ones that were friendly.

It was easy at night to be a shadow, a thin blade cutting through the night, down alleys, behind trees, in and out of garages. He never stole anything. That wasn't the point. But he looked at stuff. He watched people through windows. Sometimes he went to the edge of town, where the trees began on the mountain, and sat there in the silence and listened to nothing. He didn't know why he did it. It was satisfying. It got him out of the fetid air of that house where his parents snored and twitched and dreamed. That's what mattered.

He remembered sitting there listening to the silence. He

must have been listening for messages even then, without realizing what he was doing. He must have been selected for something, even then.

He sat up suddenly. There were voices, coming towards the house. He rolled over, stood up with difficulty, limped to the door, and eased it open, stood in the doorway. He waited, listening. It sounded like Stan and some other guy. They'd see the dishes he'd left and know someone had been here, unless they were too pissed to care. Someone came to the top of the stairs and called down. It was Stan's voice. Matt didn't answer. Footsteps clumped on the stairs. Matt shut the door and eased himself quietly away from the house, across the tall grass and under the rustling giant maple trees at the edge. The ground was covered with leaves that crackled and split under his feet like gunshots. He shuffled his way through them. Beyond them was an overgrown thicket of dying junipers that reached out with clawlike branches to snatch at his clothes and skin.

He fought his way through and out to the edge of the road. He began walking, not sure where he was going, staying in the middle of the road away from the tangle of leaves, tall grass, and fallen branches at the edge of the road.

He went back up the hill towards the centre of the town. It was quiet and cold. There might be frost by morning. A dog was barking somewhere far away. A coyote answered the dog, yipping from some hilltop.

Matt looked up at the sky. The stars were hanging like crystals on strings, swaying and dancing to some giant universal wind. He stood staring. Far away, across the horizon, a shooting star flashed and was gone, then another and another. He put his head back.

A winking green-and-red light moved slowly across the sky, followed by another and then another. He waited but he couldn't hear anything.

He put his head down and began walking again, staring at the faint sheen of starlight on the pavement, the even fainter sheen left by people's feet over the years. When he looked up, he saw without surprise that he was at the edge of the school grounds. The trucks were still there. He could hear a generator humming, but there were no lights showing. He waited, but he couldn't see anyone moving.

He went carefully around the edge of the school grounds, thinking that he could at least get closer to the trucks, but halfway around he heard something moving in the grass. He froze into the shadows, waited. There was enough starshine that he could see whoever it was was on hands and knees, coughing, then struggling to his feet, staggering towards Matt.

When the person got closer, Matt was finally sure enough to step out of the shadows and in his way.

"Magnus, man, what happened to you?"

"Beat up," Magnus mumbled. The skin around his eyes and mouth looked black in the starlight. He had his arms wrapped around himself like he was holding himself together.

Matt moved towards him and Magnus crumpled into his arms.

"You need help, you need a doctor," Matt said. "We got to get you somewhere."

"Go home," Magnus mumbled. "Get Mom."

"I'll get you to the clinic," Matt said. He lifted Magnus's arm, put it over his shoulder.

"No," Magnus said. "Not safe. Home, got to get home, everyone will be worried. Not safe in the clinic."

"Where's the truck?"

"They've gone . . . gone home."

But Magnus seemed to be drifting in and out of consciousness. He mumbled something Matt couldn't catch.

Matt tried to think, but it was hard. His head hurt and he was scared. He didn't know where the soldiers might be, if they were still patrolling, if they were watching him right now. He didn't even know if the clinic was open, or if there was a doctor available. Darlene would know, but he couldn't go there. He couldn't risk wandering through the town.

He bent over, swung Magnus's warm heavy weight onto his back, staggered a few feet and almost fell, then got his balance and began to limp down the hill, keeping to the pooled shadows under the trees.

He headed north, out of town. Lia's place was closer than the commune. He'd head there. He was groggy himself from lack of sleep and food. He thought he might get out of town, find a place to lie down, and sleep until morning. Then he could leave Magnus to rest, go to the farm, get some help.

He began counting the steps, measuring the distance he was travelling by the faint shadows of things going past him. He kept promising himself he'd stop when he got to that corner, that stump, that faint sheen of old white paint on what was left of the concrete. But he didn't stop. He was panting, his back ached, his arms. Pain howled through his leg and he tried to move his mind somewhere else so he didn't have to think about it. He tried to think about that other man, the one he had dreamed about, but nothing came.

Sometimes Magnus mumbled something, moved around on his back so that Matt lurched, almost fell.

He began to sing to himself to pass the time, any songs he could think of, old tunes from his childhood, from bands long gone, long disappeared. He remembered a period in his teens when all he thought about was the lyrics from rock songs. That was the period when drugs got so bad, so scary and lethal, that nobody would take them anymore.

That was when life started getting meaner and meaner.

Hardly a rave or a dance or a get-together went by without someone getting hurt, stomped, beat up, cut with a bottle, run over. It started to get dangerous to even go to a party. There was some kind of lust for cruelty that took hold of people. In his crowd they had all sobered up after one kid was burned to death in an old cabin where he'd been left, tied to the wall.

Matt had lost a lot of friends while they were still in school. Some ran away or took drugs or smashed up cars when they still had cars or fell off cliffs or drowned in the lake. One had murdered his parents and taken off into the woods and disappeared. It was like none of them believed they would grow up.

He'd started working so early that maybe it had saved his life. Maybe it got him out of the whole drugs, booze, cruelty scene. There'd been a terrifying edge to it, as if people were using other people to kill themselves, to commit suicide. Christ, at least the men he had worked with were still trying, still doing their best, supporting their families, keeping their lives together.

His breath by now was whistling in his throat and he was taking one step to every three breaths. He had to stop; he knew he had to stop, but somehow he kept going. He noted with relief that things didn't hurt anymore. His body was far away and disconnected from his mind, which was making pictures for him that didn't seem very connected to anything. Bits of dreams flashed and were gone; faces, voices came and went. Somehow, although he knew he had decided to stop, his legs were still going on somewhere far away without him.

They were amazing, those legs, how they went on, step by step, picking up, flopping down, muscles, joints, his foot bones spreading and compacting. He was wearing the same old pair of boots he'd worn for years now. The leather was full of cracks and small tears. He'd mended them himself a few times with an awl and bits of leather and some glue. Fascinated, he watched as the boots continued to rise and fall, far away, disconnected. He realized the rest of his body was disconnecting as well. His arms were doing the job he'd assigned them, holding onto Magnus; his eyes and ears were off looking and listening for things, his eyes noticing that the black shapes beside the road were taking on the faintest shade of grey, that birds had begun to whistle from every bush and treetop. He realized his body would go on without him, just walking and walking down the road until he got to wherever he had to be, until he could finally stop, and though he didn't know when that would be, he was as sure as anything that this was a journey he would complete.

24

LIA WAS SITTING cross-legged in the rocking chair, her hands clasped over her belly, drinking tea. She and Ama had just gotten up, but neither of them had slept much. Lia was groggy from lack of sleep. Ama was pacing. She had stayed at Lia's house, not wanting to go home until she knew what had happened to Magnus.

"You saw those guys. It's happening now. We're going to have to decide what to do."

"I'm not moving," Lia said.

"What do you mean?"

"What the hell has it got to do with me, any of it? I'm here, I've got my corner of the planet, now I'm going to survive on it."

"You can't just ignore what's going on."

"What am I supposed to do? I've got nowhere to go."

"We have to think about it. You saw those guys. They're evil."

"We don't even know who they are, what they want. They haven't made any real threats, just noises about buying the land. Then they went away."

"They're the enemy. That's obvious. Just look at them. White uniforms. No insignia. Not even numbers. That's the point. They're here to let us know what's going on. They're in charge and we'd better bow down and behave ourselves."

"They'll go away again and we'll stay."

"And what if they decide they want your land? What if they decide they know how you should live, how your child, my grandchild, should live? Then what will you do?"

"It hasn't happened yet," Lia said, but she looked frightened. She kept on rocking and rocking in the chair, staring at the fire through the glass door of the stove.

"Where the hell is Magnus?" Ama was still pacing the floor, staring out the windows. Sunlight covered everything. "He should be back by now. We shouldn't have left him there. It wasn't safe. Magnus is so fucking naive, he thinks everybody is his goddamn friend. He just has to smile and they'll fall over at his feet."

"He was going to talk to those guys, see what he could find out."

"Why didn't you stop him?"

"It's his trip, Ama. He likes to talk to people."

"Those aren't people, those are robots."

"You don't know that."

Ama turned to stare out the window again. "Oh Christ," she said and ran to the door.

She met Matt staggering up the driveway. He was going sideways as much as up, didn't seem to know where he was or what he was doing. His eyes were almost shut, his face turned to the sky. When Ama and Lia eased Magnus off his back, he fell down like he'd been shot, simply lay where he was, breathing in and out in shuddering gasps, his eyes closed.

They left him there and half carried, half dragged Magnus up the rest of the long driveway to the house. They put him on the bed, on the faded red nylon cover of the ancient sleeping bag that they used for a quilt.

"Magnus," Lia said. "Magnus, wake up. Tell us what's wrong."

"He's unconscious," Ama said. "He's covered in bruises. Maybe something is wrong inside."

They stood side by side, staring at Magnus. Ama grabbed her hair, shook it.

"What can I do?" she whispered. "I don't know what to do. I need help."

"I'll go get Sam," Lia said. "I'll take the truck." She wasn't even sure why she said it. She ran out of the house, away from the sound of Magnus's harsh breathing. On her way down the driveway she passed Matt, still lying on the grass.

He opened his eyes when she stopped beside him. He held up his hand, palm out, then let it flop over his eyes.

"You should have taken him to a doctor," she said.

He took his hand off his face. There were tears in his eyes. He stared straight up at the early morning sun.

Lia was crying as well. "What did you think you were doing? What if he dies without a doctor? It'll be your fault."

"He wanted to come home," Matt said. "We're all family now, he said. We should stick together."

She turned her head away, stared out across the yellow field, past the tall jagged black firs, the bright yellow cottonwoods by the river, the chain of pale blue mountains marching north. She crumpled to the ground.

"I'm sorry," she said. "Ama is just standing there. I'm going to get Sam and Mairi, people to help."

Matt tried to sit up but fell back. He lay there, breathing. Finally he turned over on his hands and knees, levered himself, panting, to his feet, and limped his way up to the house.

When he came in, Ama was sitting on the bed beside Magnus. She was cutting his clothes off. Matt put his arms around her and she leaned her head on his shoulder.

He told her about the soldiers, a little bit about the walk but not much. Then they both turned to stare at Magnus again. He looked terrible, his face white except where the bruising showed through.

"He's hurt inside. I'm afraid to touch him, to move him, even to take his clothes off. I'm afraid he'll stop breathing. It seems to hurt him to breathe. He won't wake up. I've called his name but he can't hear me."

"Lia thinks he needs a real doctor, a hospital, surgery."

"And where do we get those?"

He waited a moment and then went out in the kitchen, where, thank God, a kettle was boiling on the wood stove. He searched in the cupboards, found tea, bread, honey. He stood at the counter, wolfing the food down so hard that he choked.

Ama came out while he was eating, poured a bowl of hot water from the kettle, got a cloth, and vanished silently back into the bedroom.

He ate his food, stared at the driveway. After a while he lifted his head enough for his eyes to flick around the room. The floors shone, the wood stove clicked away to itself, there were curtains on the windows, the table was covered with a clean cloth. His whole body ached. He stretched his leg out in front of him. It hurt like hell but it still worked. He was proud of it. It had got him here. He couldn't really remember how. He just remembered walking, dreaming, walking, a dream like being on fire. He shuddered. He didn't want to remember.

He bent over, untied his boots, eased them off, eased off his socks, and then flexed his toes, stretched them out to the warmth from the fire. There was no sound from the bedroom. His eyes got heavier and heavier. He didn't want to but he couldn't help himself. He fell asleep.

When he woke up, the room was full of people. No one talked to him, no one even looked at him, although they talked together, their tones hushed, anxious.

Ama came out of the bedroom. She had aged in the past few hours, her hair hanging in her face, which was desperate, white, lined.

"He might be bleeding internally. I'm not sure. If he is, I can't fix it. What can we do? What are we going to do?" She stumbled forward, started to fall, but several hands caught her, eased her to a chair.

She looked at Matt but didn't see him. "What are we going to do?" she said again.

No one answered. No one had an answer. Then several voices spoke at once.

"Are you sure? Shouldn't we wait?"

"We'll have to drive him back to Appleby."

"Do we know if those guys are still there?"

"Or what they'll do?"

"Bring the truck up to the door," Ama said. "We have to try."

"For Christ's sake," Matt said, "you can't go there. It was those guys beat him up. You're gonna take him back there? Are you nuts?"

They all turned to stare at him as if he had just materialized from thin air.

"You shut up, asshole," said Sam. "You're just a fucking troublemaker. I should have kicked your ass the first time you ever showed up."

"I brought him here," Matt said. "I carried him."

"That's right," Lia said. "He did."

They were all silent at that.

"For what?" Sam said bitterly. "You should have stayed in town, found a doctor, got him some help. Carrying him all the way here. That's insane. You probably killed him yourself, doing that."

Matt opened his mouth, then shut it again. He stood up, his fists clenched at his sides. He went outside, slamming the door behind him, went and sat on the ground, staring north again. What the hell. He should leave. The air outside was cold after the warmth of the kitchen. He started to shake again. He felt sick. He wrapped his arms around himself, put his head on his knees.

There were footsteps behind him. He raised his head and Lia sat down beside him.

"I want to thank you," she said. "I want to ask you if you'll stay here for a while. Even if Magnus makes it, he's not going to be strong for a long time. I want you to stay here and help take care of him and me and the baby."

"All right," he said. He lay back on the grass, fell asleep again.

When he woke, the sun was notched between two mountains. The sky was a windy pageant of gold and pink.

He stood up, had a long and luxurious pee, then went behind the house, past the pile of wood, to where the chickens scratched and clucked at the ground. They came running when he showed up, so he guessed they were hungry and went back to the porch where he found a pail of compost, dumped it on the ground for them, went along the path to the garden.

There was an ancient rusting wheelbarrow standing in the garden among the corn stalks, stiff yellow broccoli flowers, and the green bellies of squash under broad-handed leaves.

He filled the wheelbarrow full of wood and shoved it to the back door. There was a porch at the back of the house, full of junk. Patiently, he began piling the spread-out mounds of junk in one corner, clearing a space for the wood. In among the junk he found an old green plastic slicker, torn and mildewed. He spread it on the floor and put wood on it, one piece at a time, then went back for another load.

After that he began loading the wheelbarrow with squash.

There was cabbage as well, rotted and worm-eaten on the outside, but still all right after it was stripped down, and carrots and potatoes that needed digging. She'd need a root cellar. He'd have to start building one as soon as he could.

He worked until dusk. Hunger and the smell of cooking pulled him back inside. A pot of soup simmered on the stove. He helped himself. Ama, Lia, Sam, and Mairi were eating, talking in low voices. They turned to look at him.

"I brought in them squash and cabbage," he said to Lia, and she nodded. He ate his soup and went out again. He stood for a long while, looking down the hill and across the lake to the mountains. He thought he had never seen an evening so lovely. There were piles of white clouds sitting on the shoulders of the mountains. Gold light slanted upwards through them. The air was still warm. The lake was a deep royal blue, almost black in places.

When he went in the house again, the three women were sitting silently at the table, holding hands and crying. There was a candle burning in the middle of the table, several other candles burning in parts of the kitchen, bits of dried cedar smouldered in a dish.

He sank into an old chair in the corner by the stove. The silence stretched on.

Finally Ama rose. She turned to look at Matt.

"I owe you my son's life," she said. "Thank you for what you did."

Matt nodded. Shadows danced in the room from the firelight, the candlelight. The moon came up. He watched the white moonlight coat the fields like dust, and after a while he dozed in the chair.

A rumbling woke him. The white trucks were trundling along the road in the moonlight, heading north. There were three of them. They had no lights. They made almost no sound except for their tires on the rutted broken pavement.

When they had gone, he lay down on the pallet of blankets that Lia had left for him in the corner and fell into a troubled sleep.

25

WHEN MATT WOKE, he heard Ama and Lia talking in hushed voices. He got up and left the house as silently as he could. He went in to look at Magnus, then left. He trudged slowly along the mountain to his house site, taking a trail instead of the road. As he walked, he cursed steadily, softly, under his breath.

When he got to the tent he made a fire, put water on to boil, and went about his regular activities with a kind of desperate savagery. He had taken a jar of soup from Lia's house. Now he wolfed it down without bothering to heat it.

He worked all afternoon on his house, losing himself in measuring, sawing, cutting, chipping wood from the grooves in the logs with a small axe. He paused to take off his shirt, then went on working until he was bent with exhaustion. He used a peavey to roll logs into place, ready to be hoisted onto the rock foundation.

When he stopped to eat, he noticed how silent things were. For some reason the birds had gone quiet, and even the squirrels had stopped quarrelling. A raven flopped onto a tree branch near him but said nothing. Matt lay down to sleep but got up several times, put wood on the fire. Something was prowling the woods, something was keeping everything scared and quiet. In the middle of the night he heard a tree crash to the ground. When he got up to look there was nothing, only the same brittle silence.

When he woke the next morning, frost coated the grass around the tent. The sun burned it off finally and he spent the day measuring, cutting, trimming. He knew Ama would send word about Magnus. There was nothing more he could do.

By the end of the week he had the first of the logs ready to be hoisted into place. He was exhausted and gaunt and completely out of food. He trimmed his beard with scissors, heated some water, washed his hair and face, and headed over the half mile of mountainside trail to the commune.

When he came in the house, Ama was bent over the stove, stirring something.

"You look hungry," she said.

She dished him out soup that was hot on the back of the stove, and while he was eating that she took out the bread that was baking and cut him a slice. She sat down beside him while he ate.

"You look like hell," she said.

"You look about the same. How's Magnus?"

"He's hanging on. But he's bad. There's something wrong I can't fix." She put her face in her hands. "I thought we were safe here. I thought it was safe to have a child."

Matt stood up. "Them trucks kept on north," he said. "Guess we're okay for now."

"What if they come back? What will we do?"

Matt lifted his hands, stirred restlessly. He couldn't handle being the one to try to give advice to Ama.

"Lia's pregnant. Magnus is crippled. I'm useless. I can't think. I always know what to do. Now I don't."

"I've got to finish my house," Matt said.

"Your house?"

"I got no wood, no food."

"And you've come here begging."

"Yeah, guess so," Matt said. He hung his head, stared at his hands. There was a long silence. "I do what I have to. I carried Magnus on my back. He's my friend. I'd have done anything to save him."

"I know that," Ama said. "But maybe you should have got him to the nurse at the clinic. You could have gotten him some care right away."

"Those guys were after me. Luke made a deal with them. They were hunting me."

"I know," she said. Finally she added, "Go find Sam, talk to him. We'll make a date, come over and do a house raising. I'll put together some food for you."

Sam was stretching wire over by the pasture but he was glad enough to take a break. He didn't like Matt and Matt didn't like him, but they spent the afternoon amiably enough, bent over the table with paper and pencil, drawing plans.

Matt wanted the bones to be part of the walls of the house. He had grandiose ideas of stone walls and towers.

"You want to build a fucking palace, man, not a house."

They argued and drank coffee. Ama ignored them except for making the occasional caustic comment. In the late afternoon, other members of the group came in, drank tea, stared over Matt and Sam's shoulders, made suggestions.

Matt went in to see Magnus, but he didn't stay. Magnus opened his eyes and held out his hand, but he was too weak to talk, and Matt left despite Ama's half-hearted invitation to stay for supper.

The next day he trudged the long and weary distance into Appleby and limped up the hill. Darlene's house was dark. He tried the door — everything was locked. He went around it, trying to figure a way in. Finally, he shrugged, slammed the door with his shoulder until it gave, the boards splintering and tearing in protest while he shoved his way in. Things looked normal, the furniture intact, everything in place. The only thing missing was Darlene and the kids and some clothes, as far as he could tell. There was even food in the cupboard. Surely Darlene would have left him some word. He checked obsessively, but there was nothing, no note, no word, no message, no sign of where she had gone.

The solar panels on the roof were still hooked up and there was life in the batteries. He was able to cook some food before everything dimmed and the battery alarm went off. He turned out the lights, crawled into his cold bed in the back room. Tomorrow he'd look around the town. Someone must know something.

But no one did. If they did, they weren't talking.

"Dunno, man," Soapy said when Matt tracked him down in the bar. "Had those weird army guys here, then they went. Luke's gone too, folded up his business, parked his machines, left town."

"How the hell could he shut things down that quick?"

"Just left it. Up and walked away. Left a bunch of guys holding debts. Left a bunch of us in the lurch. Fucking bastard. If you find him, tell him don't bother coming back."

Matt wandered around town for a while, looking at things. He looked at the houses, at how they were built. He looked at foundations and windows and doors and dormers and the angles of roofs. He looked into backyards. He looked at gardens and fruit trees and rock walls. Dogs barked at him. A couple of times people opened their back doors and stared at him. Once a woman yelled. It was like walking through a field of stories. The town held his life, such as it was.

He ended up back at the small park where he had met Star. He sat on the weathered bench. The sun was almost warm and he was sleepy. He sat and dozed with his head thrown back. The sun shot arrows into his eyes. When he moved his head, colours flashed and bounced around inside his head like so many tiny strobe lights. He started to float. He knew he was still on the bench, but he could feel himself floating, could feel himself rising higher and higher until the light became piercing, all-enveloping, until he was dissolving in light.

"Maybe I'm dying," he thought, and realized that his fear of dying was abruptly gone. It would be easy, easy to die, to float away into the light. Only he couldn't quite go, he couldn't hold onto it. The light faded, slowly seeped away, like water draining into sand, leaving him back on the bench, desolate.

He sat on for a while longer, trying to decide what had happened. Was that God taking a hand? After a while he got up and went back to Darlene's house. He sat for a long time by the window, looking out at the town. The sunset filled up the sky with red and purple and salmon-coloured clouds. It was so beautiful he wanted to weep. He put his head down on the table. He never thought a human being could be so lonely and live.

"I'm sorry, Darlene," he said out loud. "I'm so god-damned sorry."

It was his fault she'd run. Now there wasn't a thing he could do about it. She'd made her choices. She'd be all right. Luke would look after her. What he had to learn to do was endure. He had to take this loneliness into himself and learn to live with it. The only problem was, he didn't know if he could, or if it would just blow him apart, leave him drifting through the universe in fragments like random particles of light.

26

IT WAS A LONG WINTER, with Magnus slowly recovering and Ama a shadow of her former self. The commune was rife with suspicion and gossip. People pulled into themselves, stayed in their own houses. Hardly anyone came to dinner at the big house anymore. Quite a few people left. Lia stayed at her place. She worked hard. It was enough to do, just staying warm and fed. Ama tried everything she could think of to persuade Lia to move back to the commune, but Lia was in love with her house. She only went to the commune when she needed food or warmth or company, but the minute she got there, she began planning how soon she could leave.

Magnus began to recover. He was weak and white and spent most of his days by the fire sleeping, but he was alive and eating. Ama hovered over him like an anxious bird. Lia did too, when she had time.

Mostly she stayed in her house, cooked and cleaned and watched the bare spent ground. This winter, for some reason, it refused to rain or snow. The temperature stayed above freezing day after day. By Christmas the apple trees were struggling into bud, the blunt spiked daffodils were poking small mounds of earth above the ground.

Nothing felt right. Lia started a few seeds in dirt in pots on the windowsill, but it was half-hearted. More and more she found herself sitting at the window, staring down the hill, waiting for something to happen. Nothing did.

They celebrated Christmas at the commune and people tried to stop bickering and have fun. They had a party and even Magnus stayed up late. There was lots of food and drink. Lia sat by the fire holding Magnus's hand, stroking the delicate top of each finger, one by one. He put his hand on her belly and left it there. They watched people dancing, little kids running in and out of the crowd, stealing food, jumping on and off the furniture.

"I feel old," Lia said. "I feel grown up."

"I feel like shit," Magnus said, but he smiled. The words came out with difficulty. "When spring comes, we're going out, find a doctor, pay whatever it costs, do some trading, figure out what comes next."

"Can you stand the trip?"

"Have to, won't I? We need the money we get from trading. I need an operation, Mom says. Plus half the people in the commune are thinking of leaving. Idiots. Where do they think they're going to go?"

"Wherever. In the old days they say people used to travel all over, just get on a plane or a boat and go somewhere. Imagine, eh? When I was in Vancouver there was always rusty boats sailing towards the harbour with people clinging onto them. They'd start dropping off and swimming for shore when they were still miles out in the ocean, or they'd launch rafts. Then they started bombing the boats before they could come ashore."

"Where were they from?"

"Anywhere, all over the place. China, Japan, Africa, India."

"I always wanted to go to India. I always wanted to travel. We had a bunch of old CD-ROMs when I was a kid, and this ancient computer. One of them was about India. I used to watch it over and over. I'd forgotten that. Did you ever want to travel?"

"No, I just wanted to get home," Lia said bitterly. After a while she said, "Where would we go? Everything is so crazy. Plus it costs a fortune."

"I heard once there were small solar-powered sailing ships you could get work on. They're always looking for crew."

"Maybe," Lia said. "I heard about that. The kids from the squat were always talking about it. One of the kids hid out on a ship and the last thing we heard he was in some slave camp, planting trees in Africa. Remember when they were always trying to get people to volunteer to plant trees in Africa and India? It was supposed to stop all this weather stuff. Obviously didn't work too good. But they called it volunteer because they paid you shit and worked you to death. Yeah, right. Volunteer to save the fucked-up planet that they fucked up. Jeezus."

"Do you want to go with us, in the spring? You could maybe find some of the people from the squat. Remember how you always wanted to take them food?"

"I want to stay home," Lia said. "I want to put in a garden and plant some new trees of my own and look after the baby. I want you there too."

"It's going to be too hard on your own. Why won't you just stay here?"

"You know why," Lia said. "I want what's mine. I'm not afraid of work or being alone. That's the least of my fears. I gotta go. It's late and it's dark and my fire will be out."

She wrapped herself in a coat and shawl and took her stick from beside the door. She could feel Magnus watching her. Outside, she called the half-grown dog that Ama had given her. Most of the dogs on the commune were a mixture of border collie and black Lab. They were an intense breed. She called the dog Cousin.

It was a clear, cold night. Getting Cousin had been a good idea. He trotted ahead of her on the road. It was a very long walk. Privately she admitted to herself that Magnus was right. Living by herself was crazy, especially when she was pregnant. She didn't know anything about being pregnant. Ama assured her everything was fine, but what if it suddenly wasn't, or if she fell or hurt herself somewhere?

Well, she wouldn't, that's all. Somehow she felt calmly confident that everything would be fine. Although sometimes she vaguely resented this stranger in her belly showing up now and disrupting her life, that usually passed. She would do what she wanted and to hell with all of them, Ama and her worried face, Magnus holding in his pain and sadness, crazy Matt dithering around with rocks and bones on his piece of mountain.

She was about a mile down the road when she saw the light moving slowly across the sky. There were always strange lights in the sky, but this was a star, only much brighter than a star, blazing like a comet, trailing a tail of light and sparks. She realized as she stood there watching that it was falling, falling, falling, only very slowly, getting steadily brighter and brighter until it lit up the sky and the ground beneath it. She waited for an explosion but nothing came.

Frightened now, she began to walk quickly, tried to jog, but a stitch in her side stopped her. She had to stop several times and lean over, panting, before she finally got to the hill leading up to the house. She panted her way up the hill, made it into the house, slammed the door, and realized that the safety of the house was a mad illusion if something really was falling out of the sky and about to decimate them all.

She was exhausted and needed to sleep. Her whole body cried out for sleep, but her mind wouldn't rest. She kept going out in the yard, looking up at the sky, but the thing only grew bigger. Gradually it edged away to the south quadrant of the sky and slowly, slowly, slowly disappeared. The southern horizon brightened and glowed as if the moon was rising.

Lia finally curled up under the mound of blankets and shawls in the middle of her bed, curled around the baby that kicked and kicked against her bladder and belly, and finally she slept, although even in her sleep she kept rubbing her belly, trying to coax the restless baby into sleeping.

27

MATT SAW THE LIGHT and knew it was another sign. He got out of bed and built up the fire. He had a stove in the tent now, but he liked the fire outside as well. He heated up some of the stew Ama had given him and ate while he kept his eyes on the sky. He was hungry all the time now. He had taken to showing up at the commune two or three times a week at dinner. Ama laughed at him but fed him nonetheless.

"You're like an old dog, hanging around," Sam said to him. But Matt ignored him. He didn't have time to worry about getting food for himself. He was working as long as there was light. His house was beginning to get some shape to it, but he needed so much and he had no way to get a lot of the supplies. He'd taken to scavenging boards, lumber, old plywood, windows, and solar panels from abandoned houses up and down the lake. He'd made himself a barrow and attached it to a bicycle so that it looked something like a rickshaw. The pavement was rutted and covered with gravel, leaves, occasional tree branches and downed trees. There were places it was beginning to wash out, places it had washed out, and he had to leave the bike and inch his way down and up the side of washed-out gullies. The commune people and the other remaining families along the lake had fixed most of these washouts with log bridges, but the road was getting less and less stable.

He was making a floor with logs flattened on one side. He was glad it was staying so warm. He sat in the sun every day and worked at flattening the logs with an axe, an adze, a chisel, and a draw knife. It was slow work but the kind he liked. Every day the sun shone out of a clear sky with a hazy glare that made him dizzy by the late afternoon. It was so dry he kept a bucket of water by his campfire, and he had cleared the brush and forest floor litter from around his tent and around the house site.

It was a spooky winter for sure, with the heat and the flies still staying around, practically a plague. He often wondered what was happening in the rest of the world. When he went into Appleby, he checked out the NewsNets, but their stories were wildly conflicting. According to some, the weather was improving, scientists had fixed everything, the way ahead was clear as a bell, and everywhere there were opportunities for people working in what was called "new energy."

Other Nets were full of apocalyptic stories of despair, conspiracy, and predictions of the imminent collapse of governments, nations, economies. Wars, plagues, floods, an endless litany of bad news.

None of it seemed real or made sense. The mountains ringing the valley shut everything out. The only thing real was what was in front of him, what he had to deal with every day — feeding himself, building his house.

And yet there was something he was supposed to do, some mission for which he had been chosen but which he didn't yet understand. He was sure of that. He was waiting. It would come to him.

He watched the fire in the sky until it was out of sight over the southern horizon, but the glow in the sky remained for a long time. When dawn came he tried to work, but some spirit of perversity had gotten into his tools, into the wood, into the air. He jabbed a chisel into the palm of his hand, he broke the handle of his peavey heaving at logs, he scraped his knuckles on the raw pitchy surface of the log. When the sun began to burn through his shirt, he threw down his tools in disgust and went along the trail to the commune.

"What the hell is going on?" he said when he came in the door. "It's the end of December and I'm getting a goddamn sunburn."

Everybody was sitting down to lunch, and Matt helped himself without being asked.

"Anybody else see that damn fireball?"

"We all saw it," Sam said. "We were up half the night watching it."

"Anybody go to town, check the Nets?"

"We're going in after lunch," Ama said. "We want to know where that thing hit, what it did."

"But what was it?"

"Who knows? Asteroid, satellite, some piece of space junk. They got so much stuff floating around up there, some of it's bound to come down. Maybe that space station thing they had to abandon a while back. Remember when they used to talk about space travel. What a load of crap."

"I think it's a sign of some kind," Matt said.

"What are you talking about now?" Sam said. "Jeezus, sign of what?"

"I don't know. That's what I figure we're due to find out. But you know, I been thinking and studying on all this. Ever since my accident I been reading and studying this out. People knew for years things were getting bad and no one did nothing. Then everyone got scared all at once and the Green-Pros took over, only they were worse than anyone. Now you got the corporations running things, and us little folks stuck in the middle, and the weather just getting weirder and weirder. How's it all going to come out?"

"Weather is weather," Sam said. "No one can figure it out."

"That's not true," said Mairi from the end of the table. She was determined to stick around, she said, just to see how it all came out. "I got it figured. I been around here a long time and I figure the earth must be turning over. Everything is moving around."

"Look," Sam said, "as long as I can plant corn and corn comes up, and there's enough rain to turn it into food for the winter, I ain't worried about signs or disasters or the end of the goddamn world. Let the world look after itself. I got stuff to do."

"That's not enough anymore," said Elizabeth, another commune person who was sitting with her husband and their two kids. "That's what we thought too. We thought we'd be safe here, but it's not true. If the weather changes too much, if we can't grow food . . . that's why me and Will are thinking of leaving. It's too isolated here. It's too lonely. Anything could happen and we'd never know about it. We got kids. We got to think about their future."

Her voice had a hysterical edge to it. They were all silent for a moment.

"So any guesses as to what that thing really was?" Matt broke in. "Maybe a UFO?"

"Probably an asteroid," said Ama decisively. "A big one. If it had hit anywhere near here, there would have been an explosion, so there's nothing to worry about. It has nothing to do with us. Matt, you think everything is a sign, but life is just as normal as it ever was."

The conversation turned then to other things. The warm winter was pushing things into leaf and bud when they should be dormant. The level of creeks coming into the lake was low. Even the lake itself had dropped far below its normal level.

"Gonna be a hell of a dry spring if this keeps up," Sam said. "We'll be fighting fires all summer instead of farming."

"Wonder if we'll get any help this time? Last time there was a big fire, up Coal Creek, they just let it burn itself out."

"Everything is going to hell," Will, Elizabeth's partner, said. "Shot to hell. I don't know why you people can't see it. You're just strung out here like sitting ducks. Any goddamn thing comes along, who's gonna help you? What if those white guys come back in the spring?"

"We don't know anything for sure except we've still got each other," Ama said. "That's the whole point. We've had each other to lean on, but the more people leave, the harder it is for the rest of us. We need you guys."

The room went silent again.

Will and Elizabeth stood up and gathered up their kids. They left the room without a word, without a backward glance, and after a while everyone else left as well.

The winter wore on. In late January it suddenly turned bitterly, shockingly cold. The premature buds on the trees froze and withered. In the creeks, what little water there was froze to the ground. It was cold without snow. The ground looked shrivelled — dry, frozen, cracked, all at the same time. Long yellow grass lay matted and flattened like hair over an ancient skull. Even the fir and pine trees looked dusty and withered.

Word came that the town had settled down again after all the excitement of the white army, as it was now called, coming through. There was a second new preacher in town, and people seemed to be dividing up between the two. People who didn't go to one of the two were getting hassled. There was a feeling around town that if you didn't go to one of the churches, you weren't safe, you were just floating some-where, you didn't belong. Belonging had become important.

Ama tried to have a mediation session, but it was a disas-ter. People lost their tempers, yelled at each other, said unfor-givable things. It was after that session that people stopped coming to the big house, stopped talking to each other.

When Will and Elizabeth left, almost no one talked about it, except Ama complained to Matt.

"Why now?" she said. "What the hell did I do wrong? We were getting along here for years, then it all falls to pieces. Why? I can't figure it out. Nothing big has changed — it's just little things. You go along, you don't notice the little things, you think everything is fine. Well, that's what I thought. Then one morning you wake up and everything you thought was white is now black."

"People are scared," Matt said. "New people will show up. Things change, but not that much."

"That's what you don't get," Ama said bitterly. "Every-thing has changed. It won't go back."

"When you going on this big trip?" Matt said.

"Soon," Ama said. "Soon as the passes open. That'll be early. There hasn't been any snow to speak of. Sam says he's gonna try planting early this spring. Might as well."

Ama had changed as well. She fretted over every little thing, especially over Magnus, who was too thin and pale and stayed in by the fireplace, wrapped in blankets, reading or staring at nothing.

The next day when Matt came over, they'd gone.

Magnus, Sam, and Ama had packed and gone in the night. "Getting worse," Mairi said. She was now presiding over the kitchen. She gave him food, but the place felt hol-low and cold without Ama there, and he left again.

His house was growing like some live thing. He had put the floor down and now he was ready to start hoisting the logs on, using a tripod, ropes, and any other tricks he could think of. He knew he'd need help when he got up to the roof level, but until then he worked by himself. He rolled out of his blankets in the freezing tent at first light, lit a fire in the tin stove in the corner, heated water, and made some tea from one of the mixes Ama had given him. He'd have a cursory wash, then make himself pancakes using the coarse ground flour from the commune. The pancakes weren't too bad, eaten hot with jam. Sometimes, if he was lucky and the commune had killed a hog or chickens or a steer lately, he had some bacon or a bit of beefsteak. He had a crock of honey for the tea, and Mairi kept him in bread. Still, it was hard, dirty living, and he spent a lot of time thinking and worrying about food.

But the rest of the time he spent glorying in his house. He liked the way it was situated, perched on a rock so that the cliff fell away in front of it. Behind the house was a flat area full of small trees and brush that Matt had plans to clear away. Beyond that, the mountain rose into a curtain of black trees. It made a secret clearing, almost like a fortress. The trail to his house curved along the mountainside just below the cliff, so he could see if anyone was coming. But best of all was looking out over the lake at the dreaming blue distance of mountains. He found himself, several times a day, staring without thinking.

He got to see, as he had never seen before, the slow advance of the season, of spring coming. He got to feel it on his skin, on the thin tender skin between his hard, calloused fingers, on his cheekbones above the place where his beard wrapped his chin in warmth. He half expected to wake up one morning with a thin green layer of moss growing on him. He felt he was growing into the mountain and the mountain, in turn, was growing into him, tendrils sneaking into his heart and mind until he began to feel not so much one with the place as an outgrowth of it, a bearded moving hump of flesh and blood crawling over the skin of the mountain, where the granite banged hollow beneath his footsteps.

Then one morning, when he woke up, he heard a truck go by on the ruined road below his house. At least he was pretty sure it was a truck. Vehicles were so rare on the road now that he sensed them long before he heard them. They sent a vibration ahead of themselves.

He left for the commune right away, anxious for any news. He began to trot along the mountainside trail, perspiring in the unnatural heat. There had been almost no snow all winter, and the land had a parched desperate look. The level of the lake was lower than he had ever seen. The lake used to be controlled by dams, but Matt had heard rumours that the dams had been abandoned to run wide open all the time.

When he got to the commune, everyone had gathered in the big house. Magnus was sitting in a chair, but his face was bright, there was colour in his cheeks, and both he and Ama were talking, full of what they had seen. Lia was making coffee in the kitchen, her belly bulging huge under her worn smock. The coffee smell was so rich and enticing it almost made Matt nauseous.

"It's wild," Ama said, "worse than we figured. We didn't make any money. It cost almost everything we had just to get drugs for Magnus on the black market. It's so weird. Outside the hospital there's all these booths and little tables and shops. You can buy damn near anything there, if you got the money — stuff from all over the world."

"Yeah, I remember that," Matt said, interrupting.

"It's crazy," said Magnus. "Exciting, in a way. Lots of rumours, but it's hard to say what's true. We heard more about those white army guys. Apparently they're some independent army, mercenaries I guess you'd call them, hire themselves out to whoever. No one seems to know who is behind them — one of the big corporations, maybe. But there's other independents as well. Some of them are printing their own money, setting themselves up as enclaves. You got to belong to the right group to get inside.

"Vancouver is so changed. There's no trees left. People have chopped them all down for firewood. But they've planted all the parks into gardens, torn up the streets, made paths. Blackberry vines all over everything. Place looks like a jungle. There's animals, farms. Lots of beggars too, lots of little kids running around full of hell. There's money around. Lots of it. But you got to know someone to get your hands on any of it. Lots of fighting.

"God, they're even growing rice out in the valley. Got all these little farms diked off, growing all kinds of shit. People are amazing."

They drank the coffee and ate the sandwiches that Mairi and Lia provided. Magnus and Matt wandered out into the bright sun.

"Christ, it's so warm. You should see Vancouver. All kinds of flowers. Nothing dies out anymore. They've got cockroaches the size of chickens, giant marigolds, hibiscus, weird stuff. A lot of stuff has gone wild. Things have gotten out of greenhouses and taken over. It was kind of neat. Lots of music and street theatre. I had a great time, once I started to feel better. I'd like to go back, take Lia."

They wandered down to the garden and back. Sam had been planting before they left, but the soil was dry. He had made channels beside each row, and small trickles of water ran through these notches in the thirsty ground. Green curled fronds poked through the dried crust.

"It's too early for this," Magnus said. He bent and scraped away the soil from around one struggling seedling.

"Hey, when is Lia . . . ?"

"May," Magnus said. "Three more months. Then I guess I'll have to decide where to live. I'd move over there now, but she doesn't want me. Drives me crazy. How can she be so damn stubborn and independent? I get scared for her all the time. What if something happened and I wasn't there?"

"Whyn't you just go over there?" Matt said. "Plunk yourself down. Move in. Say you've come to stay. Christ, it's your damn kid."

"It's her life," Magnus said cheerfully. "She's got a right to do what she wants."

Matt just snorted. They went on wandering, looking at the work that wasn't getting done. Things looked neglected.

"Jeez," Magnus said, "guess Sam can't do it all. No one is helping out much anymore. Gotta get my lazy ass in gear." He grinned and his white teeth flashed. A lock of hair fell over one eye.

"What about the surgery?"

"Yeah, I still got stitches. Gotta wait until those come out. No heavy lifting for a while. But I guess I could do some planting and weeding, maybe some of the pruning. Those raspberries are starting to look like a damn jungle."

They wandered over and stared at the raspberry canes, which looped in fantastic arches over top of one another.

"How's it all going to come out, eh?" Matt said. "I think about it and think about it but I can't figure it in my head. How's it gonna come out?"

"Who says it has to come out?" Magnus said. He looked astonished. "Nothing comes out. It just goes on and on, same old shit."

Magnus laughed. Nothing seemed to worry him. He peered at the ancient apple trees, checking under their bark, looking at the buds ready to burst into leaf and blossom.

"I've known these trees all my life," he said. He looked like he was ready to hug them. "They're really old, we figure maybe over a hundred years old. It's like they're my grannies or my aunts or something. They're so beautiful, don't you think?"

He turned and Matt saw, to his horror, that Magnus was crying.

Magnus saw the look on Matt's face and started laughing. "Hey, I was sick a long time, man," he said. "I feel like I just got reborn or something. I been bursting into tears every five minutes. I started crying the minute we started climbing the hill out of Hope and I've barely been able to stop. God, I love it here." He turned back to the trees.

"Yeah, it's a great place," Matt said after a while. "You're right to love it."

"It's not that," Magnus said. "It's more than that. It's like this place made me, like I couldn't live without it. I'd curl up and die. I need to see these apple trees just as much as I need to eat or breathe." He stopped, embarrassed. "I guess it sounds silly."

"Don't worry about it," Matt said. "I know what you mean. When I was in that hospital in Vancouver it felt like I was holding my breath the whole time — no air."

They began walking back to the house.

"You staying for dinner?" Magnus asked.

"I been working on my house full time. It's looking pretty good. You'd better come over and have a look."

"So take an evening off," Magnus said. "Won't kill you to have a decent meal and stay and visit."

"Yeah, guess you're right," Matt said.

2 8

IT WAS A BEAUTIFUL morning when Lia's baby came squalling her way into the world, beating her fists against the air and squinting at the harsh light of morning that was blasting through the curtains.

They'd all stayed up most of the night. Magnus had crouched beside the bed, holding Lia's hand, neither of them saying much. Matt kept the fire going, chopped wood, sat outside staring at the stars. Ama somehow managed, in her brisk and businesslike fashion, to be coaching and coaxing Lia through her labour while simultaneously making food for them all, surreptitiously cleaning Lia's kitchen, and giving orders to Sam and Matt that would keep them busy outside and out from underfoot.

Lia paced around the small house, hanging on to Magnus's arm. She seemed very concentrated and far away. Finally, at four in the morning, she lay down on the bed and closed her eyes. Ama leaned over her.

"Lia," she said. "Lia, what's happening?"

"I'm okay," Lia said. "I'm just busy. Leave me alone. I want all of you to go away and just leave me alone."

Magnus picked up her hand and she snatched it away.

She got up again and began roaming around the room, holding onto the walls, stooping over and holding onto her belly with her other hand. Around and around she went, her hair in her eyes, sweat dripping off her face. She had her eyes half closed, roaming the room like something trapped. Magnus stayed just behind her. Everyone else pressed themselves into corners. Even Ama stopped rushing around and simply sat on a chair in the corner, her head drooping, her eyes also half closed, but attentive, as if she were listening. With every contraction, Lia would stop and hang on the wall, panting and moaning just under her breath, an odd drone. When it eased off she'd start walking again.

Finally, as a dim grey light was beginning to seep in the windows, Lia stopped roaming.

"Something's happening," she said.

Ama was by her side in one smooth movement. "Lie down," she said. "The baby is coming. Lie down now."

Lia let herself be led back to the bed, where the baby came suddenly in a rush of blood, water, and mucous.

They all took turns holding the baby.

Lia named her May. Her full name was May Flower. When Sam asked about a last name, Lia laughed. "No bureaucrats. No paper. No regulations. No government is ever going to know about this person — her name is never going to be registered. When she gets big, she can call herself whatever she wants."

Looking down into that small wrinkled face, Matt felt he should promise something, but he didn't want to make any promises he couldn't keep. He stared at her for a while and she opened her intensely bright blue eyes and stared back. It scared him, that look, and he passed the baby to Sam. Sam had once had children of his own who had left the commune when they were grown. Their mother had gone with them. He held the baby for a long time, rocking her. Then Lia took her back, began nursing her, and Sam and Matt stretched and stood, went outside, stood companionably peeing beside the woodpile.

"Guess I'll go home and check on things," Sam said.

"I'll stick around for a bit, do the chores, then guess I might as well go home, get to work again on the house." He laughed uneasily. He knew Sam's opinion of his house.

"Yeah, you do that," Sam said.

Matt's eyes were heavy and by the time he'd fed, watered, and let the chickens out of their pen and put some scraps down for the dog, all he wanted to do was sleep. The walk home seemed impossibly far. He lay on the grass under one of the apple trees and slept until the hot sun woke him in the afternoon. He went back inside to find everyone else sleeping, the baby on its back beside Lia and Magnus, side by side, both of them smiling slightly in their sleep. Ama was on a mat on the floor, wrapped in an old blanket. She looked pitiful and small, curled up like that, and Matt could hardly stand to see her.

He built up the fire in the wood stove and put the kettle on to boil. By the time he had the tea made, had sliced some bread and toasted it, heated up the leftover soup, everyone was stirring. The baby slept on and on while they gathered in the kitchen, slurped down the hot tea, ate all the toast and made more, everyone yawning and moving slowly. Lia was wrapped in an old dressing gown, the back of her hair matted and the rest of it flopping in her eyes.

Cousin came running in when they opened the door. He'd been shut out all night and resented it. The new smells inside the house made him crazy. He ran from corner to corner, sniffing, until he spotted the baby. He stopped. They were all watching him by now and they burst out laughing at the expression of astonishment on his face. Hesitantly, he approached the baby, sniffing, then sprang back when it moved suddenly. He started to lift his lips in a snarl but Lia snapped, "Cousin, come here."

She went and got the baby, who was stretching and sticking her fists in her mouth. Lia put the baby to her breast, where she latched on immediately, greedy and still half asleep. Cousin watched this, sniffed the baby, and flopped down on the floor beside Lia's chair, stretched his legs out behind him, sighed deeply, and put his head on his paws.

The baby made small contented mewling sounds. Outside, the sun coated everything with a hot yellow glare.

"Be hot enough to go swimming soon," Ama said.

"I've almost got strawberries ripe," Lia said. "You'll all have to come over for strawberries and cream one day soon."

"I've got to get home," Ama said. "Sam's there, but I left everything and rushed over here as soon as I heard. I think I left a pot of stew on the counter. It'll probably be spoiled by now. Oh well, the dogs can have it." She still looked old. She bent and kissed the baby, then kissed Lia.

Matt stood as well. "I'll be going too," he said. "I'll be over soon to help out. There's some weeds out there are gonna need an axe more than a hoe."

"Yeah, I didn't get much done the last couple of months. Got the garden in, then let it go. Now I have to try and catch up."

"You have to rest," Ama said, "or you'll lose your milk and the baby will go hungry. Magnus is staying to look after things. Matt will help out whenever you need him."

"For a while," Lia said, "until I get on my feet."

"Forget it," Magnus said. "I'm sticking around."

"It's my life," Lia said. "It's my house."

"It's our baby."

"My grandmother didn't need any help raising me."

"Why are you so stubborn?" Magnus said. He raised his hands, shook them in the air.

"Because I never had a life," Lia said. "I never had a chance to have a life. I had a life when I was a kid and then

it all disappeared. I don't want anything to just . . . happen
. . . the way this baby happened. I've got to get control. I've
got to feel like it's my life and I know what I'm doing, every
step of the way. Everything out there is so crazy. When I
grow things, when I prune trees, that's real, that's something
I understand. But people, relationships, I don't know, not
even you, Magnus." She stopped, said again, "Not even
you."

"I'll stay for now," Magnus said. "We'll work it out
later."

"Whatever," Lia said and bent her head over the baby.

They were all silent. Then the baby, who had been falling
asleep, jerked and gave a tiny cry.

"Lia, just remember, we're your family now," Ama said.
"We won't surprise you, we won't hurt you, we just want to
help, you, the baby, my grandchild. My first grandchild. If
you think we're going to go off and leave her and you alone,
you're wrong."

Ama's voice shook. She was crying now. So was Lia. Matt
shifted uneasily by the door. Magnus picked up the baby,
and Lia and Ama hung on to each other for a long moment.

Then Ama and Matt left. They walked together along the
mountain slope. The sun was burning hot. The sky was
white with haze, so bright they squinted their eyes against
the glare. Ama slipped on the pine needles and Matt held
out his hand to steady her. Ama was still crying. He realized
she had been crying silently all the way along the trail.

"I'm sorry," she said. "It was such a long night."

She walked ahead of him and he kept his hand ready in
case she slipped again.

"Ama, you heard anything?"

"I heard from Maeve, they're still around," she said.
"They'll be back."

"What do you mean?"

She turned to face him. Her eyes were bleak, flat as the sky. "I been sitting on this knowledge for a while," she said. "I finally got a name. It took me a while to sort it all out."

"Who are they?"

"I don't really know. All I have is a name. One of those corporations that got so rich it's worth more than the country. That doesn't say much. But they just keep buying land, huge chunks of it. From what I can tell they don't seem to do much with it. They've got a lot of rhetoric about saving the environment for the future and protecting land and resources for the future, but who knows what that means." She stopped, stood looking out over the hillside, through the glare, over the black trees huddled under the sun to where the lake sparkled in the light.

"God, we're the endangered species," she said. "We're the ones who need protecting. We're the people who just want to belong here. It's too simple, somehow. And there's so little left. This is one of the last parts of the world that hasn't been dug up or chopped down or run over, and everybody wants something from it. It's survived this long because it's so far away from everywhere and hard to get to and the roads aren't worth maintaining so it's been sort of invisible for a long time. Except to us. But now somebody wants it, somebody with money and power. So what does our existence mean?"

"But it's good, isn't it, that they want to protect the place?"

"If that's what they really mean — I think they just want to preserve it for themselves, so they can have the trees, the water, the animals for whatever."

"What if you're wrong?" Matt said. "What if they're good people? What if they mean what they say?"

"How do you tell?" Ama said. "How do you tell anymore who are the good guys and who are the bad guys? All you can do is look after yourself and your own people."

She went on, stomping along the hillside, and when they got to Matt's house she left him without a word and went on towards her own place.

He watched her out of sight, then turned to walk around his house, inspecting everything, sniffing at it, peering and wandering and standing in the sun for long minutes with his head down, frowning. The log walls were up over his head now. He was shaping the house into a spiral with crazy bits of space for windows and doors and stairs.

He had created a complicated system of ramps and pulleys and ropes to hoist the logs into place. Now he had to put on the roof supports, then the roof. He'd found an ancient cedar in a piece of swampy land just to the north of his house, and he cut it down with a crosscut saw — it had taken him a whole day. Then he had laboriously sawed it into blocks, hauled the blocks down the hill to his house, and now, in his spare time, he was splitting them into shakes for the roof. He had about half of what he needed. Everything was so goddamned slow. He thought he'd be living in the house by now, but everything took twice as long as he thought it was going to.

He worked the rest of the day and then, exhausted, crawled into his bed and slept late, only waking when the sun made the tent into a furnace.

The sun was making the country into a furnace. Sam went around with worried lines in his face, dust caked in his eyebrows and beard.

"Ain't never seen anything like this," he said solemnly to Matt one day when Matt had gone over for supplies. "This keeps up, we're gonna be short of food this winter and I never thought I'd see that happen. We're gonna have to go out again for more supplies. Plus we need more people. I can't keep up with the work. Used to have five or six people to help with chores. Used to be fun, y'know, every time we had something to do, it was more like a big party. Now it's no goddamned fun, just work all the time. I'm feeling wore out. Supposed to be kids around to take up the slack. Supposed to be a community, friends, family. Where are they?"

Matt nodded, feeling guilty. He hadn't offered to help out, although he spent at least one day a week at Lia's place, working the garden, getting up firewood, pruning trees, digging ditches for water. Sometimes he simply sat under a tree with the baby lying on a blanket while Lia went off and did her own chores. They were all tired, he thought. There was too much to do. Everything was early and it was hard to keep up with picking fruit, getting it into jars or drying it or whatever, plus the garden, the animals, chores.

The strawberries, raspberries, apricots, and blackberries were all ripe at once, which had never happened before, but it was so hot they were drying on the vine as fast as they ripened. Lia was frantic to put up enough food. She had trays of berries laid out in the sun, drying.

She flopped down beside Matt and tore off her big hat. The baby stirred and opened its pink mouth and Lia picked her up and put the baby's mouth to her breast.

"Christ," she said, "I'm starving all the time. I need meat and it's too hot to butcher anything. I could kill a chicken, I guess. Or go fishing."

"I could get a deer," Matt said. "We could divide it up between all of us. Then we wouldn't have to worry about storing the meat."

"You got a gun?"

"Of course I got a gun, my dad's old rifle. I haven't used it for a while, but I used to hunt when I was a kid. My old man would take me out once every fall. Sometimes we'd actually shoot something."

"I wish I had a gun," Lia said.

"What for?"

She shrugged. "You never know. I'd just feel safer."

"You're pretty safe here. There's no one around. You got Cousin to keep away the bears or coyotes."

"I never feel safe," she said. "Sometimes I lie awake and wonder what I'd do if someone kidnapped May. I wonder how I'd stand it. I don't think I could."

After a while she said reflectively, "I'm too pissed off to live with anyone. It wouldn't be fair to Magnus."

"He just wants to look after you and the baby — make you feel safe."

"I want to make myself feel safe."

Matt shook his head. "What the hell do you think men are for?" he said.

"I don't know," she said. "I don't know much about men. They weren't around in my life when I was a kid. There was my grandma and me. Men were people who had left a long time ago."

Matt was silent. "I'll get a deer," he said. "I'll bring you the steaks. You can dry some of the meat. Then I'll get you a rifle. If that's what you want."

As the summer wore on, the valley filled with smoke. There were fires on every hilltop from the lightning that flickered and bit during the brief violent storms that came and went almost weekly. There was always some rain with the storms, though never enough to put out the fires or soak the ground. Sometimes curtains of rain hung in the valleys between the mountains but never hit the ground. The smoke made everyone irritable, and Lia was spending a lot of time trying to soothe the fretful, restless baby.

Finally, in late July, the sky clouded over and it rained. It rained for three weeks. The ripened fruit turned mouldy; trickles of muddy water ran through the garden. Sam's face got grimmer. Clouds of mosquitoes haunted their days.

Matt went on working through it all like a man in a fever. When he lay down at night to sleep, he saw instead the vision of his house, rising steep and full of air. Bones covered the walls and surrounded the tower on the north side.

He loved the idea of his house, the idea that it would stand here for years and years, maybe hundreds of years if he did his work well; that people would move in and out of its rooms, its lights and shadows; that they would live their lives, have sex, have children, fight, make up, eat, shit, sleep in his house. He wondered who they would be. Now he thought hard about leaving something, a note, a letter, somewhere that someone would find in the future — maybe a kid or an inquisitive adult or someone renovating the house. It shouldn't be any place too obscure, maybe up in the rafters somewhere. And if no one ever found it, that was all right as well.

He daydreamed about the people who would live in his house. One would be a young girl with blond hair and green eyes. She would sit in the tower he had built and look out over the valley. Maybe by then it would be peaceful and there would be people back living in the valley, farms, neighbours. She'd wonder about the bones and what they meant. Maybe she'd know what they meant and she'd wonder about the long-dead animals and the lives they had lived. It was all good to think about.

29

AFTER THE RAIN STOPPED and the sun came out again, August was like a dream of beauty. They all started meeting at the beach in the blazing hot afternoons. Lia would make a tent for the baby and they'd swim or sit in the shade of the rocks or sleep.

Matt would go fishing, and sometimes in the evenings they'd make a fire and broil trout and potatoes and corn over it, eat the food with their hands, watch the sky as the mountains changed to blue shadows, the lake darkened and dimpled with trout rising, and the mountains breathed their whispery downdraft through the tops of the fir trees, shaking the water, shivering and whispering. They'd stay until it was almost dark and then pack up and go home to sleep, getting up early with the first light to try to work before it got too hot.

Each evening the sky softened into shades of blue and cream and salmon. The light lasted behind the hills until just before midnight. The log house at the commune was too hot to sleep in, so Ama and Sam dragged their mattress out on the porch. Matt slept outside as well, but Lia refused to give up her comfortable bed in her house. Only the baby didn't seem to mind the heat. In the long afternoons she lay beside her mother, waving her hands and feet in the air and staring intently at leaf shadows.

Lia and Magnus would wake in the morning and marvel at their daughter. They couldn't get used to her. She was mysterious in a way they hadn't expected, spent her time smiling at shadows, often turned her head away from her parents to look into the distance.

"Do you think she's all right?" Lia asked Ama one day.

Ama laughed. "She's wonderful," she said, taking the baby on her lap. And it was obvious that the baby and Ama had some connection — little May always quieted when Ama picked her up, snuggled into her broad shoulder like a refuge. "You're too tense with her," Ama said. "Just relax."

But Lia had become more fearful after May's birth and held the baby too tight, checked on her several times during the night, couldn't sleep herself.

Magnus would reach out for her in the night and discover her sitting in the rocking chair, staring out the window that faced out over the orchard, the window where she could look north over the glimmering expanse of lake, the mountains like flat blue shadows under the moon's thin light.

"What's the matter?" he'd ask.

But Lia couldn't tell him. The words stayed locked in her own head. All she could say was that she felt a sense of terrible dread, of foreboding, that seemed to sift down from the night sky. It was better during the day, when she was busy. But nights were hard. Nothing was friendly then. Nothing gave way or gave peace or even gave a message of hope. There was only this folded mysterious forbidding country wherever she looked, and even the house itself was permeable, a thing of cobwebs, dust, cracks where the wind blew through, cracks where spiders and ants hid, a box that needed patching, mending, fixing up. Endless.

And what could she tell Magnus that wouldn't sound insubstantial or foolish or tangled into threads of craziness? She sat in her chair, rocking and staring out the window, thinking of her grandmother, the city, the high-rise, and the black water that had swirled and chewed endlessly around its foundations.

30

NOW THAT THE WALLS were up, Matt was desperate to get the roof on before the winter. Magnus and Sam came to help, and Ama, Mairi, and Lia showed up later with food.

They got the pole rafters up, and the stringers for the shake roof. The big difficulty was with the odd twisted shape of the house, capped by the tower on the north side. It had taken Matt days and weeks of fussing and scribing with strings and nails and fine saws to get the logs fitted right for the tower. It was two stories and jutted out from the side of the house. It had gaps for windows on all five sides, winding in a circular pattern to the roof. Sam had just grunted when he saw what Matt had done. Nevertheless, he organized the work into an efficient set of steps that meant a lot got done. They all had dinner that night outside on the flat space behind the house — venison steaks, baked trout, baked potatoes, corn, laid out on planks set on stumps. They had a fire and Magnus played guitar, but everyone was too tired to party and went home early.

Matt worked steadily away, getting the roof on. September came and the days blazed hot, but at least the nights were cool. The light changed in September. He loved the way it slanted through the trees and turned the lake the most astounding colour of deep blue, the way it leapt in the morning from tree branch to brush to the yellowing grass tips. It made him want to go wandering, but he had to finish his house and he stuck to it, working with a desperate driven urgency.

Ama came one morning, surprising him, but he stopped work, made her tea, and they settled on the rough wooden benches by his fire.

"Be pretty different, living in a house instead of a tent," she said. "Maybe we should start looking around for a wife for you."

"It's Star's house," he said, "even if she never lives in it. I built it for her."

"It's a big house for one guy."

"It's what I want. It's mine."

"What are the bones for?"

"They go all around the outside. I'm going to wire them on. Then I'm going to plaster between them so the house will be white. You'll be able to see it from all over. It'll shine in the sun."

He waited. Ama never came just to chat. She threw some sticks on the fire, poured more tea.

Then she said, "Have you seen Lia lately?"

"No. I feel shitty about that. I just been busy trying to get the roof on. I should get over there, I guess. How they all doing?"

"Magnus and the baby are fine."

"What's with Lia?"

"I dunno. She's gone broody, worrying too much about stuff. Maybe it's old stuff coming back on her. I thought if you started going over there, helping out, it might take some pressure off, make her feel better."

Matt stared at the ground.

"I gotta get my roof and walls done," he said. "I'll be over after that."

"She needs help now."

"I got my own stuff to do."

"Jeezus, Matt, you owe us. You owe me."

"I'm not saying I'm not gonna help. I just gotta get this done is all."

He didn't look up. He heard Ama's retreating footsteps, and despite his sense that time was sliding by him, he stayed by the tiny fire, poking twigs and tiny bits of needles and dust into it, watching the little tongues of flame leap and fade and die.

Eventually he hoisted himself to his feet and went back to work, but he was heavy and slow. The excitement that had driven him for weeks was gone. But he persisted. That's one thing he knew how to do, he thought to himself. At least he kept going, no matter what happened.

By late fall he had most of the bones wired onto the logs. He thought of moving into the house, just to keep warm, but he didn't want to move in until it was done. He'd made windows out of old panes of glass, made the frames and the small panels, then fitted them into an abstract pattern in the log walls. The glass was old and warped in spots, but he liked the look of it. He liked the small, multipanelled windows that made the outside world wavery and strange.

He was short of food. Since Ama's visit he hadn't been to the commune. Instead he had taken to slipping down to the lake in the evening to fish, or setting snares for rabbits and grouse. It was the other things he was starting to miss, butter and coffee and flour. A man couldn't live just on meat. But he still worked like a driven creature, pushing and hurrying. He had to figure out how to burn limestone to get the lime for the plaster, and for that he had to find a source for the limestone and a way of getting it back to his house.

Once again he trudged with the wheelbarrow, five miles to where a ledge of dolomite limestone stuck out of the mountain. It had been a quarry once, and there were lots of loose rocks and piles of limestone dust, so he had no trouble getting enough of it. But the trips were long and exhausting. When he got home he lay on the ground, holding his leg, gritting his teeth in pain while the muscles knotted and writhed under the skin. He rubbed them in long strokes until they relented and uncoiled themselves. But then at night, when he was sleeping, they would unexpectedly snap back into knots so rigid and painful he would be jerked awake, forced to crawl from his sleeping bag and limp in cursing circles until they relented again.

He decided that rather than go to the commune and face Ama, he'd have to do without eating until the walls were done. When they were done, when the house stood complete and shining and empty of everything but air and light, he'd invite everyone to visit. He'd invite them to come and wander through the rooms and look out the windows of his tower.

Now when he got up in the morning, he drank hot water until his belly was full, then went to work. Sometimes he had to stop and hold onto the logs and breathe, but it didn't matter. While he worked, the leaves from the alders and birch on the mountain drifted into golden dusty piles. He heard geese on the lake in the mornings. Steller's jays foraged in his compost. The family of coyotes that lived up the hill had lost all fear of him. The male came in the afternoons to lie just under the trees beside the house and watch him work. Occasionally a bear would wander through as well, but Matt went on working and the bear ambled on its own way. It was still hot, but the mountains shone with the slanted distant light of autumn — reflections from the water glinted and danced on the white shining walls of his house.

And then one day it was done, or as much as he could do that was strictly on the house itself. He had been living on hot water, dried meat, fish, and not much else for three weeks. Several times he had worked for eighteen hours straight.

The house stood the way he had dreamed it. It had doors, windows, floors, walls, but nothing else — no counters or furniture or shelves. The floor was rough and full of splinters; the windowsills were unplaned rough boards.

He swept the last of the dust and shavings out the door. When he was finished the sweeping, he felt strangely weak. He noticed with surprise that he was shaking and trembling. He leaned against the wall. It was Star's house and she would never see it. His heart pounded and leapt around in his chest like some wild and crazy caged thing. He slid slowly down onto the floor, his face in his hands, while his heart thrashed and pounded at a frenzied speed inside his chest.

When he woke up, he knew something was very wrong. It was dark. He was lying on the floor of his house. He could move, but only slowly. While he was lying there, he heard a sound which at first he didn't recognize, an odd soft *whup whup* like a grouse drumming, but this noise didn't speed up and die away. It just got louder.

He realized that it was a helicopter and it was coming closer. He rolled to his side, breathing hard, got on his knees, got his hand on the wall, and pulled himself to his feet. It took all his strength to stand there, but when the house stopped spinning around him he stood up straight, then slowly and unsteadily limped to his tent and pulled his rifle out from under his sleeping bag.

He set off down the trail slowly, still dizzy, moving like a drunk, weaving his way from tree to tree, stumbling a little, but keeping on, moving forward. He slung the rifle over his shoulder. As he went down the hill towards the commune, he seemed to gain a bit of strength, but he still had to stop every few feet, hang his head, and breathe. The helicopter had disappeared. He couldn't hear anything. He had no idea what time it was, only that it was dark and even darker under the trees. Then he heard a bird and saw the first faint sheen of grey on the edges of the leaves and trees. It was near dawn.

He went on walking and walking. He began to wonder if he was going to make it. He did sit down for a while. When he got up, there was a line of pearly opalescent light along the rim of the mountains behind him. He was getting closer to the commune now, coming down the hill through the fat cedar trees that squatted at the edge of the pasture. He had to struggle to open the gate and decided, after what seemed long thought, to leave it open.

He could hear voices now, raised voices. It sounded like people shouting. The voices drifted through the trees around him like smoke, like thin grey scarves draped over the black sweeping boughs, the great skirts of the trees dancing and swaying.

God, he was so tired. He could see the helicopter, sitting in the middle of the field, its rotors still turning. He wondered where the cows and horses had gone. Scared to death maybe — gone right through the fence and away. Bastards didn't care what they did, what they destroyed. The white trucks were lined up in front of the house and men were coming outside, looking around, and then going back in.

He found a place just up the hill where he could lie flat behind a granite ledge and poke his rifle through a notch in the granite.

He had to lay his head down and breathe before he could get the rifle lined up properly. The rotors on the helicopter were spinning faster. It was rising in the air like a clumsy shining dragonfly. He brought the rifle to his shoulder, aimed, and began firing, steadily squeezing the trigger while the ejected shells fell around his feet.

The helicopter lurched sideways, then flew low out towards the lake. It began to rise, rise, and then it seemed to slide down a long mottled column of air, slowly and gently tipping sideways until it went into the water with barely a splash and disappeared.

The men below were pointing to the hillside, waving and shouting. They were all outside now and he realized, to his surprise, there weren't that many of them. A small group began to run across the field towards him.

He shot the one in the lead and the others dived to the ground, then stood up and kept on running. He shot twice more and missed, then stood up. He stood up too fast and swayed as he started to run, but then he found his legs and some unexpected strength.

He ran along the mountain, back towards the trail that led to his house. Then he stopped, reconsidered, began to angle upwards. He decided to head for Lia's house and help protect her if he could. He had done all he could do here.

He could hear the shouts of the men behind him, and he forced himself to go faster, bent over double and gasping for breath as he was. The shouts were closer now, but he was already running as fast as he could.

3 I

SOMEBODY HAD PUT a marker on it years before, a single carved pole that had now fallen into the dirt and was disappearing beneath a layer of moss and leaves. May found it on one of her expeditions to the house. She cleaned off the moss and tried to stand the pole up again, but it was too rotten. In the end, she left it where it had fallen.

She had heard the story of Crazy Matt many times. It was one of the stories she had grown up with, one her parents and grandmother liked to tell at certain times of the year, often at her birthday or when her father had a bit too much to drink, which was more often than her mother approved of.

But then they were always talking about the old days. When she was little, May had never paid that much attention. She had her own world of animals, garden, woods, lake. She knew there was an outside world, but it was far away. People came from there with stories; her dad went there every year, but she couldn't picture it. When she tried, it seemed like it might be a bigger version of the farm, but with a lot more people.

She had just turned nine the day she and her friends found the house in the trees. They walked around the outside first, staring at the bones and animal skulls that gaped from the walls. That was almost enough to scare them off, but when they gathered up their courage and pushed open the door and went in, they walked around in amazement. Most of the glass from the windows had blown in, and the floor was covered with a fine litter of glass, sand, leaves, twigs, and mud and droppings from the swallow nests that lined the walls. But the walls were solid and sturdy, a soft silver from the weather. It was a house someone could have lived in but no one did. No one ever had.

They found a broom that was almost totally rotted away and spent time cleaning the floor. They moved from room to room, exclaiming, enchanted with the place. They agreed to keep their presence there a secret. Over the next few days they spent a lot of time playing there, but then something else caught their attention and the house was silent once more.

May kept going back. She didn't tell anyone, not even her mother, who was good at deciphering most of her secrets. She would walk around and around the house, staring at it, wondering why someone would go to the effort of covering a house with bones. There was still plaster around some of them, and she brought a knife and spent time chipping off whatever she could reach. One day she found a book that had been stuffed in a crack between the rafter and the roof, but it was too mildewed to read.

Often she would sit in the house on an old piece of rug she and her friends had dragged up there. They'd brought other small bits of bright stuff, a table and some cups, a cloth for the table, a jar for flowers. Sometimes May would light a fire outside and make smoky pine-needle-flavoured tea, or toast some bits of meat she'd brought from home. She never stayed long. The house in sunlight was bright and full of the scent of trees, but when the sun went behind the trees and the wind came, the house turned sad and full of shadows.

One day she asked her mother about the house and her mother came to see it. Her mother and grandmother walked around, ran their hands over the walls.

They sat outside with her and told her yet again the story of Matt, who had been at her birth, who had loved her and carried her around, who had dreamed of a peaceful life, who had fought and died. No one had a picture of him, but they described him, huge, tall, shy, a man full of dreams.

After that, May sometimes brought flowers to the house and left them. She kept it clean, swept the pine needles and bird shit off the floor. She liked the way the wind and rain came in through the holes that had once been windows. The cedar shakes leaked but stayed in place. The floorboards split and heaved in places, but the house stayed remarkably intact. Animals moved in and out — birds mostly, swallows and the occasional thrush. Skunks took up residence under the floor and the dogs learned to stay clear of them.

As she got older she came less often, but she knew the place was always there. Sometimes she dreamed of living in it. Sometimes it lived in her dreams as a kind of magic castle where she wandered through rooms and floors and passages that disappeared when she awoke.

When she turned twelve, arguments broke out around the dinner table. Her father wanted her to go outside for school and her grandmother and her mother were against it. May had mixed feelings. Her father said things had changed, things had gotten better. The world had gone through a hideous ugly time, but it was now a time of rebuilding, a new world without corporations, with real democracy coming back, and May should know something about it.

Her mother shrugged. "It might be getting safer," she

said, "but it still depends on where you go and who you know." Finally they decided the three of them would go together.

"It's going to be exciting," Magnus said. "There'll be a lot to learn, to see."

Only her grandmother remained suspicious. "You've forgotten," she said. "You've all forgotten what it was like. They tried to take our land, run us out of here. We finally wore them out. There's sure as hell something to be said for sheer stubbornness."

"But it was more than that, right, Grandma?"

May's grandmother turned from whatever she was doing, usually cooking something. Her voice was sharp and bitter. "They were evil people who wanted the whole valley for themselves. They were from the south, just over the border. They called themselves the Militia. They had money and weapons. They had an army, lots of fancy toys, but there wasn't that many of them and they weren't prepared for a real fight. They thought we'd just fold and disappear, but we didn't.

"And we had help. Maeve and her people came that spring. We hid in the woods for a whole winter. We lost most of our animals. The helicopter disappearing really kicked over the applecart. Made them mad, but it scared them too. That whole winter we fought. We hid you kids. Oh, it was hard and scary. Your dad was our big hero. He even blew up one of their trucks. It was horrible. Some people died who were sleeping in the truck. Your dad will never talk about it. But we knew the land — we knew it was ours and they didn't. In the end they went away and we came home."

"Why do I have to go to school?" May said. "I don't want to go."

There was silence at this.

"We'll be together," Lia said. "We'll be learning as well."

The argument went on over dinner after dinner. May was sullen and furious.

"I don't want to leave here," she said. "You said it was terrifying. You said people were fighting."

"I want to see it," her dad said. "Putting civilization back together again. Now they've got the Barlows ... really, that's made the difference."

"What are the Barlows?" May asked curiously.

"They were people, well, the laws they passed, that finally broke the power of the corporations. A whole bunch of people took over the government, made them pass the laws they called the Barlows. I don't know where the name comes from."

"So then what happened?"

"The corporations tried to fight, but people hated them so much by then, they didn't have much of a chance. People figured that all the trouble, the environment shot to hell, the way everything had gotten out of control, was the fault of the corporations. Mind you, it was hard because by then the corporations figured they owned everything and they had their own private armies, didn't care about what any government said. So there was fighting, lots of it, but finally people just walked away from them. A corporation isn't worth fighting for, really."

"What happened to the people who wanted our land?"

"We don't know. They were using their own money, and finally that was declared illegal, so maybe that discouraged them. Things settled down outside and people stopped panicking about escaping society and hiding in the woods, thinking World War Three was going to come at any minute, or some other weird apocalypse."

"Tell me some more about Matt."

"Poor Matt. He was a good man, but he was a fool, in

love with a ghost. He practically killed himself building that house, and all for Star."

"Didn't she love him at all?"

"Matt was just a guy she met on the road. But she changed his whole life. Sad, eh?"

"What happened to her?"

"We never found out."

"Maybe it will be all right if you go for just a little while," Ama said. "I'm just not sure. I'm too old. I don't know anymore. I only know what's under my feet, under my nose. Like this bread burning right here and now." And she leapt up to go to the oven.

May went outside and sat on the steps. The new puppy, named Cousin — there was always some dog named Cousin — came and chewed on her boot toe. She was happy, sitting in the sun, thinking of her life unfolding ahead of her, full of possibilities, full of light, like flower petals catching the sun, endlessly unfurling, pushing themselves into the air in a reckless ecstasy of growth and colour.

In the morning she'd take some flowers to the house, sit there for a while. Sometimes the wind came and blew through the windows, through the bones still hanging on the walls, making the whole house into an odd, huge, magical instrument. Some of her friends thought it was spooky, but she loved the sound. It was the sound of her childhood, the sound of dreams, the sound of magic and home.